Claire Highton-Stevenson

Dedication

Family is not an important thing. It's everything.

—Michael J Fox

Acknowledgments

With love and thanks to every single one of you who has loved these characters as much as I do.

Whilst the author and editing team do all they can to avoid mistakes and typos, it is often inevitable that some will slip through, or that grammar, slang, dialogue, accents etc might be different to what you use or expect.

In the case that you do find something that causes enough discomfort that you feel the need to report it, may I ask that you speak to the author first. As reporting to Amazon can create an issue that often isn't notified to the author.

Many thanks.

Chapter One

The flowers Scarlett had ordered had arrived on time, a huge bouquet of roses and lilies in shades of red and pink that she knew Claudia would love. She'd asked the hotel to arrange chocolates, champagne, and an afternoon in the spa. Where Claudia would receive a hot stone massage and a facial of her choice.

As anniversaries went, this was pretty much perfect, except for one vital element: Scarlett. Scarlett, herself, wasn't there.

"Darling, this is all magical I just—" Claudia sighed and sank down onto the edge of the bed with the phone against her ear as her words tailed off. The huge, lonely bed she had been forced to sleep in for the last five nights and would do for potentially three more felt even bigger now.

"I know, it isn't what we planned," Scarlett answered in all but a whisper, aware that Zara was just across the hall, "but it won't be long and then we can celebrate properly." She glanced at herself in the mirror and fiddled with her hair. The scarlet tips of the past year had now faded and gone, and she hadn't dyed her hair that dark since. She wondered if she should try a new colour now that the lighter brown natural colouring was so evident at the roots. "And at least you have this morning free to go and enjoy the spa."

"I suppose so." Claudia smiled at the huge bouquet of flowers again. "I hope this isn't going to become a regular thing, if it is you'll have to schedule your clients so you can come with me."

"We can definitely look into that if you're now a high-flying executive. I really hope you can get the spa in before you head down to that meeting and show them who you are."

Giggling, Claudia said, "I am kind of a big deal."

"Oh, you definitely are. Which is why you're out there heading up this opening." Scarlett smiled into the phone as she added, "I'm proud of you."

1

Scarlett

"Thank you, that means a lot." Claudia fell backward and landed with a whoomph on the soft duvet. Five-star really was the way to go when travelling for work. "I just didn't expect to have to be here this long or foresee our first anniversary being so…distant. I miss you, and—" She bit her lip, whispering as though someone might overhear her, "I need…you."

Scarlett chuckled. "I am fully aware of that problem, and just remember, I have the added issue of your daughter and grandson sleeping across the hall, so shower time is a very quiet affair."

The mere mention of Jacob sent Claudia into a frenzy of questions. "Oh, how is he today? Is Zara alright? Did she say how long she's staying? She's going to be there when I get back, right?"

"Okay crazy lady, take a breath." Scarlett laughed, "In answer to the multitude of questions, I don't know. I mean, he is okay, so is Zara, but I've no idea how long they plan to stay. They were expecting you home two days ago."

"Hm, I just hope Diana isn't being too overbearing."

"Last time this happened, it wasn't because Diana was overbearing, it was because Diana was over Kevin, and needed some space."

"Oh yes, Kevin, such a disappointment." Claudia recalled the man-child that Diana had chosen as the first person to date after Jason, thank goodness for rebounds and she'd soon kicked him to the kerb. He was actually worse than Alan, and that was saying something.

"Well, there has been no mention of anything like that, and we both know if Zara had something to share, she would. So, I am just going with the idea that she wanted to see us, well you, but you're not here so— she's lumbered with me."

"I'm pretty sure she only comes over to see you," Claudia grumbled in an amused tone. "I could be jealous, but I'm just so glad they all love you as much as I do."

"That much, huh?" Scarlett playfully stirred the sexual tensions.

"Well, maybe not *that* much."

Scarlett continued to tease. "So, just how much more do you love me?"

Claudia's free hand slowly skimmed down her torso imagining the way her lover would touch her, pushing aside the fluffy white dressing gown, so her fingers could continue gliding across her bare skin until her fingertips reached the edges of the lace and silk that barely covered her modesty. "Not so much *more*, but…differently…" She groaned as the pads of her fingers slipped beneath the material and slid across the neatly trimmed curls until they could part her folds and ease between them with a practised move that was all too frequent lately.

"What are you doing?" Scarlett asked leisurely, picturing what she hoped was the case. It wasn't the first time that the telephone had helped solve their need for one another.

Deliberately, Claudia's fingers moved against her need. A gentle sigh escaped before she answered huskily, "Wishing you were here to do this instead?"

Scarlett chewed her lip, walking across the room to check the door was locked before she slid off Claudia's dressing gown, the one she'd been wearing throughout her lover's absence, engulfed in the scent of her.

"Tell me," Scarlett urged as her lover's breath caught in her throat and from 100s of miles away, a rocket of arousal hit that spot between her own thighs.

"I'm just so…wet." Claudia moaned. "So, very, very wet."

"Fuck." The word escaped Scarlett's lips before she had a chance to think.

Scarlett

"Mm yes, that would be just perfect but—" Claudia closed her eyes and enjoyed the sensations as she imagined her lover's touch. "I want to feel you inside of me."

"I want that too." Scarlett climbed onto the bed they shared and sat back against the pillows, her free hand drifting lower until she could feel her own arousal. *God, what this woman does to me.* "I want to be between your thighs, my mouth on you...licking..."

"God, yes." Claudia gasped, upping the speed of her movement.

"Wrapping my lips around your clit and sucking until..."

"Yes, just like that. Don't...stop."

Scarlett squeezed her thighs together. "I wouldn't dream of stopping, not when I can have the chance to taste you on my lips, my tongue...you taste so good."

A whimper mutating into a groan filled Scarlett's ear through the phone and sent her arousal spiking. Parting her thighs, she let her fingers continue to dance a rapid cha cha of their own, until finally they were both breathing heavily and grinning, unseen. "That was..."

"Yes, it was."

Chapter Two

Zara bounced Jacob in his baby chair with one foot, while holding a book in her hand, engrossed in the story. Motherhood doing little to change her, she was still the laid-back, hippy-loving dreamer she'd always been. She just looked a little more tired nowadays, hardly surprising but she had plenty of helping hands.

It did indeed take a village, in Zara's world.

Jacob's dad, James, had him two nights a week, and Diana was always available for last-minute babysitting duties. Zara's tiredness often came from a late night out with friends more than anything Jacob did.

A steaming cup of coffee cooled in front of her, with a plate of carrot sticks and celery next to it. Jacob giggled at something on the tablet Zara had set up for him to watch that was strapped to the chair with a long-armed clamp. He clapped his hands haphazardly, still working on his co-ordination. He was a cute kid, Scarlett thought. Big brown eyes and dark curls, chubby cheeks, and a toothless grin already winning everyone over.

"Morning." Scarlett smiled as she made her way into the kitchen and over to the kettle. It was still warm as she flicked the switch down and reached for a mug. "Your mum said to say hello, and I'm supposed to give Jacob a million kisses." She shrugged. "Not sure that wouldn't be considered torture to the poor kid, so let's just tell her I did, yeah?"

Zara glanced up and grinned. "Oh, no I think you should attempt it." She placed the book down and turned to her son. "You'd like that, wouldn't you Jakey?"

His clapping became more excitable, as he bounced in the rocking rainforest Jumperoo.

"See, he definitely wants Nanna Scarlett to—" She laughed as the damp dishcloth soared through the air and hit her in the face. "Okay, aunty Scarlett."

Scarlett

"You're cruising for a bruising." Scarlett smirked as she stirred the coffee.

"Aiming for a shaming," Zara threw back watching as Scarlett placed two slices of bread into the toaster. "I never realised how much fun it would be to tease you and my mother."

"Speaking of which," Scarlett pulled out a stool at the breakfast bar and sat down opposite Zara, "she wants to know why you're here and how long you're planning to stay?" She sipped her coffee and watched Zara over the rim of the cup.

"You mean she's worried that Diana and I are arguing, or that Diana has found herself another car crash relationship to entertain? And will I still be here when she gets back?"

Putting the mug down, Scarlett grinned. "That's about the size of it."

"Well, it's neither of those things, actually, I just missed you both and I want Jacob to spend as much time as possible with those who are important to me, especially now that I'm going to be working more."

"Claudia will be happy to hear that."

"I was wondering though if…" She leaned forwards, elbows on the counter as her chin rested in her palms. "Would you be able to have him for a weekend at some point, we quite fancy a girl's weekend."

"We're not invited?" Scarlett glanced at the smiling, giggling, bouncing bundle of family joy and shrugged. "I'm just kidding. I don't see why not, when was you thinking?"

"Not sure, Diana is working out the details? I could drop him off on a Thursday and pick him up on the Monday?"

Raising one shoulder, Scarlett sipped her coffee again and took another look at the happy little kid they all loved. "Sure, I know your mum isn't going to say no, but I'll double-check just in case. This new job is…hectic."

Zara's smile stretched out into a thin-lipped frown. "Is she enjoying it?"

"I think so, I mean it's only been a few months, and she likes her colleagues."

"You mean her underlings," Zara quipped.

"Uh huh. She's certainly become much more confident lately, some might even say bossy. Not me, I wouldn't say that." She pointed at her chest. "But some might."

Smiling, Zara studied Scarlett. "I think we all know who's the root cause of that, don't we?"

"Hm, I'm not complaining."

"Or blushing either, you dirty dawg."

The toaster popped and two perfectly toasted slices of brown seeded bread stuck up ready for Scarlett to butter and eat with gusto. She slid off the stool and opened a cupboard to take out a plate.

"I don't think I've ever seen my mum look this happy. Who knew all it would take was turning lesbian and dating someone half her age." Jacob seemed to like that and kicked out his chubby legs with a squeal.

Scarlett narrowed her eyes and pursed her lips.

"Okay, almost half her age." Zara chuckled. "I don't know why you're so touchy."

"I'm not touchy, I just can't understand how a teacher has such terrible maths skills." She smirked back.

"I can't understand why you're not at work yet."

Scarlett

Scarlett glanced up at the clock and shrugged. "It's a bit quiet lately. I don't have a client till eleven." She tugged at the corner of her toast and yanked a piece off. "I might have to go back to the coffee shop at this rate."

"That bad, huh?"

"It's early days. Takes a while to build a new clientele list and art therapy isn't the go-to service for most people, so—" She blew out her cheeks. "Bills to pay and all that."

"I'm sure Mum is fine with it. Especially now, with this new job."

"Yeah, she's been great, but I want to feel like I'm contributing at least, you know?" Scarlett shoved the last piece of bread into her mouth and took a swig of coffee.

"Ew, that's disgusting."

"Coming from the woman who drinks spinach and pineapple smoothies?"

Zara rolled her eyes. "That's healthy, buttery toast and coffee? That's just grim."

Jacob made a grab for his teething ring and misjudged it, knocking it to the floor with a crash, he burst into a wailing sob.

"Alright mister, no need for such drama." Scarlett smiled, bending down to retrieve it. He wailed harder when she didn't immediately give it back to him, instead walking over to the sink to rinse it of any potential dirt and germs.

"I don't know where he gets it from?" Zara said, looking up as though she were thinking. "Oh, yes I do, Diana."

Scarlett laughed as she handed it back to him and the wailing stopped instantly. "I can imagine his other mummy is quite—"

"Overprotective? Overzealous? Fanatical?" She nodded. "Yes. But I wouldn't have it any other way. She's the best aunty."

She reached forward to wipe some spittle from his chin. "He's a lucky little boy to have so many strong, independent women to boss him around and make sure he turns into a decent young man."

"Amen to that." Scarlett raised her mug. "What do you have planned today?"

Picking up her book, Zara glanced down at Jacob before her eyes rose back up to find Scarlett's. "I think we might head to the park and go on the swings."

Scarlett
Chapter Three

The small room that used to be Adams, was now a fully working therapy room, with a large table, an easel, and shelf to hold all of the pots of pens and paints. Her client had just left, and she'd already tidied everything away and had the brushes soaking in paint cleaner. It was a nice space, but impractical in the long run. Anybody with walking difficulties would find it a problem, eventually she would need a proper space to work from.

Wandering downstairs, she realised how quiet it was when everyone else was out. Technically, it was only her and Claudia that shared the space, but all too often Claudia's daughters would appear with an overnight bag and wine, wanting to hang out with them.

That was a scenario that had taken Scarlett quite a while to get used to. Her own family life was nothing like this loving, open, and encouraging space the Maddox family lived in. And she had to admit, she loved it.

Flopping down on the sofa, she swung her legs up and contemplated what she was going to do to get her new business off the grounds properly. The one thing she didn't want was to get too used to leeching off of Claudia. It was enough that she lived here virtually for nothing anyway, there was no way she wasn't going to contribute towards bills.

Flicking through the posts of a local group on one of the apps, she spotted one that got her attention.

Looking for spiritually minded, local alternative therapists to share space within a modern location.

The address was somewhere right in the centre of town, with parking available. It looked perfect if she could afford it.

Pressing message, she wrote a quick note expressing her interest.

She heard the door open and the sounds of Zara shoving the pushchair through and dumping all of their stuff in the hallway.

Mumbling to herself, or Jacob, who most likely was fast asleep and not listening to his mummy at all. Scarlett giggled to herself and watched the living room door in anticipation of Zara appearing.

A minute later, the youngest member of the family bounded in child-free and launched herself into the armchair.

"Jacob sleeping, or have you sold him down the market for a new coat and some tickets to Glastonbury?" Scarlett smiled over at her.

Zara laughed. "You think I'd get that much for him?"

"If you're haggling skills are good enough."

Stretching out her neck, Zara considered it. "Nah, I think I'll keep him a little bit longer, I'm gonna need someone to run around after me when I'm your age."

"Oh, does that mean you should be running around after me?" Scarlett laughed at the face Zara pulled when she realised she'd put herself in it. "Want a cup of tea?"

Pulling her feet up and tucking them underneath her, Zara nodded. "I'd love one actually. The park was so busy. Bit of sunshine and everyone is out for a walk, kids screaming everywhere, it's exhausting." She yawned making the point. Truffle jumped down from the sofa and wandered over to Zara, rubbing himself on the corner of the armchair waiting for her to encourage him up. "Come on, Truff." Zara patted her leg and the feline furball jumped into her lap.

Scarlett swung her legs back off the couch and jumped up with the agility of an athlete. "Coming right up," she said to Zara, before adding, "Traitor," to Truffle.

As she entered the kitchen the sound of her phone ringing from her back pocket stopped her in her tracks. She pulled it out and smiled when the screen lit up and Claudia's smiling face stared back at her.

Scarlett

Swiping quickly, she answered the call, "Hello, gorgeous."

Claudia chuckled. "Hello, you. Are you free to talk?"

"Yep, the hordes of clients are banging at the door, but I'll hold them off for you."

"How kind. Still quiet?"

Scarlett sagged against the counter. "Yeah, but it will pick up." She tried to sound optimistic about it but wasn't so sure she managed to.

"Well, maybe I can cheer you up," Claudia whispered, and Scarlett felt that familiar arousal hit her senses.

"Oh yeah, are you gonna send me pictures of the…uh, sights, again?"

Claudia laughed again. "No, something more tangible." There was a pause before she added, "I'm taking the next flight, I'll be home this evening."

Scarlett felt all of the air leave her lungs in an instant. "Oh, that's the best news. Shall I pick you up at the airport?"

"If you like. I'll be arriving at Gatwick around seven. I'll text you the flight details. I can't wait to see you."

"Me too, Zara will be pleased too. And I'm sure Jacob would care if he understood." She chuckled and waited for the gushing she knew would come next.

"Goodness, I've missed him so much. Do not allow Zara to leave. Hold her hostage if you have to, lock her in the shed, do whatever it takes, I want to see my grandson."

"I'll just tell her you're looking forward to seeing her."

Giggling, Claudia said, "Of course I am." There was a knocking in the background. "I have to go, that's my assistant. The taxi must be here."

"Okay, go, go. And Claudia?"

"Yes?"

"Be safe, but hurry."

"I'm on my way, darling. Love you."

"I love you too."

The call ended and she did a little jig and felt her heart swell. Claudia was on her way home, and that meant she had things to do. Sheets to change, cleaning, and—she tapped her head with her finger trying to remember why she was in the kitchen.

"Tea!"

She hummed to herself as she made two cups and carried them back into the lounge, only to find Zara sound asleep. Putting the cups down, Scarlett grabbed the blanket from the back of the couch and gently laid it over her.

"I guess I can drink two cups before I get stuck in and organised for your mother's return."

Zara mumbled something incoherent as Scarlett sat back down and let herself enjoy the feeling of excitement that was stirring inside her.

Scarlett

Chapter Four

Arriving at the airport, Scarlett drove Claudia's new car up the ramps of the multistorey car park until she hit almost the top floor. Finding a space was always easier if you started at the top.

She wasn't used to driving something quite so big and didn't want to risk trying to park it between other cars if she could find a quiet spot out of the way. It was her lucky day, the level she was on was virtually empty as she swung the monster around and into a spot with nothing on either side for several spaces.

Treating herself, Claudia had bought the car she wanted. She didn't have to think about the kids, or how much it cost, or would cost. The Jeep was funky and stylish. Big, black and with tinted windows and huge chrome bumpers. Nothing like the kind of vehicle anyone would have expected a woman like Claudia to own. Zara said it made her look like a Kardashian or someone equally as rich and famous, calling it 'The Beast'. Claudia had laughed her off and smiled proudly at it. And when Scarlett's car needed more work doing to it than it was worth, she got used to the idea that she could use this whenever she needed it.

She locked it with a beep, and then skipped off towards the lifts and arrivals hall to wait.

Watching the screens that hung from brackets above her head, Scarlett searched for the flight number. EJ765 from Lisbon was due to land ten minutes ago. She felt fidgety staring up at it, willing the words to change from expected 19.15 to landed.

Looking around, she checked her watch again. Even if it landed now, there would still be a wait while Claudia got through security and customs, at least she didn't have to worry about baggage. Ever efficient, Claudia had only needed a flight bag. Scarlett had never realised how much you could fit in those. A spare suit, two pairs of shoes, and three blouses for work, plus a pair of Scarlett's tracksuit bottoms to lounge or sleep in, a couple of t-shirts and underwear.

Claudia had laughed as she rolled it all up and crammed it in. "Room service will iron it all once I arrive," she'd said, pushing her make-up bag in on top.

Scarlett spotted a coffee shop and wandered over, ordering a flat white, she found a seat in the corner and gazed up at the screens again.

EJ765 Lisbon Landed.

She grinned and took a sip of her drink. "Come on, come on." Her leg twitched and bounced with anticipation and then her phone rang.

"Just landed, won't be long. Where are you?" Claudia asked.

"Waiting very patiently in the coffee shop at arrivals," she lied, with a smile on her face.

Claudia chuckled. "Hm, patiently? Is your leg bouncing?"

Scarlett placed a palm on her knee and stopped it. "I'd be lying if I said no. Hurry up. I need to kiss you."

"Right now, I need...hold on." The line went muffled for a moment before Claudia's voice was back in her ear whispering, "I need you to do unspeakable things to me."

That hit the spot. "Like?" Scarlett glanced around her, aware that right now her face was the colour of fuchsia and her nether regions had just flooded with arousal.

"I'll leave that up to you," Claudia teased. "You know," there was another pause, "my car has tinted windows for a reason."

Scarlett was well aware of that too. The minute Claudia had arrived home with The Beast, she was reminded of their last vehicular experience in the back of Jack's car the night Jacob was born.

Scarlett

"You little minx." Scarlett faux gasped, as if she wasn't already fully aware of Claudia's adventurous side. "I did park in a quiet spot."

"Good girl. Okay, I'm just coming through customs, I'll be out soon."

The phone call ended, Scarlett downed the rest of her coffee and then quickly chewed some gum. No way was she kissing her lover after all these days apart with coffee breath. She chewed until she was satisfied her mouth was fresh again, then she wrapped it in a tissue and tossed it in the bin, heading back to the hall to wait where she could see those arriving from distant lands.

When Claudia eventually emerged from the throng, Scarlett burst forward and pulled her into an embrace, instantly claiming her mouth with her own. The kiss was firm and filled with meaning and emotion and all the things she couldn't find the words for. Breaking apart, Claudia glanced around quickly in case anyone was watching. She was getting better about not caring, but that fear still lingered a little. Not helped by the idiot who'd shouted dykes at them when they'd kissed at the park a couple of months back.

"Welcome home," Scarlett said, unable to take her eyes off of her. "I've missed you so much."

"Me too." Claudia smiled when she felt Scarlett's fingers slide between her own and the weight of the case being removed as her lover took charge and took it from her. "Let's get out of here."

Scarlett took off, dragging the case as fast as she could, with Claudia tottering along in high heels, giggling at the urgency.

"Sweetheart, hold on." Claudia stopped, much to Scarlett's frustration, then reached down and pulled off her shoes one by one. Barefoot, she reached for Scarlett's hand again, and this time, it was she who sped up.

As they reached the car, Scarlett unlocked it, already lifting the case and opening the boot simultaneously as Claudia climbed into the back seat. Scarlett placed it in as neatly as she cared to worry about and then darted around the other side of the vehicle. One quick check around that nobody had seen them, and she opened the door to climb inside.

A hand reached out and grabbed her shirt, pulling her into the car headfirst and straight into a heated kiss. The door slamming shut behind her, Scarlett reached back to press the lock down just as Claudia's tongue slid into her mouth and her perfume engulfed her.

"Mm," Claudia moaned, her hands roaming her lover's body, reconnecting with it, mapping its curves and valleys. "I want you so badly right now."

"Well, stop kissing me and let me—"

Claudia's eyes widened and locked on Scarlett. She hitched her skirt up enough to reach underneath and slid her underwear down her slim thighs. Scarlett's palms slipped around her, grabbing pert buttocks, squeezing.

"What do you need?"

"You, I don't care how." Claudia smirked, but pushed Scarlett back against the seat and straddled her. "Actually, I do care...I want your mouth on me."

Scarlett grinned, sliding down the leather as far as she could, her fingers pressing into that firm backside as she inched closer and closer. The scent of her girlfriend intoxicating enough, but when she flicked out her tongue and tasted her, her own arousal almost overcame her.

"Fuck," Claudia cried out as warm lips wrapped eagerly around her clit and sucked gently. Her fingers tousling through Scarlett's hair, tightening their grip every time Scarlett found that sweet spot that would have her writhing if it wasn't for the strong hands holding her in place. "Do not...stop."

Scarlett

Chapter Five

Zara opened the door before they were even out of the car. Standing on the step, she waved excitedly.

"Hey, Mum. How was it?" she asked when Claudia finally climbed from the car still barefooted.

"Honestly, it is a lovely hotel, one of our best, but I am so glad to be home." She reached Zara and pulled her in for a hug. "Now, where's my grandson?"

"Sometimes I think I should just leave him here and see how long it takes for you to notice I've left." Zara laughed as her mother all but pushed her through the door.

"Don't be so dramatic, I'd notice." Claudia grinned as she pulled off her jacket. "Eventually."

Scarlett came through the door smiling. "We'd realise it was far too quiet." She leaned in and kissed Claudia's cheek just because she could. "I'll take this through to the utility room." She held up the case. "And then I was thinking, take-away?"

Zara closed the door and turned to them both. "Well, I'm not sure I should have bothered, seeing as you're both so rude to me, but dinner is ready."

"I always said you were a useful thing to keep around." Scarlett smirked, now fully aware of the aroma coming from the kitchen.

"Don't get too excited, it's just spag bol from a jar."

"Thank you, sweetheart, that was very thoughtful," Claudia added, her palm touching her daughter's arm. "I am famished, it's been a long day."

Dinner was a raucous affair, once Jacob got stuck into the finely chopped-up spaghetti and sauce in his bowl. His face was smothered. His hands were too, and those sticky little fingers grabbed for anything they could get hold of. There was more of it on the floor and his table than had gone into his mouth.

Claudia snapped photos on her phone, while Zara paid no attention to his behaviour as she attempted to gain control over the spoon and actually have him eat something.

"This is delicious," Scarlett said as she swirled her fork and covered it in a huge roll of pasta. Shoving it into her mouth, she chewed quickly. "I must admit, I am ravenous."

"Was your flight delayed?" Zara asked, wiping Jacob's chin. "I tried to time things, but I was ready much earlier."

"Hm?" Claudia said, still smiling at Jacob while snapping more photos. "Oh, uh...yes, yes it was uh...delayed." Technically it was, by several minutes, so she wasn't lying.

Scarlett kept her head down, her cheeks reddening as she swirled another forkful and tried not to think about the £13 it had cost to be parked for that long. Even if it had been worth every penny.

"I thought I'd hang around until the weekend if that's alright. We can all go over to Adam's together on Saturday," Zara announced, giving up trying to get Jacob to eat from the spoon.

Claudia's eyes lit up, it was only Thursday.

"I have to work tomorrow, but from home, so that will be lovely. We can have lunch together, Scarlett how's your day looking?"

"Actually, I have a couple of clients in the morning, and then I need to go to town and have a meeting with someone about sharing some space."

Claudia put the phone down and turned towards her. "Oh, that's quick."

Scarlett

"I saw the ad earlier and asked for details. They've asked if I want to come down and take a look, so…" She shrugged and smiled with a hopeful look on her face.

Reaching out, Claudia covered Scarlett's hand with her own. "I'll miss you not being around when I'm here." Then a thought hit her. "Maybe we can turn the room into Jacob's playroom?"

"Might want to let Scarlett actually move out of it first, Mum." Zara laughed. "You know, I think if I started any request with *Jacob needs*…I could get anything out of her."

Scarlett chuckled, she was definitely right there.

"Jacob needs £100 a month to spend on spa treatments for mummy," Zara continued to joke. "Jacob needs a new car."

Claudia became very serious, "Do you need a new car?"

"No." Zara laughed loudly, throwing her head back and making Jacob jump in the process. "Sorry, Jakey." She chuckled. "Myrtle is still doing just fine, we make it work, don't we kiddo?"

The little blue Mini had been a big topic of conversation since Jacob entered the word. It wasn't safe enough, big enough, reliable enough according to everyone who felt the need to have an opinion, and yet, Zara was right, she made it work.

"Myrtle?" Scarlett asked, "I was unaware your car had a name."

Zara shrugged. "Diana said she needed one, so we decided on Myrtle, it suits her."

"Interesting, I'd have gone with Mavis."

"Hm, I could get on board with that, okay, she's Myrtle Mavis from now on."

Claudia stood up and collected the empty plates. Piling them on top of one another before Scarlett stood and took them off of her. "I'll do that, you clean up that hot mess." She jutted her chin at the

20

grinning, chubby-legged, kicking, tomato-covered demon staring up at them all.

"Thank you." Turning to Jacob Claudia grinned and held her hands out. "Are you coming with granny to get all cleaned up and ready for bed?"

"He should have been in bed two hours ago, but his nap lasted a little longer this afternoon,"

"I think he must have known his nanna was coming home." Claudia gushed and unclipped him from the highchair. "Say goodnight to mummy." She held him towards Zara, who kissed his cheek.

"Goodnight, sweet boy."

"Night night, Scarlett," Claudia said for him, holding his hand and waving it at her girlfriend.

"Night Jacob, try not to let Nanna fall asleep with you."

Zara rolled her eyes. "God, do I need to use headphones tonight?"

It took a moment before it registered with Claudia, the blush instant on her cheeks, but she hit back instantly.

"I would, something loud, darling." She winked and whisked Jacob out of the room before Zara could close her mouth and find a comeback.

"She's getting a bit too good at that." Zara grinned at Scarlett, helping to take the dishes out into the kitchen. "But seriously, I know you've missed each other, and I know my being here is probably the biggest passion killer ever."

"Don't worry, I've got a gag."

Zara's eyes widened.

Scarlett

"The look on your face. Priceless." Scarlett laughed winning the one-upmanship for today.

Chapter Six

With the kitchen cleaned, dishes washed, and everything put away in all of the relevant cupboards. Scarlett headed upstairs. Entering their room, she switched the side lamp on and the main light off and grabbed a towel.

She needed a shower.

Stripping off, she stepped under the hot water that flowed instantly as she pressed the button to switch it on.

"That looks very inviting." Claudia's voice filtered through the sound of the water splashing down around her.

Scarlett swung around, opening her eyes to find Claudia leaning against the door frame watching her intently. Her eyes sweeping the length of Scarlett's body before settling back on her face.

"You look a little over dressed for our anniversary."

Claudia pushed off from the wall, biting her lower lip, before smiling and still holding Scarlett's gaze. "Well, that is easily remedied."

Her fingers moved slowly to undo the top button of her blouse, working rhythmically downward as each one popped from its cotton cradle and the gap between the material widened, a little more skin on view until all six were undone and the blouse fell open, a black lace bra just visible. "Happy anniversary."

Reaching behind her, she undid the skirt that earlier had been hiked up her thighs with such ease and shimmied it down until it landed in a pool around her feet, revealing her matching black lace panties. Scarlett watched with intense scrutiny, enjoying every moment of the impromptu striptease.

"Every morning, I would imagine this," Claudia said, her eyes scanning the naked form in front of her once more. "I'd imagine you already in the shower waiting for me." She undid the button on one cuff. "Naked and wet." The other cuff followed as she stepped forward. "Waiting for me…" She shrugged her shoulders and the silk material slid away with ease, revealing her clavicle and the straps of her bra. She shimmied some more, and the blouse slipped with no effort to land on top of the skirt.

Scarlett held her gaze for as long as she could but the need to look at all of her became too strong, and her eyes dropped to take in her lover as she stood there, confident, and sexy, turned on.

"I'm waiting now," Scarlett responded.

"I know." Claudia unclipped her bra and pulled it off, freeing her breasts, excited nipples already erect and puckered. She smiled at the arousal that caused a small shiver to visibly run through Scarlett. "Like what you see?"

Scarlett nodded. "Very much, you know I do."

"I do." She reached for her underwear and this time when she dragged them down, she tossed them to the side. The perfectly trimmed triangle between her legs drawing Scarlett's eyes.

"Get in here," Scarlett urged, no longer able to hold back her need to reach out and touch. She wanted this woman, wanted to show her in every way possible just how much she adored her. And she wanted to feel that in return too.

The water cascaded over them like it had done many times in the past year. There was something about the water that Scarlett found erotic, the way that it trickled down their skin. Small rivulets dripping to pool in clavicles, licked away by the sweeping of a tongue hungry to quench its thirst elsewhere.

Her hands gliding across Claudia's skin, electrifying their way lower to dive into the depths of her. A different kind of wet. One she would never tire of.

"I've missed this," Scarlett admitted. "I know that—" Her mouth was kissed hungrily before those lips moved on to her neck. "I know it's only been a few days…but—" She felt her chin grasped and held firmly. Claudia's eyes intently set on her.

"Right now, I just want to fuck you, so can we put this…" she waved a finger around, "conversation on hold just long enough so that I can focus on all of the things I've been fantasising about doing to you?"

Scarlett grinned. "I guess I can do that."

"Good, now—" Claudia's fingers slipped between Scarlett's thighs and pressed against her swollen clitoris. Claudia smiled as Scarlett's head fell back against the tiles, her stance widening as she whimpered. Her muscles twitching with every deft movement. "Much better…right?"

"Uh huh," was all Scarlett could manage.

Lying in bed, Claudia mewled and stretched contentedly against Scarlett's side. Her fingertips scratching gently across the soft skin of her lover in patterns that had no real design.

"So, what was it you wanted to talk about?"

"Hm?" Scarlett's eyes were closed, equally satisfied. She was drifting off to the gentle sensations on her skin, akin to someone playing with her hair, it was just so relaxing.

Claudia leaned up on her elbow. "In the shower, before I manhandled you." She giggled. "You said, I know it's only been a few days, but…" She let her fingers walk up Scarlett's torso, between her breasts, to her chin, which she once again grasped and pulled towards her. "What was the but?"

Scarlett smiled lazily. "I dunno… I missed you, I missed us."

Claudia chuckled. "I shall be making it clear that in future they will have to fly you out for conjugal visits."

Scarlett

Rolling onto her side, Scarlett's eyes opened wide. "I mean we could arrange it so that I come with you, but..." She reached out and stroked Claudia's cheek. "I don't want us to become that couple who can't do anything without each other. It's healthy for us both to spend time apart, we end up with nights like this."

"You're right. I don't know how I'll function in the morning but right now, I have never felt more fulfilled."

Scarlett rolled back, smiling she said, "You're welcome."

"But seriously though." Claudia rolled again until she was all but on top of Scarlett. "It could be a perfect opportunity to take a break, for you I mean, I'd have to work still but you'd get to explore and soak up the sun, all for the price of an airfare."

"Well, when you put it like that." She craned her neck and puckered her lips for the kiss that was hovering just out of reach.

"And I'm not working the entire time, so we'd get time apart and time together." Claudia closed the space between them and kissed her before settling down against Scarlett's chest.

"You should be in sales, you know that, right?"

"I practically am, organising this renovation and only coming in at the last moment, has been a steep learning curve."

"It's late. Go to sleep and tell me all about it tomorrow."

Chapter Seven

Jacob wailing was not the way Claudia had hoped to wake up. Her eyes were sore, her body ached. Though she would never complain about that. Her thoughts instantly returned to the night before and images of Scarlett adoring her in the way nobody else had ever managed to.

She licked her lips and felt around the bed for her girlfriend, and found it empty, but still warm. Smiling to herself when she heard the loo flush and the scrape of the door against the carpet. She breathed deeply and inhaled the scent of Scarlett from the pillow.

"What time is it?" Claudia mumbled, her eyes half open and fighting the light that blazed through the blinds they'd forgotten to close in their haste to get naked with one another.

She felt the mattress dip as Scarlett sat down on the edge.

"It's just after eight. I was going to go and make some coffee."

"Mm coffee, you're a lifesaver," Claudia said with more coherence this time, though her eyes remained firmly shut. "I'll get up in a bit."

"Stay there. Nobody here is going to snitch that you were late to work." Scarlett smiled as she leaned down and kissed Claudia's head. "I'll be back with the coffee, and croissants?"

"Mm," was all she managed before sleep took her again.

Zara paced around the kitchen bouncing Jacob on her hip while trying to boil the kettle.

"Need a hand?" Scarlett asked.

Scarlett

"God, I'm so sorry, he doesn't usually do this... I think he's teething again."

Reaching out her hands, Scarlett took the screaming demon and bounced him just like Zara had done. "Coffee, lots of it." Scarlett smiled, picking up his teething ring, "We'll be back." And with that, she wandered towards the back door and out into the sunny back garden.

His face was as red as a beetroot.

"Here you go, Jacob Michael, get your gums on that." She held it out for him. At first, he dodged it, moving his head side to side and waling even harder. "You know if you wake up grumpy Mr Brian next door, he won't be happy."

"Too late for that." Came the sharp reply over the fence along with a chuckle. The bald head came into view first before glasses and a moustache followed. "He's on one today then?"

Scarlett bounced and walked towards the fence, Jacob finally accepting the plastic ring and chomping down on it. "Yep, new tooth we think, just giving Zara a moment to compose herself and take a break, and let Claudia sleep in, though I am pretty sure the entire street is now awake, hey Jakey?"

"Oh, is she back, I need a word. These fence panels are about done for. I thought we could go halves and get them replaced?"

"Coffee's ready," Zara shouted from the doorway. "Hi, Brian." She waved at them all and grinned.

Jacob decided that the multiple conversations and faces were much more interesting than his screaming and the little whimpering hiccups subsided.

"Hi, Zara." Brian waved back before turning his attention back to Scarlett. "Just get her to give me a shout when she's got a minute."

"Will do, catch you later." Scarlett turned and bounced Jacob back towards the house. "Feeling better now?" she asked him. His wet eyelashes blinked a couple of times as he chowed down on the ring once more.

As she stepped back into the kitchen, Claudia reached out and took Jacob, kissing Scarlett in the process. "I gave in and got up. Has anyone fed Truffle?" she asked as the cat made his presence known.

"Thanks for calming him down. I found the Bonjela, it was in the bottom of my bag." Zara waved the tube of teething gel until Claudia took it and sat down with him. "I'll sort Truff."

"Only another fourteen to go." Claudia smiled up at her. Jacob's teeth were all on track and making an appearance one by one. "He's going to have a cracker of a smile, aren't you sweetheart, yes you are." She cooed at the baby.

"I don't know whether I'm glad I missed out on motherhood, or wish I'd been part of it with you," Scarlett said, watching as Claudia turned into a babbling crazy lady. Hair unbrushed, make-up free, dressing gown and slippers. She looked nothing like the woman Scarlett had first met that night in Art. And yet, she was just as stunning.

"All those dirty nappies and sleepless nights?" Claudia smiled at her. "I might have liked doing that with you too."

"Well, thank god you're both past that idea, I don't need any more siblings arriving this late in life, thank you, especially with a twenty-plus year age gap, although Jacob might like bossing his aunt or uncle around, I suppose." Zara giggled at the idea. "Fancy having a kid Scarlett?"

Scarlett grabbed an apple, biting into it and ignoring her before she said, "I wouldn't get your hopes up on that."

Claudia nodded. "This is much more fun." She kissed Jacob's chubby red cheek, "But...I need to get dressed for a zoom meeting." She kissed him again before reluctantly handing him back to Zara.

Scarlett

"Oh, Brian wants a word about fencing when you have five minutes." Scarlett imparted the almost forgotten message.

The sound of the doorbell echoing down the hallway brought the conversations to a halt. Zara looked like a startled deer in the headlights, while Claudia pulled at her robe more tightly, and Scarlett glanced at her watch. Almost nine.

"That's my first client, do you want to…" She indicated to Claudia that maybe now would be the time to go upstairs and get dressed.

"Yes, I'm on it. Have a good day, both of you." She turned and quickly exited the kitchen.

"I'll take him out for a bit, not sure him screaming his head off will be quite conducive to art therapy."

She took a last bite of her apple. "Thanks, Z. I've got two, both forty minutes, back-to-back," Scarlett explained, walking towards the door. She dropped the apple core into the bin. "So, I'll be done by eleven."

"Alright, maybe lunch after then, before you head into town?"

Scarlett pointed fingers at her. "Sounds like a plan."

Chapter Eight

Claudia worked through lunch, while Zara, Jacob and Scarlett headed into town to their favourite spot, Banjo. One member of the family came here at least once a week in various eating parties. Claudia met up with Bea and Liz. Scarlett and Diana often caught up with a coffee or drinks in the evening. And obviously, Scarlett and Claudia enjoyed date night here quite often before heading to Art for a dance and some drinks.

"I'm surprised we don't have a recognised table by now," Scarlett said, taking her seat. The wait staff knew her by name.

Zara stood waiting patiently while a highchair was brought over. "I think we should petition for one." She smiled at the waiter and mouthed a thank you as she slipped Jacob into it and strapped him in. "Oh, I meant to say, remember we did the DNA thing? I've had an email, so I'll forward your results later. "

"That's taken ages," Scarlett answered. Zara had bought them for Christmas, and they'd sent them off in the early new year. "It will be interesting to find out where our DNA comes from. My mum's family is small, and my dad has never really mentioned his so, I've no idea what my roots are."

"I already know my mum's side are Irish, but Dad's grandmother came from Hungary, escaping the Nazis during the war, so I really want to find out more about that."

Scarlett's eyes flashed animatedly. "I'm excited to see. Wouldn't it be fab if it said something exotic that you just had no idea about, although if it says anything exotic about my parents I'll be surprised." Scarlett laughed.

The building looked just as good in person as it had in the photos. From the outside anyway. Scarlett peered up at the two-storey white-clad structure and smiled. It was the kind of place you might expect to find a therapy centre.

Zara parked the car into one of the spots marked out for Spiritually Sound.

"Looks nice," she said to Scarlett.

"Yeah, it does. Just wondering how expensive it's going to be."

Switching the engine off, Zara turned to her. "Only one way to find out. Want me to come in with you?"

Scarlett shrugged. "If you want, I don't know how long I'll be though. If you wanted to get back, I can jump on the bus."

"Nah, Mum's just going to be on the computer, and if I take him back, she's going to be distracted."

"True, come on then." Scarlett climbed out of the car, went around to the back of it and opened the surprisingly roomy boot space to drag out the pushchair. She unbent and clicked it all into place before wheeling it around just in time. Zara straightened up with Jacob in her arms. His wide eyes taking it all in as she placed him into the seat and strapped him in again.

"Right little man, shall we go see a room?"

They walked side by side until they came to the automatic doors that swished open, and Scarlett stepped to one side to allow Zara and Jacob through and into a reception area. Spacious, bright and airy, a huge desk ran half the length of one side. Two smiling faces looked towards them.

"Hi." Scarlett smiled in return. "I'm here to meet Gabby."

Before anyone else could speak, a voice came from behind them, well-spoken, but not posh. A hint of excitement in her tone. "Hi, you must be Scarlett, thanks so much for coming down." She held out a hand before glancing at Zara.

"Hey, Gabby, right?" Scarlett shook the proffered hand. "This is Zara and Jacob." There was an awkward moment when no further explanation came.

"Okay, so, let me show you around." Gabby turned. "We have several different styles of therapy here, everything for mind, body, and soul. Our rooms are available on a daily or weekly basis, whichever works for you as you build your client base." She walked them down the hall past several doors. When they reached the end, she stopped. "This is the room we are releasing now. Obviously, we can provide basic furniture and equipment, anything specialised would be down to you."

She slid a key into the lock, twisted and turned the knob, opening the door wide enough to walk through and pull it all the way open.

"As you can see, all of our doors are built for wheelchair access."

Scarlett nodded and followed her in, Zara taking up the rear. The room was bigger than she thought it would be. The huge windows to the back of the building overlooked a small patch of grassed area with trees creating the boundary. Not a car in sight. A large built-in cupboard in the corner was open and she wandered over to take a look. Deep enough to walk into, it would definitely hold all of her equipment should she take the room full-time.

As though reading her mind, Gabby stepped up behind her. "As you can see there's plenty of space, even if the room was a shared venture, each of you could easily leave your daily equipment safely locked away."

That was a good solution to Scarlett not having to commandeer The Beast to carry her stuff back and forth or have to empty it out each night.

"And what is the weekly and daily rental like?" Zara piped up.

Scarlett

Gabby turned and smiled. "Well, that's the golden question, isn't it? Okay, here's the sales pitch. We have a very strong belief that therapy should be available to all. Whether that be art therapy or physiotherapy. Our set up is complex but simple. The entire building was donated to us by a local benefactor, we therefore have no rent on the building and as such, can price the rooms in a way that encourages our therapists to price their talents accordingly. Our rental fee is inclusive of all bills for lighting, heating etc., as well as staff such as those on reception, cleaners and maintenance, and insurances on the building and equipment. You will need your own liability insurance." She smiled before she continued, "we have twelve rooms here, as well as a conference room, small kitchen, and staff restroom. This room would be £13 per hour, £75 per day, or £250 per week based on a five-day working week, Monday to Friday."

Scarlett nodded, that was indeed a good price, and this room would be snapped up pretty quickly. "So, if I took it on a weekly basis, what would the contract be like? Am I locked in for a set time period?"

Gabby shook her head. "No, as you can imagine, we don't have trouble filling these spaces when they become available, so we've no need to lock anyone in. We truly believe that once you start working here under the Spiritually Sound umbrella, you won't want to leave."

"Wow, well, I guess I need to make a very quick decision."

"I have several others looking, but we run a fair policy here, you're the first on the list, so regardless of anything else, we will work down the list. If you need twenty-four hours to think about it, then that's fine, you'll have first refusal."

Scarlett looked at Zara, her brow raised at Scarlett in a what are you waiting for way. Glancing around the room once more, Scarlett nodded. "I'm going to take it."

"Excellent, well, let's head on up to the office and get the paperwork organised." Gabby beamed at her. "Oh, and welcome aboard, Scarlett."

Scarlett

Chapter Nine

"How did it go?" Claudia asked once they were all inside and out of their jackets. She closed up her laptop and got up to greet them both before taking Jacob and wandering off to the kitchen.

"Something smells good," Scarlett said, breathing in the aroma. She'd gotten used to home-cooked meals again and loved it whenever Claudia threw something together for dinner.

"It was awesome," Zara gushed. "The room is big, and bright, perfect for art."

Claudia smiled at her excitable youngest child before turning her attention towards Scarlett. "You liked it?"

Scarlett nodded. "Yeah, I did, and it's a bargain, to be honest,"

"Well, I am not going to pretend I won't miss you around the place, but I am pleased you've found a workable space that you can build from, and I think it will be good for you to be back out amongst people again instead of cooped up in here all day."

"You're right, and you're in the office more than you are at home now anyway, so, I'm excited about it."

Zara reached for Jacob. "He needs changing,"

Alone, Claudia gravitated towards Scarlett. Threading her arms around her lover's slim waist. "So, should we go out and celebrate?"

"And miss out on whatever you've cooked up, no chance." Scarlett smiled down at her. "Plus, we'd only have to rush back to celebrate in private."

"Oh, that is true. I'd best get back to it so I can finish on time. I've another meeting on zoom." She leaned up and placed a gentle kiss on Scarlett's lips. "Congratulations, darling, you're going to make a great success of it."

Scarlett watched as Claudia sauntered out of the kitchen, then she fished her phone from her pocket and found her emails, opening the one from Zara. As she read through it there wasn't too much of a surprise. She was 49% British. But the next percentage flummoxed her, 34% Eastern European. Then it was 5% Scandinavian, 4% French, 2% Italian. How many British-born people of British heritage didn't have some Scandinavian with the Viking history of invasion, same with the French and the Romans, but Eastern European? Where had that come from?

She opened the app they'd used. The one you could build your family tree but also read a more accurate description of your DNA and see if you matched with anyone.

There were several notifications waiting and she clicked the little letter icon to open and read.

You've got matches.

"Well, in for a penny." She clicked the link that opened the section where your matches were. "That doesn't make sense," she whispered as she read the first name listed at the top.

Zarabara. The name Zara had chosen for the app.

Shared DNA: 1.853 centimorgans.

Possible DNA relationships

Percentage:

25%

Relationship:

Grandparent, Grandchild, half-sibling, Aunt/Uncle, Niece/Nephew.

She scanned the next name on the list, Adamski. Same conclusion, they were related. There had to be a mix-up.

"Zara?" she called out. "I think you sent me Diana's results."

Scarlett

"What?" she shouted back from somewhere upstairs.

Scarlett wandered into the hall and shouted up from the bottom of the stairs, "I said…"

"Will you two please stop shouting, I'm on a video call," Claudia admonished, poking her head around the door, her headset still in place.

"Sorry." Scarlett silently mouthed. She took the stairs two at a time until she reached the top and found Zara in her room with the door open. "I said, I think you've sent me Diana's results instead of mine."

Zara stared blankly at her before continuing on with the task of dressing Jacob into another outfit.

"The DNA? I think you've sent me Diana's results."

"I can't have," Zara answered buttoning up Jacob's miniature-sized dungarees.

"Well, you must have," Scarlett insisted, because that was the only thing that made sense. "They must have got switched when we sent them off."

Zara tunned to face her, hands now on her hips. "I definitely haven't."

"Can you just check though?" Scarlett asked, an uneasy feeling coming over her.

"Scarlett, I don't need to check. I know for a fact they're your results, because Diana didn't do one. It was just you, me and Adam and Adam did his own, so I didn't get his results. I only got mine and yours. I set up two Ancestry accounts, one for you, and one for me. didn't have your email address, so I just used an old one of mine, but other than that, it's all yours."

"Are you winding me up? Is that it? it's a big joke, right?" She felt relief as she said it. "Honestly, you lot are so mean."

Zara's brow furrowed. "Seriously, I don't know what you're talking about, those are your results."

She held Zara's gaze, and there was no wavering. No tiny tell, or little crease in the corner of the eyes as she tried not to laugh.

Zara wasn't joking.

Scarlett felt the room start to spin, nausea rushing over her. Something was very wrong with the results because the alternative just couldn't be true, could it?

"Are you alright? What's wrong?" Zara asked, checking Jacob was safely in the centre of the bed before quickly reaching for Scarlett, and making her sit on the bed. "You look like you're going to throw up."

"I might. Have you checked the results?"

"No, I haven't had a chance, why?" She giggled. "Has it said you're not human?"

"Worse," Scarlett mumbled while Zara found her phone and opened the app. "Just…check the matches, the DNA relationship matches." Maybe it was just a glitch and Zara's would say something completely different, but as she watched Zara's face, she realised it didn't.

"What? That's impossible. How can—"

"It is, right, it's impossible. It's a glitch, they must have assumed we are the same person?"

Zara was quiet. She opened the email she'd been sent and read through the percentages on hers and Scarlett's. "No, they're different, look. I have a 33% Irish dependency on parent one, you don't. We have the same percentages for parent two."

"So, this means—" Scarlett looked up with watery blue eyes and met Zara's gaze.

Scarlett

"It means that one of our fathers is a cheating bastard, and I have a pretty good idea which one it is, given his history for it."

"I can't believe this."

Zara sat down on the edge of the bed beside Scarlett. "Look, it says here, the link *is* on the paternal side. We're clearly not grandparent and grandchild, pretty sure you don't have any siblings so we can't be niece and aunt, that only leaves one possibility." Zara's eyes widened at the realisation, "We're half-siblings."

"Half—" Scarlett couldn't take it in, what did this mean for them all, what did it mean for her? She'd never felt close to her dad admittedly, but she'd always known that was who he was, now this was suggesting it wasn't the case. Because Zara was right, it had to be that way around. She tried to do the maths in her head. She was just under a year older than Diana. And what did that mean for her and Claudia?

"You're...my sister?" Zara stated breaking Scarlett's thoughts.

"We can't be, we don't look anything alike." The room began to swim again, this wasn't real, was it? She was just dreaming, a nightmare more like. But as she looked again, she realised something she'd never taken any notice of before. They did have similarities.

Chapter Ten

When Scarlett came around, she felt groggy and confused. As her vision came back, she could see two worried faces looming over her.

Claudia and Zara.

"You just slid to the floor and passed out," Zara said explaining.

"Are you alright? Do we need to get you checked out?" Claudia looked more worried as she spoke, stroking Scarlett's face and using the back of her hand to check for a temperature.

"I'm fine…I…did you tell her?" Scarlett looked at Zara. The younger woman shook her head, helping Scarlett back up from the floor.

"Tell me what?" Claudia looked confused. Her gaze moving back and forth between the pair of them.

"I'm sure it's all just a big mistake," Zara began, but the look on Claudia's face told her to stop stalling and spit it out. "We did the DNA thing, right? At Christmas?"

Claudia nodded. She'd thought it was a ridiculous idea, but they were having so much fun talking about family histories that she'd not given it a second thought.

"Yes, what about it?"

"You might want to sit down," Zara warned. Not quite sure how she would manage with two of them passing out.

"Zara!" Claudia raised her voice. "For the love of god, spit it out." She was losing the will to live.

"Alright, I'm trying to think how best to say it." She took a deep breath. "The results say that Scarlett and I, and Adam, and I presume by default, Diana." She looked at Scarlett, who just nodded. "It would seem…that, well—"

Scarlett

"It says we're related," Scarlett finally answered. "It says that we're half-siblings and that we share DNA on our father's side."

Claudia's face went ashen. Her mouth gaped open. Slowly, she sat down on the edge of the bed and stared at the floor, her own mind running through the scenarios.

"It's probably just a mistake, right?" Zara laughed nervously. But what were the chances?

"If you were born—then that would mean—" Claudia did the mental calculations. "That you were conceived around the time Jack and I got married, and you were born around the time that I was pregnant with Diana." Her eyes sparkled with unshed tears as the realisation became apparent. "Jack is—"

"My father."

"Fuck," Zara whispered as it was finally spoken aloud.

"Uck." Jacob copied.

"Shit," Zara said at her faux pas.

"Sh," Jacob copied again. At any other moment, it might have been funny.

"What do we do?" Scarlett finally asked. "What the hell do we do?" Her fingers pushed through her hair and then lingered around the back of her neck. "You're like my—"

"No." Claudia held up a hand. "No, I am not. I have never been a maternal figure, I didn't even know you existed before we met, so no…just no."

"We need a family meeting," Zara announced. Her eyes widening at the stares she received from the both of them. "We need to tell Adam and Diana, Adam has the results too, it won't take long before he gets around to reading them and then he will tell Diana, or worse, go straight to Dad, and goodness knows what he'd do then."

"I need to speak to my mother." Scarlett got up and brushed herself down. "I need to know what happened."

"And I need to speak with Jack," Claudia seethed.

Scarlett reached out, taking her hand, and kissing the palm. "I know it's a lot to ask, but would you hold off, just till I get some answers. My mum won't lie to me, not if I ask her straight out. We should have all the facts before we upend everyone's lives."

"Science doesn't lie, Scarlett," Claudia answered angrily. How could Jack be so—she shook her head, of course he could, that was Jack, wasn't it, selfish. "You're right, I'm sorry, I'm just so angry right now. Do you need me to come with you?"

Shaking her head, Scarlett said, "No, I think given the circumstances that your presence might be a little intimidating."

Claudia stood up. "She had an affair with my husband, it will definitely be intimidating."

Scarlett looked away, uncomfortable with thinking about her mother that way, but it was potentially true.

"We don't know all of the facts, we don't know under what circumstance they met, if they did. It could just be a glitch, it could be they couldn't have kids and Jack helped out with an anonymous donation, we just don't know."

"You're being very calm about all of this," Claudia answered, aware that Scarlett was right.

"Trust me, inside my guts are churning, but I need the truth and that's only going to come if I can keep calm and we can talk like adults."

When nothing more was forthcoming, she looked up and found Claudia on the verge of tears, but it was Zara staring at her that caught her attention.

Scarlett

"What?" Scarlett asked with a little too much hostility than she intended. "Sorry."

Zara shrugged. "I just—I can see it. Now, when I look at you I can see...Dad. I can see me."

Scarlett paced the garden. Treading down the grass that needed cutting as she strode back and forth, her mind awash with so many thoughts and images. The how, was her main question. How was it possible? If it was true, how did it happen? And then came the whys. Why had nobody told her? Did Jack know? Did her dad know?

Her dad, that made so much sense now, didn't it? They'd never had anything in common. And she did favour her mum when it came to how she looked. She got her blue eyes from her mum, her frame, her smile, but she looked nothing like her dad really other than she was quite tall.

"Are you alright?" Claudia's voice broke through the fog of her thoughts, and she stopped moving, their eyes connecting, before her lip trembled and Claudia was marching across the patio towards her.

"I don't know," Scarlett whimpered. Her shoulders sagged. " don't know who I am anymore."

Claudia's arms pulled her in, one hand around the back of her head, cradling her into her shoulder. "Yes, you do. Nothing has changed, you're still you."

Chapter Eleven

Standing outside of her parents' house, without a key to the door, only reminded her how little she thought of this as home now. Thinking of Claudia's place, and how her children all still had their keys, and used them, regularly, gave her a sense of sadness that she'd never felt that level of security, and maybe she was about to discover why.

The door opened, revealing her dad, if that's who he was now, staring down at her from his lofty position of being one step higher.

"Oh, it's you," he answered. Without another word, he turned and walked away back down the hallway. Leaving Scarlett to decide whether to come in or leave, he clearly didn't care either way.

She bit her tongue and released a breath, the one that had been suffocating her for the last hour, and then she stepped up and inside, closing the door quietly behind her. Looking around her, nothing much had changed. The walls were still the same muted shade of cream, scuffed in places where furniture had been moved over the years. The carpet could probably do with being replaced but she knew it wouldn't be, not before it was threadbare and there was no other choice.

Passing the living room door, she glanced in at her dad sitting in his chair, facing the TV, watching the racing. A steaming mug of tea sat on the side table, so at least she knew her mum was home. God forbid he got up and made himself a cuppa.

Scarlett made her way further down the hallway and into the kitchen where her mum was bending over the stove and inspecting what must be that evening's dinner. Looked like shepherd's pie. Scarlett used to love coming home from school to find that on the table.

"Hey, Mum," she said when the oven door closed, and her mum righted herself.

Scarlett

"Oh, Jesus Christ, Scarlett." Her hand flew to her chest. Flustered, she wiped her hands on a tea towel before smiling at her daughter and giving her a hug. "It's good to see you, how are things at Claudia's?"

"At home, you mean?"

"Yes. Of course." She smiled uncertainly at the way Scarlett was looking at her. "It's nice to see you."

Scarlett leaned against the door jamb and studied her mum. She looked tired as usual, and it was barely three in the afternoon. And Scarlett was doing all she could to hold it together and not scream about the unfairness of everything.

"Thing is, I have something I need to ask you, and I'm not sure you're going to like it, but I need you to be truthful with me," Scarlett finally said.

Her mum looked hurt by that statement. The atmosphere thickening with every passing second.

"What do you mean? I'm always truthful with you."

Scarlett nodded, she had always thought that was true, now though, she wasn't as convinced.

Her mum's arms wrapped around herself defensively, self-soothing, sensing an attack. "Go on then, what did you want to ask?"

The entire drive over, Scarlett had considered what was the best way to say it. To ask the question neither of them would be comfortable with. In the end, she hadn't come up with anything more than to just say it. So, she did. "Who is my father?"

She watched closely at her mum's reaction. Her spine stiffened, her cheeks losing their rosy colour. Her jaw clenching before she breathed deeply and laughed nervously. Caught in the lie.

"What do mean? Where's that come from, you know who your dad is, he's in the living room."

"Is he?" Scarlett stared at her. "Is he really my father? My biological father, not the man who barely brought me up."

"Scarlett." The way her mum said her name sounded more like she was pleading than anything else. "Why…I mean, what…he's your dad." She pointed towards the man in the house somewhere, ignoring them. There was a hint of panic in her eyes, and in the way she wouldn't quite look at Scarlett anymore.

"But he's not my father, is he?" Scarlett stated, rather than asking, this time because her mother's body language and reaction were telling her everything she needed to know to confirm the DNA results. "My father is Jack Maddox, isn't he?"

"Jack Maddox? I don't know any Jack Maddox. This is ridiculous, Scarlett please." Her mum turned away, busying herself with something unseen.

Scarlett pushed off from the door frame and moved closer to her mother, ignoring the slight flinch as she gently twisted her mum back around to face her. "I need you to tell me the truth."

Her mother's tears made her heart break. She pulled her close and into an embrace that she hoped conveyed the love she had for one her.

"I'm sorry," her mum whispered between sobs. "We should have told you."

"You don't have to be sorry, just tell me the truth, tell me what happened and how Jack Maddox is my father."

Her mum slumped in her arms. "Okay, but not here." Without another word, she left the kitchen expecting Scarlett to follow. Which she did. Grabbing keys and coats, they left the house.

Scarlett

The local park was as good a place as any to have this conversation. Away from her dad overhearing and making it all about him. Walking arm in arm in silence, Scarlett tried to keep her thoughts from running away with themselves, until she couldn't take it any longer. There was a bench, and she gently led her mum towards it. Settling beside one another before either spoke.

"So, what happened?" she finally asked. Her mum looked away, across the grass towards some kids playing football with jumpers for goalposts.

"I didn't know. Not for sure, not until it was obvious." She shook her head in disbelief and then frowned. "How did you find out?"

"Zara, Adam and I, we did one of those DNA things, family history and stuff, it was supposed to just be for fun, but the results said I was a half-sibling—Jack Maddox is their dad, Claudia's ex-husband."

"Oh, Jesus, how could this happen? I mean, what are the odds?"

Scarlett shrugged. "Right now, that's not what I'm concerned about. I need to know what happened?"

Her mum sighed, closed her eyes, and remembered back to the night that would change her life.

"I'd just met your dad, we'd only been out a few times, but he was fun." She laughed at Scarlett's raised brow. "He was," she insisted with a shy smile. "He had a boyish charm and a good sense of humour; he made me laugh."

"Somehow I can't imagine that but go on."

Her mum took another deep breath. "Like I said, I'd only just met him, it was nothing serious at that point. One weekend I was out with some friends, and we were having a good time, dancing, and drinking when this group of lads came in. It was a stag do. They were all as drunk as we were and well, one of them stood out, started

48

chatting to me. His name was Jack, I never got his surname." She blushed. "I'm not proud. It wasn't my finest moment, but we were all young and living in the moment, and this was his last night of freedom—"

"So, you slept with him?"

Her mum nodded. "A one-time thing that was over in minutes and forgotten about before the night ended. I went home, your dad started wooing me with more intent and we got together, it was about four months in that I realised I was pregnant. Your dad wasn't an idiot, the dates didn't work for it to have been 100 percent his, but he agreed to take me on anyway, so long as nobody ever found out."

"And that's why he hates me?" Scarlett whispered.

Her mum reached for her hand. "He loves you, when you were born, I'd never seen anyone more in love with a baby, but…as you grew, it was more obvious you weren't his. You looked like me in a lot of ways, but you didn't look anything like him other than your hair colour being similar. When you were about four though, something changed. He wouldn't talk about it, told me I was just being stupid, but I could see it, and nothing I did seemed to make any difference. He just distanced himself."

Scarlett was silent. She was the product of a seedy one-night stand with a man sowing his oats on his last night as a free man. A man who had then gone home and married the woman Scarlett now adored. All the while the man she'd always thought was her dad, had for some reason decided he didn't want her.

Scarlett

Chapter Twelve

When Scarlett left the house. Claudia collapsed to the sof and crawled into a ball. She couldn't believe it, and yet, as she ha told Scarlett, science didn't lie. But this was unreal. It was like livin; an episode of Jeremy Kyle or Jerry Springer. Things like this didn happen in real life, did they? To middle-of-the-road families from suburbia?

"Mum, are you okay?" Zara asked, popping her head around the door.

Claudia rolled onto her back and stretched out her legs just in time for Truffle to jump up and rub himself against her. "I am— Her eyes closed as she considered the question, what was she feelin; exactly? "Honestly, I didn't think it was possible for your father to hurt me anymore than he already had. I'd processed it all and now this." She reached out and tickled Truffle's chin.

Zara came into the room and nodded. "It is a little bit ou there, right?" She sat down on the end of the sofa. "I have anothe sister," she said almost incredulously.

"Yes, you do." Claudia acknowledged properly for the firs time. "And I'm sleeping with her."

Falling back against the cushions, Zara sighed. "Diana i going to have a shit fit, and Adam—" She shook her head. "He' going to go ballistic."

"Quite," Claudia agreed.

Glancing at the clock, Zara said, "She should be at he parents by now."

Claudia silently nodded. Her own thoughts already there, an how she wished Scarlett would have let her go with her, but sh understood her reasoning. It probably was something best lef between them for now.

"Do you think we should cancel tomorrow?" Zara mused.

"Hm? What?"

Zara smiled sadly. "We're all at Adam's tomorrow, for the BBQ, remember?"

Claudia brought her hand to her head. "Oh god, I forgot all about that."

Zara hesitated before adding, "Dad's going to be there."

Swinging her legs off the sofa, Claudia stood up. "Maybe we—It's going to be impossible. We cannot tell Adam and Diana just yet, not until we're all sure of the facts. Scarlett's right, imagine Jack was a sperm doner?" Zara raised a brow at that. "It's possible, unlikely, but possible and so we should hold off until we know for sure before we accuse anyone of anything. Somehow, we need to get through tomorrow without them knowing."

"Yes, I suppose so, but remember what happened last time we all kept things from Diana?"

Claudia did remember. The fall out to discovering that she and Scarlett were sleeping together could have been a lot worse, and they'd promised each other never to keep secrets again.

"But—" She ran her hands through her hair and pulled it all up into a ponytail, tying it with a band she had around her wrist. "We need to make sure we know what we are talking about when the time comes, and we won't know that until Scarlett has spoken with her mother, and even then, it might take longer." Claudia reiterated her argument, more for her own peace of mind than anything else.

Zara looked confused. "How so?"

"Because I don't think any of us should take the word of an ancestry app. If Scarlett's mother can't or won't give her the truth, then I think—I think a proper paternity test needs to be done."

"Really? I mean, the DNA thing got me and Adam right, it linked us instantly, and there are a couple of cousins I recognise on there too." Zara blew out a breath. "I think we have to face it, that

51

whatever Letty's mother says, Scarlett's related to me and Adam, and Diana, and that can only have happened one way. Dad is her dad."

Claudia's eyes closed. She knew Zara was right, but she didn't want to face it. Because what did it mean? Her entire marriage was a sham. He hadn't just been unfaithful at the end, but at the start too. He'd cheated on her before they were even married. Which begged the question, how many other times had he cheated that she didn't know about?

More importantly, where did that leave her and Scarlett's relationship?

As though reading her mind, Zara added, "She's not your daughter, whatever happens, you said yourself, you've never been her mother figure. You're not her stepmother. Nothing should change between the two of you."

"I'm not so sure everyone else will see it like that." Claudia smiled ruefully.

"Oh Mum, fuck everyone else." Zara grinned. "We'll be the talk of the family for five minutes until Kay and Jamie kick off at the next family gathering again."

Claudia laughed at the mention of Zara's cousins. Jack's oldest brother's daughter and her miscreant husband were renowned for arguing at every event that involved alcohol or someone Kay could get jealous over.

"You're right, I just…everything was going so perfectly, I didn't see this coming."

"I don't think any of us imagined *this* coming." Zara stood up and joined her mother. "I can go out and visit friends, give you and Scarlett some space to talk."

"I think that would be a nice idea, not that I want to push you out."

Zara rubbed her palms up and down Claudia's arms. "It's no trouble."

"If you want to leave Jacob and go let your hair down, we can watch him."

The smile was infectious. "Oh, I'm not turning that offer down."

Scarlett

Walking back into the house with her mum, Scarlett felt something lift. Something freeing, but at the same time, a sadness fought for space. Following her mum into the living room, her dad barely glanced up from the tv until her mum picked up the remote and switched it off.

"Oi, I was watching that," he said, his anger already at boiling pint. Scarlett wondered if she'd ever seen him go ballistic, and whether that was likely in the next moment.

"She knows," her mum said, staring at him until he cottoned on. "I said—"

"I heard you," he replied. He swallowed whatever he'd planned to say, and looked up at them both, tears filling his eyes. "It's about time she knew the truth."

"You could have told me at any time," Scarlett answered, her voice shaking as she fought back the emotions and the tears that threatened to erupt.

He scoffed. "Don't be so obtuse."

"Enough, the pair of you," her mum shouted. "I'm just about sick of it. This constant bickering ends now, and the pair of you will speak to each other like two people from the same family who love one another." He went to speak, and she pointed at him. "Don't you dare deny it," she hissed at him. "I was there, I watched you fall in love with our baby and to my shame, I didn't do enough when you pulled away, but don't you dare deny her now."

Scarlett was shocked. She'd never heard her mother speak to him, or anyone like that before. She almost wanted to applaud but wouldn't inflame the situation any further by being an arse. Her mum was right.

He looked away, shame faced, wiping his eyes discreetly. "I'm not going to deny her. She's mine whatever the biology says," he said, jaw tensing.

"I know you never wanted to talk about it. Wanted to sweep it all under the carpet and pretend there wasn't a possibility that she was anyone's but yours, but we've done that for too long, and now it's come back to bite us all. So, we're going to sit down with a pot of tea and behave like civilised people." She turned to Scarlett. "Sit down."

And then she left to go and make the pot of tea. Doing as she was told, Scarlett sat down in the armchair opposite her dad and stared at him. He picked at his sleeve, chewing the inside of his mouth in silence. It was awkward, but no worse than any other interaction they'd had these past few years.

"How did you find out?" he finally asked, still not looking at her.

"By accident, it was one of those Ancestry DNA things, we did it for a laugh. Thought maybe we'd find something exotic and interesting in our past that we didn't know about," Scarlett explained. "Wasn't really the kind of interesting I was expecting. Despite our differences, I'd still rather it was you that was my father."

He scoffed and huffed all at once, jerking his head around to look at her. "I highly doubt that. You've wanted this since you were small."

Her eyes narrowed at him as he sunk down into the chair even further. She'd never seen him look so small and sad. "What are you talking about?"

He shook his head and looked away as he replied, "That's what you told me."

This was becoming more perplexing as the day went on, Scarlett thought. "What did I tell you? When?"

He sat forward in his chair and leaned towards her. "That's what you said. That you hated me, and that I'm not your dad." His voice cracked, emotion getting the better of him. "Oh, what's the point?" He got up quickly and ran a hand over his head in frustration.

Scarlett

"Dad, I don't know what you're talking about." She mirrored his actions bringing them face to face. "Talk to me, for god's sake."

The door pushed open, and her mum entered carrying a tray with mugs and a teapot, eyeing the pair of them suspiciously. "What's going on?"

"Ask him, apparently I told him I didn't want him as a dad and that's the reason he's been an arse all these years."

Her mother placed the tray down and then stood at the third angle to the triangle. "What are you talking about, Terry?" she asked him.

His shoulders sagged, and all the fight seemed to drop out of him. "At that party." Was the simple answer, as though they should both know what he meant. Scarlett was puzzled, but apparently her mother understood.

"When you punched Jeff?"

He nodded and at least had the decency to look somewhat contrite, but it made no difference to Scarlett, she didn't have a clue what he was talking about, and she certainly didn't remember a party.

It was her mum who spoke again. "Because he suggested she wasn't yours?"

He nodded once more and breathed loudly through his nostrils, and then he added, "After she asked the same thing."

Scarlett frowned. "Hang on, how old was I at this party, cos have no recollection of going to a party."

Her mother shook her head. "I don't know, four maybe five?"

Scarlett's mouth gaped as she tried to process this new information. Before she asked another question though, her dad was talking again.

"I punched Jeff cos it was him that put it into Jodie's head, and Jodie went and wound up Scarlett about it. Next thing, she's screaming at me that I wasn't her dad, and she hated me. Jeff came in and wanted to know what all the shouting was, that was when Jodie said what she'd heard him say, and I punched Jeff."

"Wait, my cousin Jodie, Jodie who would have been what? Ten? You got all up in your ego over the conversation between a couple of kids at a family party?"

"Why didn't you tell me that part?" her mum asked him, thumping his arm with her fist. "We could have sat her down and explained it to her then or come up with a better solution than the one you went with."

"I never stopped thinking of you as my dad, regardless of what my four-year-old self shouted, that's a bloody cop out. I was four!"

"Yes, you were four, and you looked nothing like me, and everyone knew it."

Scarlett stepped towards him. "You are the most self-centred, child of a man. I adored you. I've spent my entire life trying to work out why the man I called Dad didn't love me—"

He looked taken aback by that. "I always loved you. Why do you think it hurt so much, not being your real dad?"

"You let your ego be directed by a four-year-old's silly throwaway comment, and the jokes of a family member you barely even see." She shook her head at the reality of it all. "You are my real dad, you idiot. You're my dad, for crying out loud," she shouted at him, unable to hold back her anger any longer. "But it was also you who has made my life miserable with your homophobic bigotry. You never took any interest in me growing up, and that hurt. You don't get to now tell me you always loved me." She grabbed her keys from the table. "And you don't get to dictate my life and who I love." She shook her head at him. "When you work it out, you can come and find me."

Scarlett
Chapter Fourteen

Scarlett pushed the key into the lock, remembering her thoughts from earlier back at her parents' house. This was home now. This was where she felt loved, wanted, needed. It was here she knew who she was, and here she was glad to be right now as she stepped inside and the aroma of life with Claudia hit her senses all at once.

She found Claudia standing in the hallway waiting. Looking at her with nothing but compassion and love. Scarlett was reminded instantly that she was the person, her person, the one being on this planet that totally got her, that loved her. And she was about to potentially hurt her with a truth she hadn't known needed to be told, until a few hours earlier.

"How did it go?" Claudia asked, not daring to move until Scarlett indicated she wanted her to.

Scarlett swallowed, pulled her jacket off and hung it. "I got the answers," she said sadly. She just stood there, facing the wall, arms limp by her side.

Claudia licked her lip before tugging the lower one between her teeth, releasing it slowly. "Do you want to talk about it now, or take some space?"

"I don't know what I want to do." Scarlett smiled sadly as she turned, wiping her eyes for the umpteenth time on the back of her hand. Her eyes were sore. Itchy from all of the crying she'd done on the drive back home. "Where's Zara?"

"She's gone to see a friend, I said I'd watch Jacob for a few hours. I thought it would give us some time." Claudia spoke gently.

Claudia breathed a sigh of relief when Scarlett finally moved towards her, and they could embrace. Scarlett breathed her in, the scent that reminded her that everything here was safe. Safe enough to finally let go of the emotions and sob it all out, but she didn't. She wasn't ready. The tears that had seeped out on the drive home had just been enough, but more was to come, she was sure of that. Emotionally, she was a wreck.

"Dinner's ready, if you're hungry?" Claudia said against her ear.

"I don't know if I can."

Taking her hand, Claudia led her to the lounge. "Let's try, okay."

The dining table was already laid, candles lit, a bottle of red breathing beside two glasses, and Jacob grinning up from his highchair with bits of carrot and cheese scattered across his tabletop.

"I see someone had a head start." Scarlett reached out and tickled his cheek.

"Take a seat, pour the wine, and I'll get dinner."

Scarlett did as she was told for the second time today. She poured two large glasses of an almost burgundy Merlot. Sitting back in her chair, she sipped it before reaching forward to offer Jacob an apple slice. He shook his head side to side when it approached his mouth, but he giggled at the new game.

"Here we go," Claudia said as she swept back into the room carrying a cast iron pan filled with something that despite her lack of hunger, hit Scarlett's sense of smell and begged to differ. "Boeuf Bourguignon," she said with a flawless French accent.

Scarlett watched as Claudia lifted the lid and the aroma wafted again in a steamy cloud that actually made her mouth water. *That was a good sign, right?*

When her bowl was filled, she lifted the spoon to her mouth and blew gently on it to take out the heat before opening her mouth, and under Jacob's watchful eye, she closed her mouth around the spoon.

It really was delicious.

Scarlett

"So," Claudia began once she had her own bowl full in front of her. "You said you got the answers?"

Scarlett placed the spoon down gently and sighed. Her shoulders felt tense, the muscles bunching up around her neck. "Jack *is* my father."

Claudia didn't manage to eat anything before she too placed her spoon down. Her hands folded in her lap. She'd prepared herself for that answer as much as anyone could, but still, hearing it was like another slap to the face.

"Did she explain how?"

Nodding, Scarlett tried to smile but it died on her lips the moment she looked at Claudia and saw the hurt already there. Something she never wanted to be the cause of and yet, here she was, adding to it with every word she now uttered.

"Yes. It wasn't an affair," she said quickly, hoping to alleviate some of the pain, "She barely knew his name." Scarlett sat upright and mirrored Claudia's hands in lap. "I am the product of a seedy ten-minute drunken shag in the toilets of a nightclub."

"Oh Sweetheart," Claudia reached out, but Scarlett shook her head.

"I need…no, you need to know that it happened when they were both drunk." That was bad enough, but the next part of the story would be the part that really stung. "And on his stag do."

Claudia sat back again, her tongue running around her teeth beneath her upper lip, the anger and hurt bubbling on the surface. Silently, she picked up her spoon and began to eat. The metal clanging just slightly on the ceramic to acknowledge her fury.

"So." Scarlett followed suit, picking up her own spoon, ready to resume eating. "I'm now a living paradox of being the thing that brings you joy and the thing that causes you pain."

This time when the spoon clanked down into the bowl, Claudia swivelled in her chair.

"Don't you dare. Don't you dare take on the hurt and pain my ex-husband causes me, that's on him. Not you. You didn't ask for any of this, and neither did I and we will not...I repeat, we will not allow this to come between us, am I clear?"

Pressing her lips together, Scarlett nodded, but the tears she'd been holding back began to well.

"There is nothing seedy about you, or us. Regardless of how you came into existence." Claudia's tone softened. "I love you. Nothing has changed."

When Scarlett looked up through her lashes, blinking back the tears, she said, "I love you, and I...I'm going to need some time to get my head around all of this."

"I think we all will but right now, let's just eat and enjoy the evening with this one." She indicated Jacob. "And in the morning we can work out a plan going forward, and I can decide how I am going to kill Jack."

Scarlett's lips curled. "Please don't go to prison because then I'll have to do something criminal so that I can join you, and I'd be a terrible prisoner."

Claudia laughed. "Fine, I'll just kick him in the balls."

"He'd probably feel that."

"It would be karma, that's for sure."

Scarlett

Chapter Fifteen

It was 2 a.m., and Scarlett lay in bed wide awake, doing all she could not to toss and turn and disturb Claudia, but sleep wouldn't come easy tonight, not with the way her mind was jumping from thought to thought.

Zara hadn't come home until after all of them had gone up. Scarlett had heard her sneaking up the stairs and doing her very best not to wake her son. Which Scarlett was grateful for. A screaming Jacob wasn't a fun event, and it had taken long enough to get him to go to sleep earlier as it was. Eventually, he'd fallen asleep in Claudia's arms, but it had taken several verses of hush a bye baby and quite frankly Scarlett was not in any kind of mood for that level of patience again.

In Claudia's arms was exactly where Scarlett had ended up once they'd showered and climbed into bed together. Tucked into Claudia's side, wrapped up in her. It had been comforting and she'd probably still be there had it not been for the fact that her arm went dead.

Scarlett rolled over and pushed the cover off just enough to poke her leg out as Claudia pressed up against her back and a sense of relaxation began to settle on her. The warmth of her lover's body feeling calm and familiar. When Claudia's arm snaked around her waist, Scarlett smiled to herself.

"Are you going to lay awake all night?" Claudia whispered.

Scarlett turned her head back over her shoulder. "Probably. Sorry, did I wake you?"

Warm lips pressed against her shoulder. "Maybe, I'm not used to you having a sleepless night."

"Yeah, I can't seem to switch off from it."

Claudia rolled away, switched on the bedside lamp, and then rolled back into place. "So, what can I do to help?"

Scarlett chuckled as Claudia's fingers began to tease her skin.

"Just being here helps."

"Really, nothing else I can do to take your mind off of things?" Her lips connected with Scarlett's shoulder again. This time lingering a little longer, her fingertips dancing along the underside of her breast. Her mouth moving as she lifted up and kissed warm skin until she found Scarlett's waiting cheek. "I'm sure...I ...could...help."

Scarlett twisted underneath her, allowing Claudia the room to find her lips and kiss her properly once she'd finished adoring her neck. "Yeah, maybe..."

"Maybe? Is that a challenge?" Claudia smirked down at her. "I like those."

"Maybe..." Scarlett chuckled more loudly.

"Well, in that case..." Claudia pushed her leg between Scarlett's thighs, making room until she could squeeze herself into the space, kissing her way down, eyes locked on Scarlett's face. "Just breathe, let your mind focus on me," she said, slowly moving down the bed, and then her mouth connected with Scarlett's clit. Her arms reaching around to harness her lover's thighs when Scarlett's hips bucked up urgently.

"Fuck," Scarlett whispered.

But as Claudia went to work, doing all of the things that Scarlett usually reacted to, she couldn't switch her mind off and focus. Every time she got her head into it, another thought would float in and ruin the moment. Scarlett squeezed her eyes shut, willing herself to let the sensations take over, to climax and enjoy the moment but she couldn't.

Claudia stopped. Crawled her way back up the bed and settled beside Scarlett. "It's alright."

Scarlett

"No, it's not," Scarlett cried, tears streaming down her face as she sat up and swung her legs off the bed. Claudia got to her knees and scooted in behind her, arms wrapping around Scarlett's shoulders.

"We're going to get through this, alright?"

Scarlett silently nodded.

"No matter what happens, I have your back, just like you have mine."

"Okay. I just..." She twisted around. "Do you know how many times growing up, I wished he wasn't my dad. That somehow, I had this father elsewhere who would have loved me, if he'd just known about me. And that one day, he would ride in and save me from my miserable existence?"

"Oh, Sweetheart."

"And now, I found out that I did, I did have a father out there, and I look at Zara, and Diana, and Adam and I realise something..." She wiped her face. Claudia patiently waiting for her to finish. "I realise how much he loves them...despite being a prick of a husband, he loves them, and I...I." She fell backwards into Claudia's embrace and sobbed. Anything else she said was nothing more than an incoherent garble of half words.

Claudia moved around the kitchen like a woman possessed. Kettle boiling, coffee machine growling, toast popping and the fridge door slamming every time she opened and closed it.

"Morning," Zara said hesitantly as she slid Jacob into his highchair and strapped him in.

"Hi," Claudia said abruptly before stopping in her tracks, taking a breath, and turning back to face her daughter. "Sorry, good morning. Did you have a nice time last night?"

"I did, yes. It was good to catch up. Everything alright here?" She pulled the side of her lip between her teeth.

"Well, you officially have a sister."

Zara sucked in some air and let it out slowly. "Wow, I mean, you know I kind of thought that, but it being confirmed is— wow. How's Scarlett taking it?"

"Upset, hurt, angry and I can't blame her. Her entire life and who she thought she was, has just been thrown up into the air overnight."

Zara nodded. "And what about you, this impacts you too. Any idea how it happened?"

"I suppose I'm feeling the same way, I just—" She blew out a breath. "I'm battle weary where your father is concerned." Drinking from her mug, she allowed the warm coffee to slide slowly down her throat as she calmed. "Do you want tea?"

"Thanks," Zara answered while opening the jar with Jacob's breakfast. "Is there anything I can do?" Jacob squealed excitedly and clapped his hands, making them both smile.

"I don't know, it impacts all of us, you included. We'll all need to talk about it, but I want Scarlett to feel more settled with it first, is that okay with you? Can you keep it to yourself until then?" Claudia gazed imploringly at her youngest, the one who everybody knew couldn't keep a secret, though she had to admit, she was getting better at it.

"Yeah, of course. But just remember that Adam has this information too. We have no idea when or if he might access it."

"God, it's all such a mess."

Zara was silent for a moment before she said, "Although, watching Diana work out that she's no longer the oldest is going to be a little bit fun." There was a mischievous smile on her face.

Scarlett

Claudia's eyes narrowed. "You're really not upset about all of this?"

She shrugged. "I mean don't get me wrong, I am very upset with dad, and he's going to hear about it, but we've all grown to love Scarlett. She's already part of the family, and this...well, doesn't really make any difference, does it? She's already aunty Scarlett." She smiled down at Jacob. "This just makes it all more official, and you don't even have to marry her to do it." She winked.

"I guess so."

Chapter Sixteen

"I don't know what to do for the best," Scarlett said, perched on the end of the sofa. "I mean, I can't just ignore it, that would neither be healthy, or possible because the cat is out of the bag. Zara already knows, and Adam will undoubtedly open that email one day. We can't just sit on it and wait until that moment arrives."

"So, what do you suggest?" Claudia asked. "Because I know I'd like to go around to Jack's and—"

Scarlett took her hand. "I know, and you have every right to be so angry with him. But it's not about him right now, it's about your kids and telling them. I think they have the right to know first."

Claudia sighed. "I guess you're right. But how are we going to get through today?"

The BBQ was just hours away. A big family day designed to get everybody together, including Jack and Maisie. Adam had been excited about it and had even bought a new BBQ just for the occasion. It was supposed to be fun.

Scarlett shrugged. "I could just skip it, pretend I'm not feeling well."

Claudia shook her head. "No, I don't want that, maybe we can both skip it?"

"But then everyone will worry, and Zara will be left to her own devices and if someone says the wrong thing, or Adam has seen it?"

"So, we have to go."

Nodding, Scarlett grimaced. "I think we do. I can handle it. It's not like Jack and I are best buddies anyway, and then tomorrow we tell Adam and Diana." She noticed Claudia's lack of enthusiasm for that. "Unless you think differently?"

"I just…I was thinking maybe should we tell Jack first?"

Scarlett

"I mean yes, but if I look at the bigger picture, who do I see myself having a solid relationship with?"

"I understand that. I'm just thinking that the moment they know, he's going to get bombarded, and as much as I have little empathy for him right now, I do have to acknowledge that he has no clue that this is happening. No offence, but he most likely has never thought about your mother since that night. And I wonder if it would be better for you two to talk first, and for the children if he was prepared for it."

The children, Scarlett considered that. None of them were children any longer. And wasn't she now part of that description. It felt odd. She'd never had any siblings before. These family dynamics were very different to what she was used to.

"I guess. It's fucked up. Whichever way we look at it, we upset someone."

"*That* I cannot disagree with, and if we're going to upset anyone then let it be Jack." Claudia attempted a smile but gave up and kissed her instead. "Let's just wing it and work it out as we go along. I'm not sure there is a right way to do this, only the best way and that will show itself as the day goes on."

"I hope so. I don't want to be the cause of this family being ripped apart."

"A little dramatic, darling." Claudia did now grin. She rubbed Scarlett's knee before getting up. "Come on, let's get ready."

The sun was high in the sky and the smell of coal burning already floated in the air as Claudia and Scarlett arrived with Zara and Jacob. As predicted, the baby was swarmed by Sunnie and Diana the moment he was unbundled. Zara happy to hand him over so she could annoy Adam.

Scarlett's gaze darted around the garden looking for any sign of Jack. She relaxed when she realised that he wasn't here yet. Claudia's fingers squeezed hers just as Diana almost bounced across the grass towards them.

"Hey Mum, Scarlett." She leaned in to kiss each of them on the cheek, smiling warmly. "What a great day for it, hey?"

"Yeah, it's a really lovely day," Scarlett answered, now looking at Diana in a totally different way. Trying to work out the similarities between them that she hadn't noticed before. It was the nose and mouth area. Glancing across at Adam, she realised how similar in height they were, and their frame, and the nose. With Zara it was the eyes, something similar in their shape and distance apart. *How had she never noticed any of that before? But then, why would she?*

Scarlett smiled as Claudia let go of her hand and wandered over to the blanket on the grass where Jacob would be entertaining his harem for the best part of the day. Her world fell into silence as a multitude of thoughts roamed her head wanting answers.

Was this what she had missed growing up? All of this, family, people hanging out because they wanted to spend time together. She'd have been running around a garden like this, chasing her sisters and brother. *God, I have a brother and two sisters.*

But then something else filtered through, *and you'd never have had this with Claudia.* She shuddered at the thought of Claudia as her stepmother rather than her lover. It didn't bare thinking about. *Maybe things had worked out for the best.*

"Beer?"

"Sorry, what?" Scarlett blinked several times, turning to find herself face to face with the man who had helped create her. Jack was standing beside her holding a box of beer in the crook of his arm, a bottle in his other hand. *When had he arrived?*

Scarlett

She stared at him. His greying hair close cropped around the sides, framing the bald spot that he'd had for years. Eyes hidden behind sunglasses.

"I said, did you want a beer?" He smiled at her, and she saw it, her own smile right there in front of her, on his face. "Or something else? Sorry, I didn't mean to sneak up on you."

"No, it's fine. I was just..." *Wondering about you.* "In a world of my own." She took the beer. "Thanks." Glancing around, she caught sight of Claudia gazing over at them, already half standing as she prepared to come over and rescue her. Slowly, she shook her head.

She didn't need saving.

"Bloody traffic held us up, otherwise we'd have been here ages ago." He laughed, "Well, I'd best do the rounds. Good to see you again."

She unscrewed the cap and took a swig of the beer as she watched him walk away, laughing at something Adam said as they exchanged a word or two by the BBQ. The way he walked, was that how she walked? How he stood, one leg slightly out to the side, just like she did.

She'd only ever looked at him before as the idiot ex-husband, now though, she was seeing something else: a father. Her father.

He patted Adam's shoulder, and she noted the look of pride that filled his face. They might bicker and Adam might be angry with him often, but there was love there. Regardless of it all, love wasn't ever the issue.

"You alright?" Zara sidled up beside her. Both of them staring at *their* father and brother. "So, just remember, Adam might be your brother now, but he will always be a dick." She winked and chinked her own bottle of something non-alcoholic with Scarlett's beer.

Scarlett chuckled. "Okay."

With the burgers cooking and the sausages being served up in buns with onions and mustard, it was actually a nice afternoon. Everybody sat around on the grass on blankets, or in chairs at the garden table, chatting easily, smiling, and laughing. For a moment it was just one big happy family and Scarlett almost forgot about the episode of *Eastenders* she was currently living.

When Jack stood up suddenly and called for everyone's attention, Scarlett felt her innards churn. *Did he know?* But then he held his hand out for Maisie to stand and join him. Scarlett winced when Claudia groaned, her forehead landing dramatically on Scarlett's shoulder.

"Shoot me now. If he proposes, just shoot me," Claudia whispered quietly.

Scarlett chuckled at that, though it did look like he was about to announce something important. He ran a hand over his head and looked somewhat nervous as everyone gazed up at him.

"While we have you all here, I thought it might be a good time to share our news." He glanced at Maisie who was blushing furiously under the scrutiny. "I know everyone thinks I'm an old man and should get out there and find someone my own age." He smirked before looking at Claudia. "Well, everyone except your mother, obviously." He winked like the confident bastard he usually was. "But the truth is I've found something I didn't think I would again, and well, I guess there's no point hiding it any longer, Maisie and I are having a baby."

"A baby?" Claudia exclaimed, *oh the irony*, her eyes almost popping out of her head.

Adam put his plate down and walked away, Diana stood there open-mouthed, but it was when Zara reacted that shit really hit the fan.

"A baby?" Zara glared at him. "You couldn't even deal with the four you already have, what the hell are you thinking bringing another child into this world at your age."

Scarlett

Maisie burst into tears. Claudia looked startled and Scarlett felt sick.

It took a moment.

And then Diana asked, "Sorry, four?"

Chapter Seventeen

The moment it was out, Zara covered her mouth. She turned to Scarlett and her mother and mouthed. "I'm so sorry."

"What's going on? This is supposed to be a joyous moment for Maisie." Jack was saying but Diana had other ideas and shushed him.

Staring at her sister, she moved in like a wolf ready to tear into its prey, repeating the question, "What do you mean by four?"

"Nothing. I didn't mean anything." Zara tried to backtrack. "I meant three, obviously."

"No, you meant four. You said four. Four and three are very different and you absolutely said four."

Claudia turned to Scarlett. "It's up to you, there's never going to be a good time."

Jack stepped in, "Diana, clearly there are only three of you, Zara obviously just misspoke. Let's not make a big deal of it on such a happy occasion."

Zara glared at him.

Standing up Scarlett had a decision to make, speak up or walk away, but either way was going to create chaos. Was it better to just get it out there?

"Actually," Scarlett started. "The thing is—" She ran a hand through her hair and looked down at Claudia for help. "I—"

Claudia got to her feet and turned to Jack, her words venomous as she spoke. "You actually do have four children, Jack."

His eyes narrowed at her as though she were completely barmy. Maisie cried louder and Sunnie went to her, ushering her into the house and away from this latest Maddox family drama. She must have said something to Adam because he stomped back outside and looked between them all with a mix of curiosity and disgust on his face.

"Claudia, I understand that this might be a little hurtful and you—" He was cut off with a roll of her eyes as she continued.

"The kids did a silly Ancestry DNA thing they bought each other at Christmas. The results came back and linked them both to someone else. Someone who would be their half-sibling," Claudia explained.

Adam looked aghast. "What?"

"If you bothered to read your emails you'd know," sneered Zara.

"I do look at my work email—" he tried to say before he too was cut off.

"Look, what are you all talking about?" Jack intervened trying to make sense of everything. "This is madness, I don't have any other children. I'm pretty sure I'd know about it if I did." He laughed nervously.

Claudia reared up on him. "You don't remember the casual little fling you had in the nightclub toilet on your stag do, no?"

His eyes widened. His face flushing a red none of them had seen before.

"Uh huh." Claudia nodded. "All coming back now, is it?"

"Claudia, I don't rem—"

She stepped closer, her anger growing with every second she had to look at him. "I think you do. I think you remember it like you remember all the other times you cheated on me, that I've yet to find out about. And I probably never will, but this one has come back to bite you on the arse, hasn't it?"

Diana moved, her gaze softening on Scarlett as she closed the gap. "Are you alright? You look a little pale."

"I—" Scarlett couldn't find her words. *How the hell did she say it?* "I'm your sister," she blurted.

For a moment, Diana stood very still, then she laughed. "Good one." Her laughter continuing until she realised that her mother and Zara were not laughing. "What are you talking about, that's impossible... Dad?"

Scarlett swallowed, realising all eyes were now on her. "I'm...me...it appears that..." She looked from Diana to Jack. "You are my biological father."

Before anyone else could speak, Adam swung a punch and hit Jack square on the nose, blood gushing down his striped shirt and spreading like a psychological ink text.

"You utter bastard," he said before storming back into the house.

Claudia watched silently from the window. Zara stood beside her doing the same while Diana was still pacing the lounge carpet. Adam had stormed out of the house altogether, needing a walk to cool off.

In the garden stood Scarlett, and Jack, who was still dabbing his nose with the cold compress Sunnie had given him.

"Do you think we should have stayed out there?" Zara asked, completely absorbed by what was happening, and hating every second of not being able to hear the conversation taking place.

Sunnie wandered over with Jacob in her arms and glanced out before turning away again with a disinterested disdain. "I'll go check on Maisie."

"No, I don't," Claudia answered when Sunnie had moved away. "They need to talk."

Scarlett

"Yes, well so do we." Diana huffed with contempt from the other side of the room. "Don't we get a say?"

"Of course you do, and you will." Claudia turned to face her. "This isn't the time for one-upmanship, Diana."

"I just can't—it's one thing after another, Mother. Maybe Adam is right, maybe he is irredeemable."

"He's still your father."

"And everyone else's apparently too," Diana retorted petulantly.

"For god's sake, Di," Zara joined in. "Whatever has gone on isn't our fault, and it's not Scarlett's either."

Diana stopped pacing, put her face in her hands and wept. "I just—who am I now?"

Zara looked to Claudia, who looked equally perplexed by the statement. Claudia turned away from the scene outside and moved across the room towards her eldest daughter, taking her into her arms.

"What do you mean? You know who you are,"

"Do I? I was the oldest, and now—"

"Oh my god," Zara exclaimed. "You're really going to get jealous about your spot at the head of the clan? Just because you bullied us into following you as kids, doesn't mean we think you're in charge, you know."

"I don't think I'm in charge, but there is a responsibility for the eldest, and I've lived up to that…"

Zara snapped back, "Well now you don't have to, do you, you can delegate it to Scarlett."

"Oh, stop it the pair of you," Claudia shouted. "Like this isn't difficult enough without you both returning to your five-year-old selves."

Scarlett
Chapter Eighteen

Arms wrapped around herself as Scarlett fidgeted and moved from one foot to the other, feeling every bit as uncomfortable as she looked. The silence between them both was as loud as any noise she'd ever heard. Jack stood motionless, his face ashen as he contemplated all of the information she had just given him. A lonely burger remained scorched and charred on the BBQ still smouldered and bringing the stench of burnt meat wafting across on the breeze, which at least gave Scarlett something to focus on and ground herself.

It was a weird sensation for Scarlett. She was looking at her father. The man who had helped create her, and yet, she felt nothing. In her mind, he was just her lover's ex-husband. But now, that felt even more of an ick than it had done before. She was sleeping with, and in love with, the woman her own father had discarded. Her father, who was the father to her lover's children. God, it was all such fucking mess.

"I—" he started but stopped, looking around the garden as though he might find the words he needed sprouting up like weeds amongst the flowers. "This could be—it could all just be—"

"A coincidence?" she finished for him. "My mum just happened to have sex with a man named Jack on his stag do thirty-odd years ago around the same date, and who's children's DNA matches mine? Yes, I guess it could just be a coincidence."

The silence reared up again. She could feel the eyes on them from the house, understandable of course, they were probably all going through some kind of shock at the revelations.

"So, what do we do now?" he asked, as though she would have all of the answers.

She stared blankly at him. Because she didn't. She had no answers at all, and why should she? She was just the by-product of his seedy little life, wasn't she?

He sighed. "What a nightmare…"

"I guess so." She turned to walk away. If that was his response, then what was the point?

"Scarlett, that's not what— I didn't mean you, just…the situation." She stopped walking and turned back to him as he continued, "What with Maisie being pregnant, I'd…I wasn't expecting to have any more children, and now—if I'd known."

"If you'd known? What? You'd have been my daddy?" She walked towards him again, tilting her head as she took him in. All forlorn and flustered.

"Yes, of course, I'd never have—" He huffed.

"You'd probably never have married Claudia, and you'd never had your other children."

"Of course, I'd have married Claudia. She was the love of—" He stopped himself from saying anything more and looked away towards the house where he could see Claudia staring at them from the window.

"The only way you'd have married her was if you didn't tell her about me, and that would have meant you were never my dad. I'd have been the dirty secret."

"That's not true, I—"

"It is, that is exactly what it would have been. You're the most predictable man I've ever met. Always thinking what's best for you, what angle you can work to get what you want. Claudia was never the love of your life, she was the love you needed in your life, until you tired of it and found someone else to replace it."

"And now you have her." He stepped forward. "Now she's yours."

"She's not a possession to own. She's with me because I love her and she loves me, nothing else."

Scarlett

"Is that what this is about? You want to hurt me because hurt her?"

She shook her head at him. "Go and read the science. I can' make it up or change it to fit a scenario just to hurt you. And why would I bother, like you said, she's with me." And then she turned away again and started to walk.

"I want a paternity test."

She raised a hand, middle finger extended.

Adam had returned and sat with Diana and Zara at the dining table. Claudia sat at the head of it while Scarlett stood by the door not quite sure where she fit in but ready to run the moment it got too much.

Jack had left, taking Maisie home to rest after, *the shock of i all was too much apparently.*

It was Diana who spoke first. "So, do we get the full story now, or do we have to guess and fit the pieces together by ourselves?" She glared at her mother, then Zara, and finally, Scarlett.

"I have to agree with Di, we need a full and prope explanation," Adam concurred.

"What's to tell, Scarlett is our sister, that's the simpl answer," Zara countered.

"I am well aware of the simple answer, Zara, however, I thinl we are entitled to the more complicated one. Our entire lives have just been turned on their heads," Diana snapped.

"Mother?" Adam said with annoyance.

Claudia turned to him and sighed.

"Your father—"

Scarlett interrupted, "He met my mum in a nightclub on his stag do, they were both drunk, had sex and nine months later I came along. My mum was dating my dad by then, and he took me on, under the proviso that nobody knew I wasn't his. Your dad had no idea about me." Scarlett moved away from the door and took a seat beside Claudia. "And none of us would be aware if it hadn't been for the Ancestry thing tagging us all together."

"His bloody stag do?" Adam jumped up in anger. "I was feeling regretful for hitting him but now—"

"I know, it's not the most ideal situation." Claudia tried to calm the situation, but Adam was having none of it.

"He was cheating on you before he even walked you down the aisle, he's a bloody disgrace."

"I am shooketh," Diana interjected, shaking her head slowly.

"Really? Dad cheats and you're shocked by it?" Zara asked. "It's not like he doesn't have form."

"So, what happens now, with you and Mum?" Adam asked his eyes moving from Scarlett to Claudia and back again.

Claudia narrowed her eyes at him. "Nothing happens, this has nothing to do with me or our relationship."

"You're our mother, sleeping with our sister." He continued, "That's a little bit…incestuous, isn't it?"

"Don't be such an idiot." Zara glared at him. "They're not related, we are."

"Yeah, but you have to admit, it's a bit—" He shrugged.

"No, it isn't a bit—" Zara imitated him.

"I have never been Scarlett's mother figure. I was already divorced from your father when we met, so I've never in law even been her stepmother. We are two people in a relationship, that's it," Claudia concluded. This was not a topic of conversation she was going to allow to continue. "As far as I can see, nothing changes. Scarlett was part of this family before and now she's just a little bit more a part of this family."

Scarlett followed up with, "I don't want— I mean, I understand that this is difficult and that thinking of me as your sister is probably not something—"

"I already think of you that way." Zara smiled. "And if she's honest, so does Diana." She stared across at her sister.

"Well, yes, but that was before…I mean, this is different. Now you really are my sister, and that's…Oh I don't know." Diana covered her face with her hands.

Adam pushed his chair out and stood up. "I don't know about you, but this is going to take more than a quick conversation to work through. I'm not unhappy about it, I think the world of you, Scarlett, and how you've changed Mum's life and made her happy, but I didn't think I'd be discovering new siblings at my age, and we've not even touched on the fact Maisie is pregnant." He looked to the ceiling as if in prayer, hands on hips. "So, I suggest we do what this family does best, and we get back outside before we miss all of the sunshine and enjoy the BBQ we came together for."

Claudia stood up too. "I think that sounds like a wonderful plan."

Chapter Nineteen

Scarlett climbed into bed and faced the ceiling, staring up into the shadows dancing from the lamp. It still felt surreal, her life in that moment. Lying beside the woman her father had been married to. She couldn't quite get that out of her head. It had never bothered her before that Claudia had been married. Everyone has a history, a list of past lovers, and Scarlett had never thought about it with any previous partner either, but this, this was different, wasn't it?

"Do you want to talk about it?" Claudia asked as she too slid in between the sheets. The aubergine-coloured silk nightdress contrasting against the white sheets was usually Scarlett's favourite, but not tonight.

Scarlett glanced up, smiled quickly, before looking away again and back to the ceiling. "I'm just—I dunno, it's been a lot."

Claudia cuddled up beside her, her head laying on Scarlett's shoulder.

"It has, yes, but nothing has changed."

"Hasn't it?" Scarlett answered, turning her face towards Claudia.

"What I mean is, obviously I—" She leaned up on her elbow, her face just inches from Scarlett. "We're okay, right? I know this is all—"

"Weird?"

"No, not weird…it's different, of course, but—"

"I'm living with my father's ex-wife, sleeping in the bed he shared with you. Having sex with my sibling's mother, no, nothing at all weird about that."

"Well, when you put it like that. But he never slept in this bed. I replaced it the moment he moved out, so that's one less weirdness for you to think about."

Scarlett

Scarlett tried not to laugh.

"And if it makes you feel any better, I hadn't been sexually active with him for three years before we separated, and we've been divorced for almost two years. So, I was practically brand new again when you and I met."

This time Scarlett did laugh, as she twisted around and grabbed hold of Claudia, moving them both until she was straddling her lover's lap and hovering above her.

"And..." Claudia continued, wriggling beneath the weight of Scarlett. "He never touched me the way that you do. I never felt safe the way I feel with you."

Scarlett held her gaze, deciding something for herself in that moment. She leaned lower until their mouths were almost touching.

"Can we agree that we never talk about him in our bed ever again?"

Claudia smiled up at her and licked her lips. "Talk about who?"

"Exactly, now kiss me and make it all better."

"You know what would make it all much better?" Claudia wriggled free until she was more upright.

Scarlett's head tilted, her eyes narrowing. "What?" she asked slowly, noticing Claudia's grin grow bigger.

Claudia nibbled the edge of her finger. "Put it on," she whispered, before biting her lip in anticipation. "Go on, it's been ages, not that I'm complaining..."

"You," Scarlett pointed a finger at her, "can't be quiet enough for that."

"Please...I promise. I'll be quiet."

Scarlett raised a brow. "No chance. Zara is literally twenty feet away."

Moving in closer, Claudia's voice dropped to that husky sexy tone that usually worked so well with Scarlett. "Isn't that part of the fun of it?"

"Fine, but so much as a whimper that's audible across the hall and I'm gagging you." Scarlett grinned as Claudia's eyes lit up. Climbing from the bed, Scarlett went in search of 'the box'. When she found what she was looking for, she held it aloft in victory.

Claudia watched on as Scarlett stepped into the harness and slid it up her firm thighs, fiddling with it until it was in place and the straps were tightened. She did a little jig, swinging her hips and making it jiggle up and down, a move that never failed to amuse Claudia, before slathering it in liquid silk.

"Get over here, I need you," Claudia urged.

"Yes, boss." Scarlett grinned scampering across the carpet to launch herself onto the bed. She peeled the sheet back and revealed Claudia and the silky material that covered her from chest to knee. Her fingers searched for the hem, enjoying the feel of it, skimming the warm skin as she bunched the material up. Claudia's thighs instinctively parting to make room for her lover to nestle between.

Scarlett's hand continued its pathway, up over Claudia's hip, flattening out over the soft swell of her torso before it met resistance in the form of Claudia's hand, grasping at Scarlett, tugging the warm palm to mould against her breast. Their lips met once more, urgent and firm as need overtook the events of the day in an effort to push it from their thoughts.

Breathing heavily. Scarlett's husky voice said, "Turn over."

Claudia didn't need telling twice, bouncing on the mattress until she was on her front, and then her knees, bent forward grasping the headboard. She moaned softly, her head dropping forward when

Scarlett

Scarlett pushed her nightdress up and slid her fingers between her thighs, teasing her.

"Don't make me wait." Claudia all but begged. Gasping a she felt the nudge of something hard push against her until it sli inside and the air in her lungs expelled in a swirl of bright lights tha lit up a path ahead that she was sure might be the end of her. "Fuck."

Scarlett's hands wrapped around her waist and haule Claudia upright until she was resting back against Scarlett's chest Hard nipples pressing into her back as her own nipples wer squeezed and pulled with practised hands, her breasts fondled an caressed with the firmness she loved so much. Scarlett's hips movin slowly, creating the most delicious sensation. Every nerve endin pulsed somewhere deep inside because it was just so fucking good.

Claudia felt a hand enclose around her neck. The grip jus firm enough to hold her in place without constricting her need t breathe.

When her mewling became whimpers, and her whimper threatened to turn louder, she found her mouth covered with the paln that had been around her neck, Scarlett's thrusts harder and faste now. The hand that had smothered her breast now moved and hel firm against her stomach. She could barley move as she focused o every stroke until the climax built to a crescendo that even with he mouth covered, the moan was load enough to pull Scarlett over th edge with her.

Chapter Twenty

Sunday morning came too early for both Claudia and Scarlett, the sound of Jacob's wailing cut through the peaceful silence and woke them both with a start.

"Bloody hell, I thought someone was being murdered," Scarlett said with a breathless sigh the moment she flopped back down against the pillow. Awareness of the situation seeping into her exhausted brain.

Claudia chuckled. "The joys of parenting."

"Any time I think he's cute and how it might have been fun to have one, remind me of this moment."

"Did you ever want a family? I mean, we've never discussed it, have we? I just assumed—"

Scarlett turned to her, smiling at the serious look on her face. "Do you want more kids?"

Claudia thought for a moment, sucking her lower lip between her teeth. "Not really, I mean, we thought about it after Zara, but decided three was enough, and since then I always assumed I'd meet someone my own age who either already had children, or was past the point of wanting one." She reached out and stroked Scarlett's face. "So, do you? Is it something you want to explore?"

"No, I decided a long time ago that unless I met someone with kids already, it wouldn't be something I wanted. I don't think my own family experience really lends me towards it." She chuckled. "And I'm quite content with what we have."

"I'm glad we're on the same page." Rolling across the bed, Claudia slid naked from the sheets and grabbed her robe. Tying it around her waist. "I'll go see if there's anything we can do to help."

"I guess that's my cue to put the kettle on then." Scarlett smiled, following her out of the bed. She pulled on a t-shirt and reached for some joggers. "Do you want to go out for breakfast?"

Scarlett

As Claudia opened the door, she glanced over her shoulder. "That might be nice."

Across the hall, Jacob was making his feelings known still. Claudia knocked lightly on the door before opening it to find Zara pacing the room with her son in her arms. His face raging red, little fists clenching and grasping at her hair.

"Are you alright? Anything I can do?"

On the verge of tears herself, Zara smiled apologetically. "Got any miracle cures for teething? I tried giving him the teething ring, but he won't take it, keeps launching it across the room. The Bonjela works for a bit but then he's screaming again."

"Have you massaged his gums?"

"Yes, and he bit me." Zara looked as though she were on the verge of a tantrum herself.

Claudia chuckled. "Oh dear, well, one thing that used to work with Adam was a cold carrot."

Zara raised a brow at that.

"I know it sounds crazy, but the cold helped, and he can suck on it, or chew on it. You just have to be careful in case he chomps off a larger piece than he can handle."

"Right now, I'll try just about anything." Zara sounded exasperated as she followed Claudia out of the room and down the stairs, Jacob's wail accompanying them the entire time.

Scarlett was already in the kitchen boiling up the kettle and brewing coffee from the pods she liked. She could hear their impending arrival and turned to greet them.

"Morning." She yawned. Jacob had quieted with the movement from up to downstairs, his attention now focused on what was going on and who else was in the room.

"Sorry," Zara sheepishly answered. "I know it wasn't the best way to wake up on a Sunday morning."

Scarlett slid a glass of orange juice towards her. "Don't worry about it."

"I think there are some carrot sticks in there." Zara nodded towards the fridge.

Claudia swung the door open and produced one with a flourish that seemed to entertain Jacob enough to get a giggle from him at least. "Here we go, want to try chewing on this, Jacob?"

He took it, eagerly shoving it into his mouth.

"At least he is quiet for now." Zara yawned.

"Do you want to leave him with us while you go shower?" Scarlett asked, reaching tentatively for him in case the movement set him off again. Zara handed him over without even thinking about it.

"That would be great." She turned and left before anyone could change their mind.

"Where do you want to go for breakfast then?" Scarlett asked while Claudia continued the coffee and tea making. "I was thinking Banjo, but I realise we go there a lot. What about Nicoletta's?"

"I don't mind, we could try something different."

The doorbell rang. Before anyone moved, there was the sound of the door opening, and then closing. Scarlett poked her head around the kitchen door and looked down the hallway to see Diana striding towards her with purpose.

"Heads up," Scarlett muttered quickly to Claudia. "Hi, Di."

"Morning," she responded miserably. She'd been offered the opportunity to stay over the night before but had chosen to go home instead, and much to her annoyance, Zara hadn't come with her. "We need to talk."

Scarlett

"Okie dokie." Scarlett handed Jacob over to Claudia. "Do you want a coffee?"

"No, I'm fine, thanks."

"Diana, are you alright?" Claudia asked,

"No, not really." Came the curt response.

"Right, let's sit down and talk about it then," Scarlett answered, taking charge of the situation, and meeting her head-on. "Living room or kitchen?"

"Living room, I guess," Diana replied, a little less abrasive than before.

One by one they filed out of the kitchen and into the lounge. Diana chose the armchair, while Claudia and Scarlett sat beside one another with Jacob bouncing on Claudia's knee.

"So, the thing is…I'm angry." That part was obvious, Scarlett thought as Diana continued, "Not with you, I'm getting my head around that part, I mean it's such a strange place to find us all in, isn't it? These things don't happen to people in real life, it's the stuff of drama on TV or those awful reality shows." She scrunched up her nose at that idea.

Scarlett and Claudia listened silently.

"But I *am* angry, I'm furious actually, all of the lies and the bad behaviour, and I'm not sure how I move forward with Dad."

"I think you have every right to feel that way," Scarlett answered, "You both do, this has come as a shock for all of us and it's going to take time to work through it and find—"

"I'd like to kill him," Claudia said quietly. "I know that sounds dramatic, and of course, I never would, but actually, now that Diana has voiced it, I feel angry too."

"Right, well, yes, it's a very—" Scarlett was cut off again.

"He is the most selfish man, no." Diana held up a finger. "The most selfish *person* I have ever known. And I can't get over the fact that he's my dad, and I've realised, he's the reason I keep falling for arseholes."

So, this was going to be a therapy session, Scarlett thought. She kept quiet, allowing the space for them both to speak.

"I'm sorry," Claudia began. "I should have divorced him a long time ago, and I should have realised the impact he would be having on you all."

"It's not your fault, Mum."

"Isn't it? I always had an inkling he was cheating on me, I just didn't want to believe it, so I ignored the red flags, until I couldn't ignore them any longer because, well, it was so obvious."

Scarlett reached for her hand. "I'm sorry."

"Oh, it's fine, I'm alright now, I've got you and the kids, and my career, everything turned out fine, and he wasn't a horrible man, we had many happy times, and he wasn't a bad father." She looked to Diana. "He had his issues with our marriage, but as a father, he did his best."

"That's what is so disappointing, and so difficult for me to process. I have this image of this great dad, and yet, I have the logic of knowing what a monumental prick he is."

"I feel cheated," Scarlett added to the conversation. Both Diana and Claudia turned her way. "I grew up with a man I called dad, whose ego was so upset by a comment I made as a four-year-old that he washed his hands of me, and the entire time there was a man out there who was really my father, and he was a good dad, and I didn't get to share that."

Diana looked as though she might cry. "I never thought of that. I'm sorry. I didn't stop for one moment to think how this would feel for you. I guess I am as selfish as he is."

Scarlett

"Oh, Diana, you're not," Claudia interjected. "This situation has—it's been a huge curve ball for all of us and we all have to deal with it in whatever way works, and the first thing is always going to be how it affects us individually."

Diana nodded. "I know, I'm still struggling with who I am in the grand scheme of things. And you can all laugh, I don't care but I've been the oldest my entire life and now, you trump me."

Scarlett chuckled at that idea, regardless of their age, Diana was always going to be the older child. "I get that I'm older, but the way I see it, I've always been the only child. I don't have any experience with hierarchy and family dynamics, I'm not interested in trumping your oldest child status."

"You're not?" Diana seemed astounded by that. "So, I'm still in—"

"In charge? Sure." Scarlett grinned. "Your relationship with Adam and Zara shouldn't change."

"But you're our sister now."

Scarlett nodded, that was still a weird thing to hear. "I know and I'd like the opportunity to develop that relationship, but I'm not sure I'll ever comfortably fit into the dynamic you three already have cultivated."

"I see." Diana nodded, accepting the situation. "Maybe I need to have it out with dad?"

"I think a conversation probably needs to be had," Claudia agreed. "But maybe take a few days to decompress and process it all a little, let the steam of it dissipate and get what you want to say clear in your mind before you launch into it."

Diana shrugged. "I guess so. Anyway, I thought I could stay for lunch and then I'd take Zara home. It's lonely without her and Jacob."

Chapter Twenty-One

The first few days of the week had kept Scarlett busy, which was good. She'd been given the go ahead to paint her room at *Spiritually Sound* and after spending almost all of Monday picking colours and having paint mixed until she had the perfect shade, she'd then been up and down the ladder with rollers and paintbrushes changing the colour to a warm and healing sage. It was starting to feel like her space.

Interspersed with having to head back home, get changed and ready herself for the few clients she still had coming to the house, it had been exhausting. But by Thursday, she was a little bit impressed by herself. The room was looking like a great space to work from, and she'd done a good job of ignoring her personal life, keeping her mind busy and focused on the task at hand.

Not that she was entirely avoiding the whole *Jack is your father* drama, but she'd needed a breather from it and every conversation about it. All completely understandable, but still it had started to feel like an episode of Jeremy Kyle whenever a conversation sparked.

She was packing everything away when there was a gentle knock on the door. Frowning, she checked her watch. It was late, and she wasn't expecting anyone.

"Come in," she called out as she shoved wet paintbrushes into sandwich bags to keep them from drying out. When she looked up, the last person she expected to see was standing in the doorway, one hand still holding the handle, looking every bit the casual, easy-going guy, everyone thought he was. Beige chinos held up with a fancy belt that probably cost more than Scarlett earned some weeks. The perfectly pressed shirt and comfortable but stylish brogues, all gave an air of importance he thought he deserved, and maybe he did in some circles, but not here.

Jack.

Scarlett

"Zara said I'd find you here," he said, running a hand across the bald spot on top of his head. "Can I come in?"

Scarlett dropped the paintbrushes and stood up, wiping her hands down the old pair of jeans she'd worn to decorate in.

"Yeah, of course." There was something in her that wanted to smile in this moment, a little girl's hopes of a father who cared, but she held it back, out of fear of the man he might not be. Because he most definitely wasn't the fantasy figure she'd created over the years.

Stepping inside, he closed the door gently behind him. He took a moment to look around and take in his surroundings, gathering his courage and the words he wanted, even though, she was sure that he would have practised this in his head over and over on the journey.

"I have to admit that this situation isn't something I ever contemplated," he began, and she waited, silently listening. He locked eyes with her as he continued, "I was a terrible husband. I didn't know a good thing when I had it, always looking for something else, something exciting, and always ending up in situations I didn't even really want to be in." His eyes glazed, shiny with emotions. "I remember your mum. That night. I was terrified. I'd met Claudia and fallen in love, or at least what I thought love was meant to be, and we'd made a plan, and a commitment to one another, and I was determined to go through with that, because one thing Jack Maddox isn't, is a quitter, but it scared me, to be a grown-up and tied down to something for the rest of my life." He smiled at her quickly. "I don't regret it, we had a good life for a while and we had three amazing kids together. I'll never regret that, but in hindsight, I should never have married when we did, I wasn't ready for that level of responsibility."

"Why are you telling me all this?"

He stepped closer, fiddling nervously with his cufflink.

"Because I want you to understand that had I known about you, I would have claimed you. I'd have risked my marriage to do it, I wouldn't have left you without a father."

"I had a father," Scarlett answered, though she knew that was a terrible answer.

He looked away, hurt? embarrassed?

"And I'm grateful to him for stepping up when I—"

"Listen, if this is going to be some woe is me, happy you had a good life speech, then save it. I had a father, he wasn't a dad, he wasn't the man I needed, or wanted, but he was there, and it was his money that put food on the table, and clothes on my back, but that's all he did. And I got used to a life where I didn't have a man I could rely on to be there like a father should, so don't go getting all sentimental thinking that I'm going to start calling you daddy and inviting you into my life, because that's not going to happen." She stared him down.

He nodded slowly. "I understand that, but whether you like it or not, I am your dad."

"No, you're the man who provided half the ingredients to create me. I've never had a dad, and I don't need one now. Especially one who was married to my girlfriend."

An ironic chuckle bubbled out. "Yes, that does make things a little—"

"It doesn't. This has nothing to do with Claudia and I."

He held his hands up in surrender. "I didn't come here to fight, or create problems, I came because…you're my daughter. My flesh and blood, and I take that seriously."

"Last time we talked, you demanded a paternity test, why the big turn around? What are you expecting is going to happen here?"

He shrugged and smiled. "I don't know, but I hoped we could start by opening the door to at least discussing it?"

For the first time in her life, Scarlett felt torn. The urge to tell him to just leave was being fought by the urge to run to him and throw her arms around him and put all of her hope into finally having a man in her life who wanted to be her father.

"I appreciate that…and maybe." She sighed. "Maybe we can try to work something out."

His smile grew. "I'd like that."

If she was honest, she liked that too.

"So," he looked around the room at all of the DIY stuff lying around on the floor, "can I give you a hand with anything?"

She followed his eyes around the space and shook her head. "Nah, I'm pretty much done."

"Okay, well, I'll leave you to finish off and," he slid his hand into his pocket and pulled out his wallet, fishing through it he found a business card and held it out for her, "if you need me."

She hesitated, before finally stepping forward and taking it from him. She was sure she could have gotten the number from Claudia or Zara, or Diana, even Adam, but she didn't say anything to ruin the moment.

"Thanks."

Bea sauntered into the kitchen and plonked herself down on one of the stools while Claudia opened the bottle of wine she'd arrived with.

"So, what's occurring? New job still the best job in the world?" She grinned.

Claudia smiled, but not the all-reaching, eye-sparkling one she usually threw in Bea's direction. "Oh, you know, plodding along."

Eyes narrowed as Bea stared at her. "Hm, and what are you not telling me?"

Silently, Claudia uncorked the bottle and poured two glasses, pushing one across the counter towards her friend.

"Have you ever had something happen in life that leaves you feeling as though you're living an episode of Jeremy Kyle?"

Bea grinned. "Other than dipping my toes into the lesbian world of dating?"

"Yes, other than that," Claudia said seriously. Bea sat up straighter, something big was happening if Claudia wasn't even making the tiniest of jokes at her expense. "It appears that, well no, not appears, it's a fact, it's an actual fact, that Jack is…"

"An idiot?"

"Yes, and Scarlett's father."

The speed with which the wine burst from Bea's mouth and landed on the counter was most likely a world record. "What?" She grabbed for a cloth. "Sorry, but…what?"

"I said what I said." Claudia sighed. "Zara, Adam and Scarlett did one of those DNA things for shits and giggles apparently, and the results have been nothing but shits and none of the giggles."

"But…how?"

Claudia topped up Bea's glass. "Well, it would appear that infidelity in our marriage didn't actually require a wedding certificate, he was happily sharing the love before we even made it up the aisle…on his stag night."

"The mother fuck—"

97

Scarlett

Holding her hand up to stop the rant that was coming Claudia smiled sadly. "Yes, he's all of that and I am really angry about it all, but—"

"You don't want to make things more difficult for them?"

"Exactly. Scarlett is dumbfounded. Her dad's an arse, and now she discovers she has another father and he's an arse too. And as for the kids, well…" She threw her hands up. "Diana doesn't know who she is anymore, Adam punched him, and Zara doesn't get why anyone is upset because she loves the idea of another sister."

Bea blew out her cheeks. "Wow, I gotta admit, I never saw that one coming."

"No, me either." She took a long swig of her wine and checked the clock. "Scarlett will be home soon."

"Alright, I won't bring it up, but does she know you're telling me?"

Claudia nodded. "Of course, we don't have secrets."

"So, what do you need?"

This time Claudia did smile. "A punchbag?"

Chapter Twenty-Two

"I'm home," Scarlett called from inside the door as she kicked off her shoes. She'd changed out of her painting clothes at work and dropped the bag by the door as she slid her jacket off and hung it next to half a dozen others.

"We're in the kitchen," Claudia called, but then appeared in the doorway.

Two things struck Scarlett as she checked her out. Her hair had grown and was so often pulled up into a ponytail for work that she'd almost forgotten what Claudia looked like with her hair hanging loosely around her face. Gorgeous was the word for it. The baggy cotton dungarees and long-sleeved collarless shirt underneath gave her an air of laid back, chilled and relaxed, but Scarlett could tell by the clench of her jaw and the firm stance that she was anything but chill. The other thing was the smell. Something amazing was cooking.

"You alright? Had a good day? Something smells good." Scarlett closed the gap and kissed her cheek as she entered the kitchen and waved. "Hey, Bea."

"Scarlett," Bea replied, raising her glass.

Scarlett turned back to Claudia and tried to read her; she looked tense. "Are you—?"

"Yes, I'm fine, honestly," Claudia answered too quickly.

"I don't believe a word of it but okay. We'll talk later," Scarlett said quietly, before turning back to Bea again. "Got a glass for me?"

"Only if you're opening another bottle." She grinned, waving the almost empty one in the air.

Claudia leaned against her back and hung an arm around her already holding another bottle.

Scarlett

"Thanks babe, you know, for someone who makes a living out of paint, there is no way I'd ever make it as a decorator." Scarlett smiled, unscrewing the cap, and pouring it into the glass that Claudia also slid in front of her without the need to ask for it. "I'm going to go grab a bath."

"Dinner won't be long," Claudia offered, following her to the door.

"Okay, I'll be down shortly. Are you joining us, Bea?"

Bea quickly responded, "Nope, I have a hot date."

Scarlett's brow raised. "The same woman?"

"No, I'm not the settling down type." Bea grinned. "At least, not yet."

Scarlett laughed, and Claudia rolled her eyes. "Alright, give me a shout ten minutes before you plan to serve it up and I'll come down." She kissed Claudia quickly on the lips and turned away, heading up the stairs towards the long overdue bath she'd been thinking about for most of the day. She had muscles where she hadn't known she had muscles, and all of them were creating merry hell with every move she made.

She placed the glass down onto the edge of the bath, leaned in and pushed the plug down before twisting the taps and pouring a big dollop of Claudia's fancy bath bubbles into the gushing water.

Stripping off, she threw all of her clothes into the laundry bin and then perched on the edge of the tub sipping the wine while her free hand dangled into the water to test the temperature.

She heard Bea shout up a goodbye and hollered one back, and when she deemed the water to be perfect, she stepped in and slowly slid down into the suds. Letting out a loud groan of approval.

Her eyes closed and she enjoyed the warmth seeping into her bones, so relaxed was she that she didn't hear the sound of the door swishing open, or the footsteps that padded across the carpet of the bedroom and into the bathroom, but she did notice the sudden smell of something delicious.

"Did you bring me food?" she said, her eyes still closed.

Claudia chuckled and covered the toilet lid with a towel, placing the plate down on top of it. And the bottle and her own glass chinked on the edge of the bath. "I figured it was just as easy."

Scarlett opened her eyes and grinned up at her lover. "What did you cook?"

"Calzone. With salami, ham, and far too many cheeses to be healthy." She peeled off the straps of her dungarees and let the outfit fall to the floor. "And I thought, it's a takeaway kind of meal, so…" She lifted her shirt off and revealed that she wasn't wearing any underwear. "I wondered if maybe… I could join you?"

Sloshing the water as she moved, Scarlett sat upright and made space for Claudia to climb in and nestle between her legs. When she was comfortably lying back against Scarlett, she sighed.

"I guess I can eat it cold then." Scarlett smirked, cupping water in her hands and spilling it over the bare torso within her reach. "Hard day?"

"Somewhat. I couldn't focus during a meeting earlier and I think I've annoyed a co-worker."

"They'll get over it." Scarlett kissed the back of her head and tugged her closer. "Relax."

"I want to, I just…I'm angry, Scarlett."

"With Jack?"

Claudia nodded. "Who else?"

"You have every right to be."

Scarlett

Twisting to face her, Claudia pressed her lips together before she answered, "I know, I'm just processing why, and what I'm going to do about it."

"What did Bea suggest?"

Claudia chuckled and settled back again. "She agreed with a punchbag, with his face stuck on it."

Scarlett smiled. "It's not the worst idea." They sat quietly for a moment before she added, "He came to see me today."

"Oh." Claudia shifted and the water slopped around them. "What did he want?"

"He wanted to open the door to having a relationship with me, as my father."

"And what did you say to that?"

"I told him I don't need a father, that I'd never had a dad, and there wasn't space for him in my life like that, but—"

Claudia turned to face her again.

"I said I would think about maybe discussing things further."

"As rubbish a husband as he was, he isn't a bad dad."

"If I was twelve, maybe that would mean something but I kind of think I'm past the need now. I've had so many years being used to not having that *man* in my life who will always have my back, and I'm not sure I can rely on your ex-husband to be my supportive father while I have a relationship with you."

"Well, I'm not going anywhere," Claudia said firmly before settling back into her spot once more. "But maybe you should explore the opportunity."

"And maybe you need to tell him how you feel."

"Yes, I guess you're right."

Chapter Twenty-Three

Claudia Maddox hadn't walked into Jack's office for almost a decade. She'd stopped the moment she suspected he was engaging with his staff in ways she wasn't then prepared to deal with. The last thing she had wanted was to be subject to the sniggering voices as she walked through the corridors.

The building was the same, the office still in the same place, but everything else had changed. His secretary was no longer the hot young thing she always was when Claudia was his wife. No, Maisie wasn't a silly girl when she'd insisted on that little change to things around here.

"I'm here to see Jack," she said confidently to the woman in the grey suit who was much nearer her own age than Maisie's. And much more school head mistress than potential mistress.

The woman eyed Claudia up and down before checking his diary. "I'm afraid Mr Maddox is busy at the moment, if you'd like me to make you an appointment for tomorrow, I can—"

Claudia huffed and rounded the desk, heading for his door. "That's fine, I'm sure he will see me."

"You can't just—"

The door was open, and Claudia stepped inside before his secretary had a chance to finish her sentence. "Jack, we need to talk."

"Claudia?" He looked perplexed as he stood up from the pile of paperwork on his desk. "Is everything alright, are the kids— is it Scarlett?" He waved his secretary off. "It's fine, Martha. Close the door please."

Martha stared indignantly at Claudia for a moment before finally nodding. "Of course, Mr Maddox." She closed the door behind her, but not without one last glance at the woman ruining her secretarial reputation.

"The kids are fine, Scarlett's fine, I'm not here for them."

Scarlett

"Okay," he said slowly, coming around the desk to perch on the corner of it. "Take a seat."

"I'll stand if you don't mind."

He smiled casually at her. "I don't mind. What can I do for you?"

"You can stop being so bloody cool about everything for a start. I'm so angry, with you," she said as calmly as she could manage under the circumstances.

Jack stared at her for a moment. "I can imagine you are. I've been an utter bastard."

Claudia's eyes widened, because that wasn't the response she had expected at all.

"I owe you an apology, Claudia." He stood up and walked towards her, his hands that had once been the only hands to touch her, felt cold against her flesh when he placed them on her biceps. "I'm deeply sorry for the way that I behaved throughout our marriage, it was selfish, and underhanded, and cruel. It came from a place of never quite accepting that I was loved, and that was never on you. I know that all you ever did was try to love me and I didn't respect that."

She blinked rapidly as she took in the apology, an apology too long overdue, and if she were honest, totally unexpected, but it didn't alleviate her anger. "I did try, I did. I absolutely did love you and you ruined it. You threw us away without a care, put our kids through all of that turmoil, and for that I'll never forgive you," she snapped and looked away.

He was nodding when she brought her gaze back to him. "You're right, I threw us away. And I put you all through so much hurt and for that I am deeply ashamed, but I'm working really hard to try and come to terms with my behaviour. I don't need you to forgive me, I absolutely understand that it's not something I can ask of you—"

104

Claire Highton-Stevenson

"Where is the real Jack?" she asked, bemusedly looking around the room. "What have you done with him?"

This was not how she had foreseen this conversation going. In fact, that almost made her angrier. She had wanted to give him what for, and instead, he was taking all of the heat out of her with his humbling apologies.

He chuckled and stepped away, back around to the other side of the desk.

"I've been in therapy for the past few months. Actually, it was you moving on that made me realise everything I'd caused, and Maisie made it very clear that if things went that route with her then she was gone, so here we are." He held his hands out, palms up. "We were too young, both of us, but I wouldn't change it. We had some good times, and we have three great kids to show for it." He smiled at that thought. "But I've started to look inward, to understand that my selfishness has caused so much pain for so many of the people I love—"

"Sorry, you've what? Been in therapy?" she interrupted him. If there was anything more astounding than this, she was lost, even him being Scarlett's real father was less shocking than the idea of Jack Maddox in therapy.

"I know. I didn't think I'd get anything out of it, but I promised Maisie I'd try." He held his hands up in that who-knew kind of way. "And so, I went along, and well…it was eye-opening."

Claudia felt a little deflated. All of the anger she'd barged her way in here with had dispersed as she looked at her ex-husband with new eyes. Until she thought of Scarlett and the betrayal that had caused that issue.

"I'm glad that you're finally working things out and turning yourself into a better version of you, I am, really, I am, but that doesn't negate the absolute fury I feel. You cheated on me before we were even married. On your stag night, for fuck's sake, Jack." She threw her hands up in the air. "And you created a child. A child who

Scarlett

has grown into a beautiful, wonderful, amazing woman, and honestly, I feel torn from wanting to throttle you..." she breathed in deeply, releasing it slowly, "or thank you, because in her, I have found the most wonderful partner and I wouldn't be without her."

"I admit. It's been a shock. And again, I can only apologise for the hurt I've caused you. I know it probably means very little, but I mean it, I'm being sincere. I didn't plan to hurt you. And as for Scarlett." She watched him speak. The way his voice caught in his throat, his eyes wet with emotions she hadn't seen in him in years. "I can't pretend I'm not stunned to discover I have another daughter, and she is the woman my ex-wife is in love with, but I'm not unhappy about it. I'd like the opportunity to get to know her better. If she'll let me, and if you are agreeable with that?"

"That's something only Scarlett can decide, I won't influence her either way," she held his gaze, "but I will support whatever decision she makes including if she wants nothing more to do with you."

"Thank you, that's probably more than I deserve."

"It's not about you anymore, Jack. It's about her, and our children and what is best for all of them."

"Yes, of course."

"Right, well, I've said what I came here to say so..." She looked around the office as though she expected to find something familiar, but there was nothing. "I'll—" She pointed a thumb over her shoulder towards the door, feeling suddenly awkward.

"Thank you, Claudia. For everything."

She nodded curtly at him, there was nothing more to say.

Chapter Twenty-Four

Diana fussed with the table settings, lifting the placemats, and brushing imaginary crumbs away before placing them back exactly where they had been a moment ago. Zara watched with amusement from the armchair. Her legs swung over the arm, one bouncing in time to the music playing in the background.

"What are you doing?" she finally asked her elder sister. Jacob looked up from his playmat with little interest to keep him from returning his attention to the plastic block he'd been chewing on. "Not you sweetheart, mummy can see what you're doing, mummy is talking to aunty Diana, who is being a great big nervous numpty."

"I am not." Diana huffed, before flicking away imaginary fluff from the tablecloth with a sweep of her hand.

"Then why are you being a twit?" Zara asked, sitting up and pulling her legs around until her feet hit the floor and she could stand up. "You've had weeks to get used to this."

"I am not being a twit," Diana insisted, almost but not quite stamping her foot as her voice raised an octave. "Okay, fine, I don't know. It all just feels…weird still."

Zara nodded. "Yeah, but it's a good kind of weird, right? I mean, we liked Scarlett when she was just your friend or Mum's girlfriend, so she's still the same person."

"I suppose so. I just…I feel a little intimidated. She's the oldest now and that means—"

Zara grinned. "She can boss you around, yes, but we established she probably isn't going to do that. You still hold bossing rights, sis."

"I am not bossy."

Zara chuckled just as the doorbell rang and interrupted the banter. "Okay, whatever you say. Are you going to get it, or shall I?"

Scarlett

When Diana didn't move, Zara's smile widened and she wandered off in the direction of the hall, towards the front door. She swung it open and grinned at their visitor. Scarlett stood on the doorstep holding flowers in one hand and a bottle of something in the other, looking equally awkward.

"Hey, Sis." Zara giggled.

Scarlett blushed, like Diana, caught off guard, she was still not used to the familial situation yet either. "Uh, Hi. You, okay?"

"All good, come in. Diana is cooking up a storm, I think she thinks royalty is coming for tea."

"Oh, has she gone to a lot of trouble? I mean I'd be happy with beans on toast."

"Are you kidding, when she had Mum's cooking to compete with for your approval."

Scarlett frowned. "She doesn't need my approval."

"I know that, and you know that, but alas our idiot sister hasn't worked it out yet." She turned and headed back to the lounge. "Di, Scarlett's here," Zara called out as though Diana wasn't expecting her.

Appearing seconds later, looking as perfect as perfect can be, Diana greeted them from the doorway. "Hey." She smiled a little hesitantly.

"Di." Scarlett stepped forward, handing off the flowers and bottle to Zara. She pulled Diana into her arms. "It's good to see you." While they were close, Scarlett whispered, "Please don't over think this, we're good, alright, nothing changes."

"Doesn't it?" Diana laughed nervously.

Scarlett shook her head. "No, we're sisters, we can't change DNA, but how we fit into this new knowledge is not to change anything. We just need to be ourselves and organically allow this to become whatever we all need it to be, okay?"

"I guess," Diana said without any real conviction.

"So, what's for dinner then?" Scarlett grinned. "I'm starving."

Zara moved in past them both, dropping the flowers down onto the table as she passed, along with the bottle. She bent down and lifted Jacob, placing him into the waiting highchair. "Do you want a drink, Sis?"

They both turned to look at her and Zara giggled, but Scarlett didn't miss the confused look that came across Diana's face.

"Sorry, I was speaking to Scarlett, but obviously, if you're in need of a top up, Di?"

Diana glanced across the room at her half-filled glass. "No, I'm fine, thank you. I'll be in the kitchen."

Scarlett followed her. "Diana? Can we talk some more?"

Busying herself at the stove, Diana nodded. "Sure."

"I know that this is difficult for you, for us both, I guess, but particularly for you. And I just—" she stopped for a moment wanting to choose her words, "how do we make this easier? What do you need?"

Slowly, Diana turned around to face her, her eyes averting away as she blinked back unshed tears. "I don't know. What I do know is that everything feels so jumbled and—you were my friend. And I liked that, I like having my things separate from—not that you're a thing, I just—"

"I get it."

She stared right at Scarlett. "You were my friend and then you were mum's girlfriend and now, you're my dad's daughter, and my sister, and what used to be simple is now something I never dreamed I'd have to deal with." She turned back to the stove and

stirred the pot with a wooden spoon. "I'm also angry." She glance
back over her shoulder at Scarlett.

"With me, or the situation?"

"All of it," she answered honestly. "I'm angry with Da
obviously. And I'm angry with Mum for putting up with him, and fc
stealing you. I'm angry with Zara because she finds this all so eas
I'm angry with Adam because he's able to vent with his fists, an
I'm angry at you for being born first." Her voice had gotten angri
as she spoke until in the end she spat out, "And I'm angry with n
for being so bloody resentful of you all."

"I'm sorry." Scarlett stepped towards her, but Diana flung h
hands up and Scarlett stopped moving. "I'm here to listen if th
would help. Maybe it would do you good to vent more and get
out?"

"It's not really me, is it?" Diana smirked. "But that
probably another part of my resentment, it's changing me, and
don't like it."

"That's true, you've never been very good with change."

"I just need time usually, but this—it's hit hard, Letty. And
know that for you it must be just as difficult, if not worse. I can
imagine discovering my dad wasn't the man I thought he was."

"Actually, that's probably been the easiest part." Scarle
smiled. "You know I never really got on with my dad."

"Have you spoken to him since?"

Scarlett nodded. "I have, yes, and he's just as ridiculous s
nothing much has changed."

"Do you want it to?"

"I'm not sure, maybe. Not right now. Right now, I want to f
things with you and make sure that moving forwards, we're alright.
grew up without siblings, so I'm not expecting much—I just thoug
that maybe it's something we—"

"Yes," Diana said quickly. "Yes, I want that."

"You do?"

"Hm hm, it's just going to take me some time, that's all, and I need something from you."

"Go on," Scarlett urged.

"You might be almost a year older than me, but I can't lose my position. I've always been the eldest, the leader, the one they look to, it's a huge part of who I am and I—I don't know how to be a middle child."

Scarlett tried not to grin, but the corners of her mouth lifted a little. "As I said before, I don't want your spot, Di. I think I'm too independent to fall in line behind too, but I'm not going to fight you for the role."

"See, I told ya." Zara winked as she came into the room, eavesdropping on the conversation.

"I might also add." Scarlett grinned. "I'm probably going to abstain from any sibling arguments. I'll be the voice of reason."

"Yes, good luck with that." Diana laughed.

Scarlett

Chapter Twenty-Five

Hanging artwork to dry at the end of a session, Scarlett smiled to herself as the sun shone in through the window. She had a hot date with Claudia later and was planning a late night. Their world recently had become a little manic with both of them ploughed under with work and Claudia's kids' drama. She stopped what she was doing and reminded herself that it was her sibling drama. She couldn't quite get her head around that completely, but she was trying. Zara, Adam, and Diana had always been Claudia's but now, now they were hers too.

The phone buzzed from inside the drawer on her table, but she ignored it and finished the task. Her client's images were dark and a little sinister, but that was kind of expected with everything he'd been through in his short life. Eventually, she would see the colours change and the images soften, but for now, this was the thought process. She pegged the last one on the line and was just about to reach for her phone when there was a knock at the door.

Before she could answer, it swung open.

Jack.

He looked a little awkward as he stood there, just like he had done a few weeks ago. His face evened out from a little apprehension to a smile she recognised as her own.

"Jack," she said confidently. "What brings you here again?" She winced internally for adding the again, as though his being here was unwanted and an inconvenience to her, which she wasn't sure wasn't the case, but still, he was at least making an effort, even if she wasn't and it was more of an effort than the man she did call dad had ever made.

"Hey, I was just passing, and I wondered if you wanted to grab lunch with me?"

"Lunch?"

He chuckled. "Yeah, that meal between breakfast and dinner."

She smiled at him. Thinking back to the man she had first met, almost a year ago, Claudia's ex-husband, it was hard to fathom who this version of Jack was. Her opinion of him had been that he was an arsehole, but this man in front of her was trying. And according to Claudia, he was in therapy, so shouldn't she be applauding his effort?

"Uh, I—"

"Of course, you're probably busy already." He turned towards the door. "I should have—"

"No, I just, I wasn't expecting you." She rubbed her hands down her thighs and checked her shirt didn't have blobs of paint on it. "Okay, why not."

His face broke out into a wider smile. "Really? That's great. I was thinking there's a nice place just around the corner."

The only places Scarlett could think of around the corner were the kind of places she didn't frequent, because her mum had always taught her that if there were no prices on a menu and you had to ask how much before you ordered then you probably couldn't afford to eat there.

"Right, I just…I'm not sure I'm dressed for those kinds of—"

"I've always found that the kind of places that turn people away for how they're dressed, really should try and understand that the bill gets paid from the wallet, not the shirt and how much has been spent on it."

She kind of liked that analogy. "Yeah, I guess so. I need to lock up and let them know I'm out of the building."

"I'll meet you in the car then?"

Scarlett

She nodded and watched as he turned away, the door closing gently between them. Was she really about to go to lunch with her father?

Joie was a chic restaurant on the corner. With bistro tables outside, it felt very much like a Mediterranean eatery, especially with the sun shining high in the sky like it had been for days now. It was a little out of the way and didn't get the same kind of footfall as many other places did, but it was always busy, which told a story of its own, and Scarlett wondered if they'd get a table.

"Ah, Mr Maddox, how good to see you again, your usual table?" The waiter spoke excitedly, and Scarlett smiled at him. Clearly, Jack was a regular here.

"George, thank you that would be great." He waited for George to move, and then for Scarlett to follow, his hand touching the space between her shoulders and not the small of her back made her feel protected. Where had that thought come from? She'd never needed to feel protected by anyone.

They took their seats at the window, and George passed menus while talking rapidly about the specials and the choice of drinks on offer. All of it went unheard as Scarlett contemplated this moment. The first time she would eat a proper meal with the man who helped create her.

"So, how are things going?" Jack asked once George had taken their drinks order and left them to peruse the menu.

Scarlett looked up and found Jack staring at her. "Good, I guess. You?"

He smiled. "Yes, well. Maisie is blooming and work is good, the business is doing well, so no complaints."

She kept forgetting that Maisie was pregnant, and another brother or sister would soon enter her life. *That was weird, wasn't it?*

"Yes, not long to go now. Do you know if it's a boy or a girl?"

He shook his head. "No, we decided to wait and let it be a surprise. What would you prefer, a new brother or another sister?" He looked at her hopefully, and she felt a pang of guilt for not caring.

"I uh, I hadn't given it much thought," she answered honestly and felt the guilt ramp up when she saw the look of sadness on his face. "I mean, I'm still getting used to the idea of Zara being my sister, and being an aunt to Jacob. I guess at my age, I never expected to be—"

"Of course, I get it, it's all still a bit of a shock, I just…I'd hoped maybe by now things might have settled a little and we could forge ahead. I want to be the father you didn't have."

George reappeared looking eagerly at them as he placed drinks down onto the table. "Have we decided?"

Jack slowly moved his eyes away from her, looking back at his menu quickly he said, "The steak, medium. Thank you."

"And for you, madame?"

Scarlett winced, madame? She really was getting older, wasn't she? "I'll have the country salad."

"Good choice." George beamed and took the menus from them before turning away and leaving them to it.

"The thing is, I don't know what you, being *the father I didn't have,* looks like," Scarlett explained. "I don't know that that's what I need from you. What do you see happening here?"

He sat back, relaxed, and confident as he considered the question.

Scarlett

"I'd like it if we could do this more often. Spend some tim getting to know one another, spend time together as a family with m other children. I'd like to be someone that maybe in time you fe able to call when you wanted to. Speak to for advice maybe?"

"I have someone for that. And if I needed advice about her, think it highly unlikely you'd be my first port of call."

"I understand. Claudia will always be an off-limits subject, get that, and I'm in total agreement, it would feel quite odd speakin with my daughter about my ex-wife."

She sipped her drink.

"How do you do that? How can you so easily call me you daughter?"

He shrugged. "Because you are. I only have to look at you t see it, and despite my reputation, I'm not actually the bigges arsehole most people think I am. I take my parental responsibilitie seriously."

"Just your marital ones that didn't matter?" She knew onc she'd said it that it was a low blow. "Sorry, that was—"

"Fair." His smile thinned out across his lips. "I was a horribl husband, that's true."

George returned carrying an oversized tray ladened with large plate of steak and frites, and a fancy bowl of green vegetables all of which he placed down onto the table in front of Jack. "Tha looks amazing, George."

"Thank you, Mr Maddox."

In front of Scarlett, he placed her bowl of fresh leaves an warm chicken. She had to admit, the steak looked more appealing.

"This is my daughter, Scarlett," Jack added proudl introducing her. "I'd like it if you made sure her name is added to m account."

"Of course, lovely to meet you, Ms Maddox." George bowed, actually bowed at her, which was awkward and amusing all at once.

"It's Taylor, Scarlett Taylor," she corrected. When George was gone, Scarlett picked up her fork, ready to eat. "I don't need to be on your account."

"Why not? The others are, and believe me, they take full advantage of it." He chuckled, mirroring her actions with the cutlery. "Especially, Adam."

"I just don't know that I'm comfortable with it." She took a bite, it was delicious.

"Then don't use it, but it's there if you want to." Jack cut into the steak and popped a piece into his mouth, chewing instantly. Unable to stop the sound of gratification that came with it.

"Claudia tells me that you've been in therapy?"

"All true." He continued to slice and stab and chew.

"Finding it useful?"

He placed his knife and fork down, wiped his mouth with the linen napkin, and looked up at her. "Yes. The old me would never have managed this situation, and it's been helpful to talk about it with him, my therapist. Having to accept the root cause of my behaviour has really helped me to rethink and relearn a lot of things. I'm still a work in progress, but I think I'm on the right track."

"That's really good, Jack."

"It is, isn't it?" He grinned, proud of himself for once.

And she had to admit, she was quietly impressed. "Yes, it is."

Scarlett

Chapter Twenty-Six

Claudia was late. The candles on the table had burned almost halfway when Scarlett finally blew them out. She'd tried calling but it just went into voicemail each time. It was almost nine now and Scarlett was really starting to worry. Heck, who was she kidding, she'd been worrying for nearly thirty minutes. It wasn't like Claudia to not come home on time, or to at least not call her in advance, even though this new job was taking up more and more of her time recently, Claudia never failed to call and explain she would be late.

Scarlett pulled the curtain back and checked out of the window for the fifteenth time. The shadow of The Beast on the drive not helping to remind her that Claudia wasn't home because The Beast was far too big to park at her new office block. She searched both directions of the street, hoping for headlights on the uber Claudia would be travelling in.

Her heart skipped a beat as a beam of lights swung around the corner and got closer, her heart sinking when the vehicle drove straight past without slowing down.

"Where are you?" she muttered under her breath, dropping the curtain, and turning back to face the room. She picked up her phone again and pressed Claudia's number.

"You've reached the voicemail of…" She switched it off. What was the point of yet another message wondering where she was. She opened the contacts list and called Zara.

"Yep," her sister's chirpy voice said quickly.

"Hey, have you heard from your mum?" Scarlett ran her hand through her hair as she twisted back and forth on the spot, phone pressed tightly to her ear.

"No, why? Isn't she at that meeting today?"

"Yeah, it's just we had a dinner date at home planned and she's not turned up, her phones off and—"

"I mean, she's probably just ran out of battery and on her way," Zara said absently before her voice muffled and Scarlett heard. "It's Scarlett, Mum's not home yet. I think she's worried."

There was a commotion before Diana's voice came on the line. "How late is she?"

Scarlett flipped her wrist and checked her watch. "Nearly two hours."

"And her phone's off?" Diana clarified.

"Yeah, goes straight to voicemail, and I've left half a dozen messages already."

"Right, we're coming over."

"You don't need—" It was pointless arguing; the call was already disconnected.

She tried Claudia once more.

"You've reached the voice…"

"Shit."

Making herself feel useful, she cleared away the plates and cutlery from the table, carrying them all out to the kitchen where the aroma of the lasagne, going cold in the oven, clung to the air and filled her nose with garlic and onions. It made her stomach rumble but the thought of eating right now soon counteracted that.

When the doorbell rang, she almost jumped out of her skin. Frowning as she checked the time, did they break the speed limit to get here? Why didn't they just use their key? Should she be as worried as Diana appeared to be? But then a thought hit her, what if it was Claudia, forgotten her key or just too tired to search that ridiculous bag for them.

She flung the door open, a hopeful expression on her face, and instead, got the shock of her life when she realised that the two figures standing there were not Claudia, or Zara and Diana, but two police officers.

"Good evening." The male officer stepped forwards, taking the lead. "Is this the residence of Claudia Maddox?"

Scarlett felt her soul leave her body and slam back in a second later.

"Yes," she stammered. Her heart rate had reached atomic levels.

"May we come in?" he continued, giving his name, but she didn't hear it.

She shook her head. "No, not until you tell me where she is. Is she alright? What's happened?"

The other officer stepped forward, her face soft and a thin smile filled with pity pressed against her lips. "If we could come in, we can explain everything."

Scarlett swallowed and acquiesced, stepping back, she pulled the door wider for them to pass inside. They waited in the hall for her to show them to the lounge.

"I'm PC—" he tried again.

"Sorry, I don't care. What's happened to Claudia?" Scarlett burst in tears. "Where is she?"

"And you would be?"

"Scarlett, I'm Claudia's partner. We live here together, now what's happened." She could feel her frustration begin to build. Why wouldn't they just answer the question? It was simple enough.

The woman officer stepped forward again, "There's been an accident on the motorway. Ms Maddox has been taken to Queen Charlotte's. I'm afraid, that's all the information we have right now."

"But she's alive?" Scarlett stared intently at the woman. "She's alive!"

"As far as we are aware, she was taken to hospital unconscious but alive, yes."

Scarlett was shaking.

"Are you alright? We can take you to the hospital."

"I'm…I'm fine, I just—I need to go." She stalked out into the hall and grabbed the keys to The Beast. "Can you stay here? My sisters are on their way over and someone needs to explain things and bring them to the hospital."

The officers looked at each other and then nodded. "Okay, though it might be advisable to wait, you're in no fit state to—"

"I'm not waiting another second. I need to be with her and they're going to be at least another fifteen minutes. I'm not going to call them with this news while they drive, so please. Just make sure they get to the hospital safely."

And with that, she was outside and climbing into The Beast, key in the ignition, engine roaring into life, seconds before she backed out and onto the road.

Scarlett

Chapter Twenty-Seven

Queen Charlotte's wasn't the local hospital to where the lived, and Scarlett couldn't recall ever having had to come here. was a good thirty minutes' drive out of town and Scarlett thanked th heavens for the in-built satellite navigating system that led h through the maze of streets and used the fastest route. She put h foot down and hoped to goodness she didn't get a ticket, but sh really didn't care right now. All of her thoughts were on Claudia.

Arriving at the hospital, she parked the car and ran until sh reached the entrance to A&E. Stammering her details at th receptionist through ragged breaths, until finally, she was being le down a corridor to a small room.

"A doctor will be with you as soon as they can. Can I get yo a cup of tea?"

"No, thank you, I'm fine, I just need to—" Scarlett tried t smile but failed, there wasn't anything to smile about was there?

"Someone will be with you as soon as they can."

Scarlett took in her new surroundings. Beige walls and plasti seats. A large couch that looked as though it must be twenty year old, and a coffee table covered in magazines that had been read by thousand sets of eyes and fingertips. She ignored it all.

It took six long minutes of pacing back and forth befor finally, the door opened and a woman in a white coat stepped insid All confidence and authority as she took in the lone occupant of th room.

"Family of Claudia Maddox?" she asked, and Scarle nodded, standing still instantly.

"Yes, I'm her partner."

The doctor smiled at her, and Scarlet relaxed just a little. "I' Doctor Hassid. I'm heading up the team treating Claudia, along wit Dr Goodhart."

Team? That didn't sound good.

"Claudia was brought in just over an hour ago following an RTA on the motorway. She was travelling in the front of the vehicle along with the driver, and two other passengers in the back." Dr Hassid sat down on the edge of a chair and Scarlett mirrored her. "From what we can ascertain, the vehicle was hit from behind, causing it to spin out of control and eventually roll into the other lane where it was subsequently hit again." She let that information sink in before continuing, "I'm told that it's a miracle anyone survived at all."

Scarlett winced.

"Claudia is currently in surgery to reset the bones in her left leg and we have already reset a dislocated shoulder. She has some internal damage caused mostly by the seatbelt doing its job. The air bags cushioned the impact and prevented a much more serious outcome; however, she has had a massive bang on the head and we're monitoring to decide whether we need to do anything more. Signs are good that it's just some bruising. She has some internal bleeding that we are monitoring. We will know in the next twenty-four hours." She smiled reassuringly. "But for now, all we can do is wait."

"She's not—" Scarlett felt her throat constrict. "She's not going to die?"

"I am hopeful that that won't be the case, but she's not out of the woods yet, okay. Do you have family, anyone who can be here with you?"

"Yes, my sisters are on their way."

"Good. We'll keep you all updated as best we can." She was about to get up when Scarlett stopped her.

"What kind of internal damage? What does that mean?"

Scarlett

"Her spleen has a small bleed but we have decided that we can wait to see if it will stop on its own rather than doing surgery. Try not to worry too much, she's in good hands."

Scarlett nodded. "And...the others, in the car with her?"

"I don't have much information I'm afraid, but I know that two of the three are here and receiving treatment."

"And the fourth?"

Doctor Hassid stood up and smiled sadly. "They didn't make it."

"Jesus," Scarlett muttered. "Thank you, thank you so much."

"I'll send someone to get you once we have Claudia back and settled, then you can sit with her." She turned ready to leave when the door flew open and in crashed Diana, followed quickly by Zara and the two officers that had broken the news to her earlier.

"Scarlett," Zara cried out and rushed to her, throwing herself into her sister's arms. "Is Mum, okay?"

"We—" Scarlett broke down in tears.

"I'm Doctor Hassid," she repeated. "I've explained to Scarlett that Claudia is currently in surgery. It's going to be a while before we know everything that we are dealing with, in the meantime, you're all welcome to use this space to wait until we can update you."

Diana stepped forward. "Is my mother going to die?"

Scarlett noticed the look of confusion register on the doctor's face. Their mother, but Scarlett's partner, and yet, Scarlett and the other women were sisters.

"We're going to do everything we can to make sure your...mum is okay."

"We have the same father," Scarlett felt the need to explain, as she wiped her cheeks dry and sniffed. "I met Claudia before I knew we were siblings. She's not my mum. She's their mum, and they're my sisters. And we have a brother, Adam." She glanced away quickly and found Zara staring at her in amusement at the oversharing of information, but also the first public acknowledgement of them all.

The doctor's eyebrow raised. "Okay, well, I'll make sure that staff know to keep you all informed. I need to get going, if you need anything, just ask at reception." She was about to leave when she stopped and turned back to them. "I forgot, sorry." Reaching into her pocket, she pulled out a clear plastic bag. "These came in with Claudia, we had to remove her jewellery in order to proceed with surgery. I believe the police will have any other personal items, but these were either on her or in her pockets." She held out her hand and Scarlett stepped forwards to take it. Noticing Claudia's necklace and rings instantly, as well as her phone.

They all watched as the doctor left the room and Scarlett heard the male officer mutter to his colleague, "Well that explains the dynamics."

Ignoring them, Scarlett turned to Diana. "Has anyone called Adam? And where's Jacob?"

"I have," Zara answered, her hand halfway in the air. "Well, I text him."

"You text him? What did you say?"

She shrugged. "That he needed to call me asap. And Jacob is with James obviously, I didn't just leave him at home."

"And has he?" Diana now butted in. "Has Adam text you back?"

Zara pulled out her phone and checked. "No."

Scarlett

"Oh, for goodness' sake." Diana sighed, pulling her own phone out and hitting buttons before she placed the speaker to her ear. "Adam, it's Diana. You need to come to the hospital." She paused. "Yes, now. It's Mum." Another pause as she paced the room. "I don't know, but you need to be here." She ended the call abruptly, turning to Scarlett. "So many questions, why can't people just do as they're asked?" She typed out a text with details of where they were and pressed send.

They all stood in silence.

Diana's wrath turning then to the two police officers. "And why are you still here? Shouldn't you be out there finding out what has happened, and why our mother is currently fighting for her life?"

The female officer looked uncomfortable but said, "I'll go and see if there is any more information." She nudged her partner. "Why don't you sort some coffees?"

"What? Oh, yeah, I'll go get some coffees, anyone?"

Scarlett and Diana shook their heads, and both muttered no thank you.

"Can I get a tea?" Zara piped up.

The three of them stood silently until the officers both left the room and then Diana turned to face Scarlett. "Are you okay?"

Zara moved in and put her arms around them both, pulling all three into a hug that Diana wasn't comfortable with but didn't make a fuss.

"I'm okay, just terrified, I can't lose her." Scarlett spoke quietly. Her voice choking. "I can't."

"That's not happening," Diana said firmly, Zara nodded along. "Mum isn't going to just give up, so whatever is happening I can guarantee, she is going to fight her way through it."

"You're right, we have to keep positive," Zara agreed. "Mum is a fighter."

126

Claire Highton-Stevenson

For the first time in her life, Scarlett felt something she had been missing her entire life, the love of family.

Scarlett

The tick tick ticking of a clock high up on the wall was th₁ only sound that broke the silence in the room. Outside was different matter with people yelling, and alarms going off every fe₁ minutes. But none of it compared to the noise inside Scarlett's brai₁ as it ruminated over every possible potential outcome. She could fee₁ her jaw clenching tighter, her fingers squeezing closed into a tighte₁ fist, and nothing anyone said made it feel any better.

When the door opened, they all looked up expectantly that i₁ would be the doctor, or Adam and Sunny, but the face that appeare₁ around it wasn't someone Scarlett had considered at all, Jack.

"Dad? What are you doing here?" Diana asked curiously a₁ she stood to greet him with a kiss to the cheek.

"I called him," Zara announced, and when Scarlett and Dian₁ both turned their gazes on her, she added with a shrug. "It felt lik₁ the right thing to do,"

"How is she?" He asked to no one in particular. Both Zar₁ and Scarlett looked to Diana.

"We don't know," Diana said slowly. "We've been left i₁ here for what feels like hours, Mum's being operated on though an₁ they don't think it's too serious as yet, but..." She shrugged an₁ teared up like the rest of them.

Jack reached out and rubbed his palm up and down Diana' bicep. "Do we know what happened?"

This time, and surprisingly, Diana deferred to Scarlett.

"She uh, they were travelling back from a meeting and th₁ vehicle was involved in a collision on the motorway. It rolled int₁ the other lane, where it was hit for a second time. Three of those i₁ the car were brought here, the fourth—" she felt her throat constric₁ "they didn't make it."

Hot tears streamed down her cheek and before she knew what was happening, arms folded around her, embracing her in a hug like nothing she had known before. She felt her cheek pressed against a strong shoulder and the sensation of a kiss being placed against the top of her head. Jack was holding her. Pulling her in close and holding her like only a father could. It felt oddly nice and weird all at once, and she pulled away, stepping back.

She didn't need a father, did she?

"I—I'm okay," she muttered, her own arms wrapping around herself instantly at the loss of his. She glanced at him quickly, noting the look of sadness that flickered across his face before acceptance took its place. She felt a pang of guilt at that.

The door swung open again, this time like a saloon door in the wild west, almost bouncing off of its hinges. "Where is she?" Adam said urgently, as Sunny bustled in behind him and the door closed with a bang. "What's he doing here?" Adam sneered at his father.

Jack raised a brow but said nothing.

Scarlett surprised herself when she answered, "He's here to support his kids in our time of need."

His kids. Our time of need. She heard the words repeat in her head and knew that she had included herself in that statement. Jack's other brow rose to match the first, as did Diana and Zara's.

"So, if we can all get back to worrying about the important person in all of this and not ourselves and our petty family grievances, I'd appreciate it," Scarlett concluded.

"What she said," Zara piped up before the room dove back into silence.

"So, how is she?" Sunny asked when the silence became unbearable.

Scarlett

Scarlett couldn't bear to go through it all again. "I'm going to go and get some air. Can you get me if there's any news?"

"Sure," Diana answered.

Walking down the corridor by herself, Scarlett glanced into every bay hoping to catch a glimpse of Claudia, but of course, she never did. These were patients that didn't need hours of emergency surgery. At the nurse's station, she stopped and hovered for a moment before finally getting someone's attention.

"Sorry, any news on Claudia Maddox?"

The woman on duty looked down at her paperwork and then up at the board behind her screwed to the wall, shaking her head. "No, sorry love. She's not with us yet."

Scarlett nodded and walked away. At the end of the corridor, she buzzed the door open and continued to walk until finally she came to the hospital's entrance and the big automatic doors slid open. Cool air hit her face and the waft of smoke that hung heavily as several people huddled in the corner with cigarettes and fruit-flavoured vapes.

She stepped to the side and leaned back against the wall, her eyes closed as she breathed deeply and tried to calm her mind. It was helping nobody by getting herself wound up when she had no idea what was happening.

"Any news?" A gentle voice she recognised broke through her thoughts. Turning, she found the female police officer standing less than a foot away.

"No, nothing yet." Scarlett shook her head. "How come you're still here?"

"Still trying to speak to those involved. It's going to be a long night all round."

Scarlett nodded. "I'm sorry if I was rude to you earlier…shock, I guess."

"That's no problem. Had worse. I'm PC Sims though if you need to speak to me at any time?"

"Right, yes." She took the business card PC Sims held out. "So, how are the others?"

"I'm not supposed to really say, but…they're no worse than Claudia."

"Except for the one that didn't make it." Scarlett sighed. "I just, I can't imagine if anything—if she doesn't make it."

"Scarlett?"

She glanced over Sims' shoulder and saw Jack. Sims smiled. "I'll leave you with your dad."

Scarlett smiled sadly and noticed that she didn't correct her.

"Hey." Scarlett spoke to Jack once the police officer had left.

"I got sent out to check you were okay." He smiled at her. "Are you okay?"

"No, not really." She tried to laugh and failed miserably as the chuckle choked up and into a sob. "I can't lose her."

"You're not going to," he said, once more pulling her close and this time, she didn't fight it. Her clenched fists rested against his broad shoulders as he held her in his arms. "And whatever happens, I'm here, for you all."

"I know," she mumbled. "Thank you."

"I'm your dad, this is what we do."

And for once, she didn't feel the need to argue that. She felt safe. Cared for, and most of all, wanted. And all by a man she had had little or no respect for over the last year.

"I—"

Scarlett

Zara running through the door and skidding to a halt when she saw them, side tracked her.

"Scarlett, Dad, come quickly, they've got an update."

Chapter Twenty-Nine

They gathered together, huddled in a small group of worry and tears as the doctor explained.

"We've reset the leg and shoulder, and made Claudia as comfortable as we can. For now, it's a wait-and-see scenario as we monitor her brain and the internal bleed. The internal bleeding seems to have stopped, so unless there are complications we won't be doing another surgery. But we are very hopeful that she is through the worst of it."

"Thank god," Jack said for them all, his arms around Zara and Diana, hands squeezing their shoulders.

Doctor Hassid smiled. "She's not out of the woods yet. She needs to rest, and the best way for us to do that is an induced coma until the swelling in her head goes down. It will also keep her spleen stable minimising the need for further intervention." Gasps around the room, meant she raised her hands for calm. "It's just a fancy way of saying she's heavily sedated in ICU. It allows the body time to recover from the physical trauma and will only be for a few days at most. We will assess her again tomorrow and decide when the right time to bring her back around is."

"Can we see her?" Scarlett asked, chewing the side of her fingernail.

"Of course, though we'd prefer no more than two at a time, and for short periods. You can all continue to use this room in the meantime."

Jack took charge. "Diana, Scarlett, why don't you go first?"

Scarlett looked at the faces staring back at her. Adam flushed and visibly upset, staring away to the floor, Sunny smiling sadly but nodding her agreement. Zara twirling her hair. They all wanted to go, she knew that, but an element of selfishness pushed its way to the fore, and she nodded.

Scarlett

"Okay, let's go." She turned to face Diana. Her sister's eye wide with fear. "It will be okay, come on."

For once in her life, Diana let herself be led. They followe the doctor out into the hall. "I don't know how—" She glanced a Scarlett. "Can you be the oldest tonight?"

Scarlett reached out and took her hand. "Sure thing."

Claudia had a room to herself. Set at one end of the sma ICU department, right next to the nurse's station. There was a larg window to the right of the door with shutters already closed. Doctc Hassid stopped them at the door.

"Just prepare yourselves, it will look a lot worse than it i Claudia has a lot of monitors and wires attached, she has cuts an contusions that will heal but for now they look very upsetting."

Scarlett felt her hand being squeezed. "It's okay, she's aliv that's all that matters." She turned to Diana. "Ready?"

Diana breathed deeply and then nodded. "Okay."

The door opened and they stepped inside past the doctor.

"Oh God," Diana muttered. "Mum." Her voice quivered a she slowly neared the bed. Letting go of Scarlett's hand. The doc closed gently behind them. Scarlett remained where she stood, sti and silent as she took in the scene.

Claudia looked so small in the bed. Beneath covers pulled u to her chest and tucked around her. Her arms free of the materia restraints, but not free of needles and tape and wires. It wasn't a sigl Scarlett had ever considered she would witness. The sound of a cha scraping across the floor brought her attention back to the beeps an whooshes.

"You alright?" she asked Diana.

"Probably not the word I'd use." She smiled briefly. "Do yo think it's okay to hold her hand? She looks so…fragile."

Scarlett finally found her feet moving as she rounded the other side of the bed and pulled her own chair closer. "Yeah, I would think so."

With permission granted, Diana reached out and as gently as she could, picked up her mother's hand. Gently running her thumb back and forth over the area that didn't have a huge needle sticking into it with a plastic tube leading up to the bag that dripped whatever medical fluid was needed.

"I can't believe it."

"I know. It's crazy isn't it. We were supposed to be having dinner. Something so mundane and—" Scarlett croaked. She reached out and gently touched Claudia's forehead, running her fingers lightly over the bruise that was already angry and purple. "I'm not leaving her."

"I know. But you have to sleep, eat, rest."

Scarlett nodded, glancing at the armchair in the corner of room. "I will, but I'm not leaving her. I'll go for some fresh air or food when one of you wants to visit, but I don't want anyone pestering me to leave her. I'm the big sister tonight, remember?"

"Of course. We'll all stay tonight. And in the morning, I'll take Zara home and we'll get organised. I'll drop by yours and pick you up some clothes and a wash bag. I'll bring in snacks too."

"Okay, thank you. Do you think you could drive your mum's car?"

Diana's eyes widened. "The Beast?"

"Yeah, it's in the car park, and I don't want to leave it there. If you or Zara could drive it home."

"How about I get Dad to drive it, and I'll drive his, and Zara can drive mine?"

Scarlett chuckled. "Whatever works."

Scarlett

Diana checked her watch. "It's nearly 3 a.m."

"Yeah, it's going to be a long night."

"I'm glad you're here, I mean…obviously not glad, but if I had to go through this, I'm glad you're here." Diana closed her eyes and shook her head.

"I know what you mean, and I'm glad you're here too, all of you. And I don't just mean as Claudia's kids, I'm glad you're here as my sister."

"I still feel like I'm living an episode of Eastenders." Diana chuckled. "Did you see the doctor's face when you tried to explain."

Scarlett glanced up and smiled. "Yeah, was kind of comical. I mean not in the moment, but now, looking back."

"It's Jacob I feel sorry for, his aunty is his nanna, his nanna is his aunty, his grandad is one nanna's ex-husband and the other nanna's dad. That kid's going to have identity issues."

This time Scarlett laughed. "Maybe we need to just keep things simple for him, I'll just be aunty Scarlett, and Claudia can be nanna. I don't think I'm old enough for the nanna label just yet."

"Fair." Diana smiled. "She's going to be alright, isn't she?"

"She can't be anything else, we all need her too much."

Chapter Thirty

Like the animals onto the Arc, they all entered and left Claudia's room in pairs. Spending no longer than ten minutes before swapping for another set of visitors who cried and talked in whispers.

Scarlett glanced at her watch, it was almost five in the morning and all of them were yawning and bleary eyed as they desperately tried to stay awake. There had been no change with Claudia. She was the only one of them getting any rest.

"We should probably all go home and get some sleep, come back tomorrow?" Diana suggested to deaf ears. "I think it would be beneficial to us all."

Eventually, Jack stretched. "You're probably right, why don't you all get going. I can stay here with Scarlett and—"

Adam groaned. "Be her knight in shining armour?"

"That isn't what I meant."

Scarlett opened her eyes and looked at the pair of them. "Can you two fight another time, this really isn't the place for it." She glared at Adam before turning towards Jack. "And thank you, but I'll be fine. When Zara and Sunny get back, I'm going to go and sleep in the armchair by her bed."

Diana jumped up with far too much energy for everyone else. "Right, that's decided then. We'll all head home and grab a few hours sleep, then if Scarlett can let us know in the morning what time to come back, we can organise round-the-clock visiting."

"You're not in charge, Di," Adam grumbled.

"Yes, I am," Diana argued, finally stepping back into her power. "Right now, someone needs to lead, and that's my job." She turned to Scarlett. "I think I'm okay now."

Scarlett nodded, her role as the eldest pushed back again for now.

Scarlett

Adam rolled his eyes.

"I'm the one you're all going to lean on at some point, so I think it's only fair that I am the one who—" Diana continued.

"For once I can't be bothered to argue." Adam stood up. "I'll go find Sunny, and we can all reconvene tomorrow."

"Great, that's what I said, glad we're all on the same page." Diana smiled victoriously just as Zara and Sunny arrived back in the room. "So, Dad, can you drive Mum's car and I'll drive yours, Zara can take—"

"Uh, I can drive The Beast," Zara butted in.

Diana smiled like a teacher with a child just learning to read. "I'm sure you could, but—"

Zara ignored her and turned to Scarlett, her hand held out for the keys. "I'll drive it."

"Zara, don't you think—" Diana was cut off.

"Di, for once will you just allow other people to organise themselves. I am perfectly capable of driving any car."

"I didn't mean to sound as though you couldn't."

Scarlett stood up, pulled the keys from her pocket, and handed them to Zara. The bickering all just a little too much. "I'm going to let you argue amongst yourselves. I'll see you all tomorrow."

She walked into Claudia's room and stared at the figure in the bed. Hardly believing that this was the same woman she'd made love with twenty-four hours earlier before Claudia had rushed out of the door, already late, and heading to a meeting she didn't really want to go to.

"I can't wait to get home again," she'd called out as she all but ran down the stairs and out of the door. "I love you."

She looked so small bundled up beneath bandages and blankets. Like something out of a sci-fi movie with all of the tubes and wires attached to her.

Scarlett moved around the room, closing the blinds, and dragging the bulky plastic-covered armchair over as close to Claudia as she could get it. She leaned over the bed and looked down at Claudia's face, cursing all of the tubes and bruises. Gently, Scarlett placed a warm kiss against the only area that wasn't purple or covered in bandages.

"Don't you dare leave me." Scarlett sniffed and continued to just watch for any recognition, but there was nothing. Not even a flicker of an eyelash, and she'd stared hard enough to have noticed.

Then she dropped down exhausted into the chair and pulled a spare blanket over herself, one hand sticking out and resting on the bed in order to hold Claudia's limp fingers.

The monitors continued to beep quietly as Claudia's chest rose and fell with each lung full of air. Scarlett cursed it all, the tubes and needles. Mostly she cursed whoever had caused this to happen in the first place, whether that was a person, or a god, she didn't care. She was angry and scared, but that didn't stop sleep from taking her away from one nightmare, into another.

A loud bang from outside of the room woke her with a start. Her eyes blinking rapidly as she came awake again. It couldn't have been more than an hour she had slept, and she felt every minute of the seven hours she was missing.

Instantly her attention moved to Claudia.

No change.

Still lying there peacefully sleeping in the same position she was earlier. Scarlett checked her watch and was surprised to find it

Scarlett

was almost eight. Three hours then. Three hours of dreamless sleep that made her feel worse than if she'd just stayed awake, but she knew that was impossible, she'd been exhausted. She rubbed her face and dragged her fingers through her hair as she yawned and stretched out the kinks in her spine and the knotted muscles in her neck.

There was a light tap on the door, and it opened slowly to reveal a smiling face.

"Morning, just popping into check on our patient." The voice was warm and jovial, a hint of Caribbean mixing with southeast London to her accent. Her name badge read Alvita and had a little smiley face sticker next to it. "We've got the tea trolley coming soon."

"Oh, right," Scarlett pushed the blanket aside and stood up, hovering close enough to the nurse that she could watch her read the charts and go through her checklist. "Is she doing any better?"

"Well, she isn't doing any worse." The warm smile appeared again. "Your being here will be a comfort to her, I'm sure."

"Really? So, you think she knows I'm here?"

Alvita unhooked the almost empty drip bag. "I think the evidence is that people always know when they are loved, and that their loved ones are around in times of crisis."

"That's good. She definitely knows she's loved." Scarlett blushed a little.

"Why don't you go get yourself something to eat? I'm going to be here for a while getting all of this sorted, and then giving her a wash down."

"I could do that," Scarlett said hopefully.

There was that smile again, "Of course you could, but who's going to look after her if you're not looking after yourself. She's going to wake up soon, and then she'll be going home and you're going to need to be at your best for all the running around she's going to have you doing."

Scarlett grinned at that. "Yeah, I like that idea."

"Okay then, so you go get yourself some breakfast, and we'll see you in a while."

Hesitating at the door, Scarlett took one more glance back at Claudia, Alvita nodding at her that it was okay, before she walked out of the room, in search of the canteen, and a much-needed cup of coffee.

Scarlett

Chapter Thirty-One

"Zara, are you getting up?" Diana bellowed for the third time that morning. It was eleven already and she planned on being back at the hospital for twelve. "We need to go soon. Scarlett needs to get some rest while we take over visiting."

The door to Zara's room swung open and the sleep deprived, dishevelled figure gripped the door in one hand and the frame in the other. "You do know what time it is, don't you?"

"Of course I do," her tone softened. "We're all tired, Zara."

"We didn't get to bed until almost six."

"I know that, and now we need to up and at 'em." Diana walked away down the hall. "Oh, and James called. I told him he needed to keep Jacob for another night."

Zara rolled her eyes, grabbing the towel that was hanging on the back of her door. She followed Diana. "Mum is going to be sedated for a couple of days, I really don't think it will kill us to—"

Diana stopped abruptly, spinning around to face her younger sister. "Mum is sedated, yes. But Scarlett isn't, and we need to pull together and show her exactly what being a real family is all about. She's spent a lifetime of being an only child, she thinks she doesn't need us."

"Maybe she's right." Zara yawned.

"You know, for someone who was so excited to have another sister, you are severely lacking in empathy this morning."

"I'm severely lacking in sleep, and it's the first morning in over a week that I haven't had to get up and deal with Jacob screaming for food, or a teething ring, so yes, excuse me if for a few minutes I lack empathy." She pushed past Diana, into the bathroom, and closed the door.

"Infuriating," Diana muttered before turning and continuing into the lounge. Her bag, the big one she used for beach days or festivals, sat open on the sofa, already stuffed with everything she thought they'd need.

She picked up her phone and messaged Scarlett.

Diana: How's mum? How's you? Will be swinging by mums on the way, Shall I pick up anything you need? Dad said he will pop by later. Adam is coming back this afternoon. I'm going to set up a rota for visiting. Do you need anything? X

She watched the screen for a moment, the little ticks remained grey, so she squeezed the phone back into her pocket and sighed. There was nothing worse than feeling useless.

Her phone jingle indicated a text and she reached for it quickly, almost dropping it in the process. Flicking the screen open, she saw a reply from her brother.

Adam: What do you mean, I can come at four? It's not a bloody rota Di, Mum is in hospital, I'm on my way now. X

She narrowed her eyes, breathing deeply. *Why couldn't they all just fall into line and make things easier?*

Diana: Fine, Adam, but don't blame me if they won't let us all in. X

Adam: I don't care. I want to be there. Sunny said do you need anything? X

Diana: Tell her thanks, but I'm all sorted here. X

She closed off the text app and growled, didn't they know she was just trying to help? Still no reply from Scarlett, Diana put the phone away.

"ZARA!"

Scarlett

The beast sat at an angle on the drive, just where Zara had left it earlier that morning, much to Diana's irritation. She squeezed her car in beside it and switched the engine off.

"Scarlett still hasn't replied, but I think we should grab her some clothes and toiletries. Can you think of anything else?"

Zara considered it for a moment before shaking her head. "Nope."

They both stepped out of the car and the doors banged closed simultaneously. Zara opened the front door and stooped down to pick up the mail.

"I guess we could take this?" She rifled through the few envelopes, mostly addressed to her mum. "Though none of it looks very important."

"Well, leave it then. Come on, let's get what we came for and then get to the hospital."

They ventured up the stairs and into their mother and Scarlett's room.

"I kind of feel like we're prying," Zara said as they both hesitated just inside the doorway.

"Yes, I know, but try to think of it like when we were teenagers and *borrowing* Mum's clothes, or Christmas when we searched for presents."

Zara turned to her and smirked. "You mean that time when we got grounded for taking things that weren't ours?"

Diana smiled back. "Exactly, only now she can't ground us." She held up the bag they'd brought. A gym bag neither of them used for the gym. "Right, you do the drawers, I'll rifle through the wardrobes. I'm thinking comfort over style, but let's keep it somewhat decent."

"Okay, and if we find anything we shouldn't then?"

Diana winced. "Oh God, don't even say that. I cannot cope with finding Mother's—"

"Sex toys?" Zara sniggered. "You can say it, it's not something illegal."

"There are things I can deal with and will happily lead on, but imagining our mother—"

"And sister."

"And sister, engaging in…no." She waved Zara off. "I will not think about it, I will not."

Scarlett

Chapter Thirty-Two

After breakfast, Scarlett had stretched her legs with a quick walk around the hospital perimeter. She found a small shop and picked up a few snacks and some drinks, and a magazine she wouldn't usually read before heading back to Claudia's room.

Alvita passed her in the hall and smiled but didn't stop to give any information. Scarlett wasn't sure if that was a good or bad thing, but it didn't perturb her. She opened the door and stepped inside, finding Adam and Sunny sitting in the plastic bucket chair on the left side of the bed.

Adam held Claudia's hand, and they both looked up at the same time.

"Hey," Adam her acknowledged first, a think-lipped smile pulling his mouth into a straight line.

Sunny smiled too, then stood and pulled Scarlett into her arms. "You, okay?"

Scarlett blew out her cheeks. "Honestly, I dunno if I'm coming or going."

"Did you get any sleep?"

"Some," Scarlett replied as she moved around the bed and dropped the plastic bag onto the cabinet beside the bed that was rapidly filling up with medical supplies. She opened the small cubby hole and shoved her snacks into it, out of the way. "Anything change while I was gone?" she asked hopefully, but with no real expectation. The doctor had already explained it would be at least twenty-four hours before they'd consider lightening the sedation.

"No, just sitting here like useless lemons," Adam responded. "If I could get my hands on whoever did this."

"I'm sure the police will find out what happened and deal with anyone accordingly. I'm hoping it's just been a horrible accident," Scarlett answered as she took Claudia's other hand and lowered herself back into the armchair.

"I guess so," Adam muttered.

"I don't know what has gotten into you lately, you can't keep using your fists to fix things." Sunny glared at him. "I didn't marry a man who thought violence was the answer."

Scarlett watched for his reaction and noted the emotion fill his eyes at his wife's words. Sunny was right, even she had noticed Adam's anger issues had been steadily growing this past year.

"I—" His mouth opened but nothing more came out.

"You what? You hit your dad, and now you're threatening what? And to who? We don't even have any of the facts and you've already decided that anger and vengeance is the answer."

"I know, you're right, I'm sorry." He turned to her and then to Scarlett. "I just feel so helpless, and protective. She's my mum."

Sunny stood up, walked behind his chair, and wrapped her arms around him. "I know, sweetie, but she doesn't need protecting, not like that anyway."

"Did you see that?" Adam asked suddenly, sitting upright, and staring across at Scarlett. "Did you feel it?"

"Feel what?"

"I could have sworn she squeezed my hand." He turned his attention back to Claudia. "Mum, can you hear us?"

Scarlett shrugged and stood up, leaning over and hovering above Claudia's face. "They say that patients can often hear those around them. Claudia, it's me, and Adam, and Sunny. Can you squeeze Adam's hand again?" She looked over at Adam's hand holding Claudia's, "Anything?"

He waited a moment before finally shaking his head. "No. But I definitely felt it, I'm not making it up."

Scarlett

"Nobody thinks you're making it up," Scarlett reassured him. "We should tell the doctor though, don't you think?"

"Yes." Sunny nodded. "I can go."

"No, it's fine, you stay here with Adam, I'll find the doctor." She grinned. "Maybe she's waking up?"

"It could just be a case of the nervous system playing tricks. Of course, it could also be that she did actually squeeze your fingers." The doctor explained when she was eventually free to speak with Scarlett. "We're going to lessen the sedation a little at a time from tomorrow anyway, and start bringing her around, so expect there to be a lot more movement and potentially noise."

"Noise?" Scarlett questioned.

"Yes, the body still functions, and pain is pain, although we are maintaining pain relief, there may be times when Claudia might groan. Her movement is restricted and that may be a source of frustration as she starts to become aware of it."

"Okay, I'll let everyone know."

Dr Hassid patted Scarlett on the arm. "Don't look so worried, she's going to be fine. Nothing that some rest and recuperation won't fix."

"That's good to hear."

When the doctor walked away, Scarlett had a sudden thought. *Bea.*

"Shit." She rifled through her pockets and pulled out her phone, scrolling to open her contact list, she hit the button that would call Claudia's best friend.

"Hey." Came the almost instant greeting. "What do I owe the pleasure, are we planning her birthday already?"

Scarlett smiled, it was true, she rarely called Bea and usually it was to plan something for Claudia. The smile slid off her face when she remembered why she was calling now. "Hey, I…it's Claudia."

"What about her?" Bea asked tentatively.

"She's been in an accident, we're all at QC."

"An accident, what kind of accident?" Bea asked, and Scarlett could hear her moving, already getting up from her seat and shuffling through whatever room she was in.

"A car accident, late last night, on the motorway. She's been in surgery and now she's in an induced coma—"

"I'm on my way. Where do I go when I get there?"

"She's upstairs on a ward, next to ICU. Text me when you get here and I'll come and meet you, we're only supposed to go in two at a time, but they're being pretty decent about it seeing as there are so many of us."

"Okay, Scarlett, I'm coming now. I'll be about thirty minutes."

The call ended and Scarlett sped up, back to the room, and to Claudia.

Scarlett

Bea's arrival caused a stir, not because she was causing an issue, but because she wasn't alone. Clinging to Bea's arm was a hot, red-headed woman in blue jeans and a plain white t-shirt that didn't look like the outfit had come from Primark, but something much more designer and stylish, and she was at least ten years Bea's junior.

Somehow, they'd all managed to sneak into Claudia's room. Adam and Zara sat on the floor against the wall, Scarlett handing over her armchair for Bea, while Diana took the other plastic chair beside Scarlett. The red head stood quietly beside the armchair. Sunny had gone for coffees.

"Hi, I'm Scarlett." She reached a hand across the bed towards the woman Bea had forgotten about in her haste to see her friend.

"Annabelle." She smiled shyly.

"Shit, sorry," Bea looked up at Annabelle apologetically. "I'm so rude, sorry, sweetie, this...well, this is Claudia, my best friend." She pointed down at the bed. "And this is Diana, Zara, and Adam, Claudia's children, and her partner, Scarlett. Everyone, this is Annabelle, my uh—"

"Girlfriend?" Zara asked with surprise, not because Annabelle was a woman, but because Bea didn't do girlfriends or commitments.

Bea blushed. "I was going to say my friend, thank you, Zara."

They all watched Annabelle's reaction, but other than a slight blush to her cheeks, there was none.

"Anyway, how is she?" Bea asked anyone who wanted to reply the quickest.

Diana won that race.

"She's as well as they can expect, it's all just a waiting game but they're reducing her sedation tomorrow, so hopefully in the next twenty-four hours we should have her back with us in the land of the living."

"That's good," Bea whispered, clearly the emotion of it all was getting to her as she wiped her eyes and took a deep breath. "I can't believe it. You must all be…"

"It's been a long night, that's for sure," Scarlett confirmed.

The door opened and Alvita came through it, stopping in her tracks as she took in the people crowded around her patient's bed. "Okay, this is—" She smiled at them. "Some of you have to go wait in the family room. I don't know how you all managed to sneak in here." She chuckled. "But you're in my way."

Adam and Zara got to their feet and Annabelle shuffled awkwardly on hers.

"Come on, let's all give Mum a bit of breathing space," Adam addressed the room. "I'm sure we could all do with some fresh air and a bite to eat."

Diana nodded and stood. "That includes you, Letty," she said, placing her palm on Scarlett's shoulder.

"Go on," Bea encouraged. "I can stay with her."

"She's not going anywhere," Alvita reassured while checking the chart at the end of the bed.

"I know, I just. If she wakes up?"

"If that happens, we'll come find you, but it's not likely with this amount of sedative. Go on, you are no use to her if you don't look after yourselves." Alvita's wise words hit home, and Scarlett nodded.

"Okay then, we won't be long," Scarlett bent over the bed and said to Claudia as she placed a warm kiss against her forehead.

One by one they filed out of the room, just as Sunny returned carrying a tray of coffees in each hand. They all made a grab for one.

Scarlett

"We've been chucked out." Zara grinned.

"Oh, is she okay?"

Scarlett took a sip of her coffee while nodding. "Yeah They're just doing whatever it is they need to be doing, we're going to get some fresh air and something to eat. Bea's staying with her."

"Bea and her hot girlfriend." Zara threw in with a wink.

"A girlfriend? Bea?"

Zara linked arms with Sunny as they walked away down the corridor. "Yep, though she's calling it friends."

"Are you okay?" Diana asked Scarlett as they followed the herd.

"Can I answer that once she's home?"

"I think that's fair. But seriously, you alright?"

"Yeah, you?"

Diana sighed. "I'm just doing what I do best, avoiding my emotions and running through the motions. So yes, I am alright."

Scarlett nudged her shoulder. "You know you don't have to do that, right? Just let it out, we've all got you."

"Hm hm. I know, I just—it's not me, but don't worry, I will let it all out once it's over with and everything settles."

"Alright, but you know you can lean on me, right? I can be your big sister while you're being ours."

Diana narrowed her eyes. "I'm getting a little bit used to that now."

"Oh hell." Scarlett giggled, feeling a little bit lighter in herself.

"Every cloud..." Diana laughed and followed Zara's lead by linking her arm through Scarlett's. "We're going to be alright, all of us."

"Yeah, we are," Scarlett said just as she looked up and noticed him, standing with Zara and Sunny.

Jack was there again.

Noticing him herself, Diana asked, "How are things going with Dad?"

Scarlett shrugged. "Okay I guess, it's all still a little weird."

"He's...he has a lot of flaws, but he's been a good dad on the whole. The last few years have been difficult with the break-up and discovering all the lies and stuff, but he tries to be there for us, and he's been doing much better recently."

"Yeah, he has," Scarlett admitted. *Was having Jack in her life really a terrible idea?*

Scarlett

Chapter Thirty-Four

Another night sleeping on the armchair hadn't been the best, but Scarlett had made do. It was certainly better than leaving Claudia and going home. Home to an empty bed and a night filled with worry. She'd at least managed a few hours sleep and was grateful for the clean clothes Zara and Diana had brought in.

She stretched out her back and stood up, leaning over the bed to inspect Claudia for any change. There wasn't any, other than a darkening of the bruises. Gently, she traced a finger around Claudia's cheek with one hand and took Claudia's fingers in her other.

"Time to wake up soon. I miss you."

Standing stock still, she waited, hoping for any kind of movement, but there wasn't any.

So, she grabbed the washbag and towel her sisters had brought in and wandered into the small en suite bathroom attached to Claudia's room. She wasn't sure she was allowed to use it, but figured nobody would know if she were quick. And she was. Stripped off, under the water, washed and out again in minutes. She dried off hurriedly and pulled on the clean clothes, almost falling over in her haste as her wet foot got caught on the material and refused to slide down the leg of the trouser.

When she came out, she felt flushed, but at least clean, and bumped straight into Dr Hassid.

"Sorry, I thought you'd gone for a walk." The doctor smiled as Scarlett closed the door to the bathroom.

"Uh, no, I just," she pointed over her shoulder at the room, "I grabbed a shower, I hope that was alright."

"Well, technically they are supposed to be for patients, but I think in this situation we can let that slide, huh?"

Scarlett smiled. "Thanks. How is she?"

Doctor Hassid considered things for a moment before she smiled. "I think that today we might try and wake her up. Everything looks good, her chart is consistent, no lingering issues with the surgery, so—"

"Wake her up? When?"

"We'll give her another hour or two, so I suggest you go and get something to eat, call around and ask that people don't bombard her initially. She needs rest. Okay?"

"Yes, absolutely." Scarlett grinned now, a sensation of excitement rushing over her.

"Go on, nothing is going to happen yet, even when I reduce the sedative, it will take hours for her to come around."

Scarlett checked her watch, it was still early, barely seven.

"Alright, I'll go and get some breakfast. Thank you, for everything you've done, and are doing, I can't…I can never thank you all enough."

"That's what we're here for."

The canteen was busy already. Scarlett queued behind doctors and nurses, patients and what she assumed were other visitors. She was surprised by the level of chatter, and how upbeat it all sounded. Even in their darkest moments, humanity found a way to light the path, usually with humour.

"Black Americano, please, and scrambled eggs on toast," she said as she reached the assistant taking orders.

"Want any sauce with that?" The woman waved a sachet of ketchup at her.

"Oh, no, thank you."

Scarlett

"Seven eighty." She held out a hand for payment, then withdrew it when she noticed Scarlett holding her bank card. "There you go." She offered the card reader and Scarlett zapped it with her chip and pin.

"Thanks."

"Number forty-three, they'll shout it out when it's ready." The woman handed her a ticket with forty-three printed in bold and Scarlett turned away with a small smile of gratitude to go in search of somewhere to sit. As she passed the cutlery station, she picked up a knife and fork, and some salt and pepper sachets, as well as a handful of napkins.

Most of the tables were for four or more people, but she didn't feel like sharing with strangers who would likely want to engage in conversation and share their stories, so she found herself walking further away from the counter, towards the row of single tables along the wall of windows.

"Might as well have a view," she muttered to herself as she sat down and stared out over the entrance to A&E. Ambulances backed in with that incessant beeping until they were lined up and jumping out to wheel yet another unfortunate person inside.

"Forty-three," someone yelled and Scarlett stood back up and went to collect her food.

It was definitely not the same as eating at Joie or Banjo, but it would do for right now. She sprinkled some seasoning and then sliced into it and took a bite as she remembered back to her lunch with Jack. If she was honest with herself, it had all felt quite easy considering she barely knew him, and what she did know, she hadn't liked. But now, she was starting to see him in a different light, which both infuriated and calmed her. His presence these past couple of days had been reassuring, comforting even.

She fished into her pocket and pulled out the card he'd given her. Studying the gold embossed lettering and the numbers that she could use to call him anytime she wanted to. Did she want to? That was the question. She mulled it over while she chomped the last of her breakfast and washed it all down with the much-needed coffee.

Pushing the card back into her pocket, decision made, Jack would have to wait. Claudia was the only person she wanted to think about right now, and being in the room when she woke up, was all that Scarlett needed to concentrate on and the only people she needed to call right now were Zara, Diana, Adam, and Bea. Her own parents had been considered for even less time. They'd not been part of her life with Claudia so far, she'd be damned if she'd turn to them now.

Scarlett

Chapter Thirty-Five

Adam arrived first. By himself.

"Sunny not coming?" Scarlett asked. They sat opposite on another with Claudia still asleep between them.

"Yeah, she just got caught up in some traffic in town, so headed up on my own. She's going to drop everything off at hom and then meet us here."

"Cool, hopefully it won't be long." She squeezed Claudia' hand.

"Did they give a timeframe?"

Scarlett gazed across at him. "Anything from a couple c hours for her to start to come around, to a day or two, but the expected it to be quick."

"I can't wait to talk to her again." Adam smiled, as he to gripped his mother's hand. "How long has it been since they stoppe the sedation?"

"Only three hours." As she spoke, she stiffened. Her hand fe it, she was sure of it. "Claudia? Can you hear me?" She looked ove at Adam again. "I'm sure she squeezed my hand."

They both stood up and hovered over the bed, looking dow as Claudia's eyes flickered but didn't open.

"Did you see that?" he said excitedly, grinning at Scarlett.

Her smile was reciprocal. "I saw it."

"Mum, it's Adam and Scarlett, can you open your eyes?"

Claudia's eyes remained closed but there was movemer behind them, and a groan of what Scarlett imagined was discomfort.

"It's okay, babe, you're in hospital. Everything is alright, w just need you to come back to us and open your eyes."

When nothing happened, Adam tried again.

"Mum, come on, you can do it."

But there was nothing, Claudia wasn't ready yet, and they both slunk back down into their seats feeling a little defeated.

"The good thing is, she's with us, and it won't be long," Scarlett reassured.

The door opened quietly, and Zara carrying Jacob ducked inside, quickly followed by Diana.

"I know we aren't all supposed to be in here, but I don't care. I want to be here when Mum comes round," Diana said before anyone else could suggest otherwise.

"Nobody in here will mind." Scarlett grinned. "She's coming round slowly. She just squeezed my hand and her eyes flickered. She can definitely hear us."

"Oh good, just in time, Jakey." Zara's voice was quiet, trying not to wake Jacob and get them sent out, but the mention of him caused another moan from the bed. They all turned towards Claudia. "Jacob," Zara said again, "is she reacting to—"

Claudia responded.

"I have an idea," Diana said, taking Jacob from her sister's arms. She bustled over to the bed and gently placed him down on Claudia's bed. Holding onto him just in case he wriggled, but he was sleeping peacefully, so she wasn't too worried. "Mum, look's who's come to see you. It's Jacob."

It took a moment, lashes flicking, eyeball sweeping around beneath the lid, but then slowly, ever so slowly, Claudia's eyes began to open.

"Hey," Diana said smiling down at her mum. "Keep trying, you can do it."

Scarlett

Scarlett, and everyone else, held their breath as they watched. When Jacob mewled and sounded like he was about to cry, Claudia reacted again, her eyes pushing open and squinting against the dim light.

"Hi. Good to have you back with us." Scarlett grinned like an idiot. Tears streaming down her face. "We missed you."

"Mmi—ss…you." Came the garbled response before Claudia's eyes closed again.

"I guess it's exhausting," Zara offered as she reached for Jacob. "She can have him back later."

"Yeah, but she's with us," Adam reiterated. "And she's speaking."

"I'll go and fill the nurses in on the news," Diana announced.

A few minutes later and a nurse arrived back with Diana. She looked around the room at them all apprehensive about being kicked out, but she said nothing and moved across the room to Claudia.

"Claudia, can you open your eyes for me?" She rubbed her arm vigorously and Scarlett was about to suggest she be a little more gentle, but Claudia moaned, and her eyes flickered again. "That's it. Open those peepers, we've got all these people here waiting to speak to you."

It took what felt like an age but just as quickly they all gasped as Claudia's eyes opened properly and she focused for the first time. Searching something, or someone out.

"Jaco—b."

"Ha, trust the kid to be the most important." Adam laughed as Jacob was passed around until he was on Scarlett's lap and staring over at his Nana.

"Scarlett." Claudia groaned.

"Can she have more pain killers?" Diana asked. Claudia's line of sight changing to move with each sound and voice.

"I'll speak to the doctor. Welcome back, Claudia. It's good to finally meet you." The nurse patted Claudia's leg. "You have thirty minutes and then we need to let her rest. That means no more than two of you at a time, alright?"

They all nodded in agreement.

Scarlett

Chapter Thirty-Six

By teatime, everyone bar Scarlett had gone home. Claudia had slept most of the afternoon, which was to be expected as the sedative's worked their way out of her system. The occasional coming to, in order to waffle some gibberish had given them all something to smile about at least.

Diana had argued that Scarlett should go and get a good night's sleep in a proper bed, but in the end, she gave up, knowing that it was a fruitless exercise. Scarlett was going nowhere.

She made sure to eat the sandwich Adam had got her and she had a cup of what was called tea, from the trolley, but she was definitely sure it wasn't any tea she knew. Then she managed another quick shower before she sat back down again in the armchair, and promptly fell asleep.

When she woke up, it was darker in the room, only the light from outside illuminated anything, but it was bright enough to notice two blue eyes staring at her.

"Hey," croaked Claudia, and Scarlett reached for a glass of water holding the sponge on a stick to Claudia's mouth.

"Hey, how long have you been awake?"

Claudia took a suck, and then another. "Long enough. Thank you." Scarlett set the glass back on the tray. "Why are you still here?"

"Uh, because you are." Scarlett smiled. "No place else I'd rather be."

Claudia smiled and grimaced.

"You gave us all a nasty scare," Scarlett said taking her hand and squeezing gently.

"I gave myself a nasty scare. It all happened so fast, and yet, I feel like I remember every detail like it was in slow motion." Her fingers gripped Scarlett's. "I was so scared."

Sitting forward, Scarlett perched on the edge of her seat, as close as she dared without climbing into the bed with her. "I can't imagine how frightening it was, but you're safe now."

"Safe, yes. Broken too." She laughed through the tears. "Leg? Shoulder? Everything hurts or doesn't move, so I can only imagine."

"Actually, you're not in as bad shape as they thought. Your shoulder was dislocated, but they popped it back in, so that pain should wear off sooner rather than later, and yeah, you've a broken leg but six weeks and you'll be right as rain again." Scarlett grinned at her. She was awake at last, and talking, and making sense. It felt almost dreamlike. "You had some internal bleeding from your spleen, but you got lucky and it stopped bleeding before they had to do more surgery."

"And…and everyone else? Are they okay?"

"Honestly, I don't know who was in the car with you. The police haven't shared too many details and they'll want to speak to you now you're awake, but—" She swallowed as considered the best way to say it. "I do know that someone didn't make it."

"Who?" Claudia tried to sit up and winced.

Scarlett shook her head. "I don't know."

"It's all such a mess."

"Right now, all I care about is you, and getting you well enough to come home where I can fuss around you and help get you back on your feet again. Everything else we can manage once we know more."

Claudia nodded in agreement. "Yes, I suppose so, I just wish I knew."

"You had a nasty bang on the head, the last thing it needs right now is for you to be overthinking. In the morning, I'll call the officers and ask if they have an update and arrange for them to come in and speak to you, if you want me to?"

"Yes."

"Or I can hold them off for as long as you need me to."

"No, I'd rather get it over and done with. I'd rather know. Claudia stifled a yawn.

"Alright then." Scarlett sat back into the chair. "So, you war to keep talking or get some rest?"

"I'm fine, I just..." And then she was asleep again, leavin Scarlett chuckling to herself.

"God, it's so good to have you back."

Scarlett woke to the sound of people talking. Opening he eyes, she realised that Claudia had a visitor: Dr Hassid.

"Sorry, we tried not to wake you." Claudia held out her hand

"You should definitely have woken me," Scarlett responded taking her hand, she looked up at the doctor. "Everything alright?"

Dr Hassid smiled down at her. "Yes, everything is goin swimmingly. We're very happy with Claudia's progress. Anothe few days' rest and I think she'll be ready to go home."

"That is good news."

When the doctor had finished her checks and left, Claudi sighed and reached for the button that would lift the back of her be more upright.

"I feel so useless."

"Get used to it, because you're not going to be doin anything more than getting up and sitting on the couch for at least week when you get home."

"I really don't think that will be nessec—"

"I'm sorry, what part of that was optional?" Scarlett interrupted with a grin. "You are going to be visited non-stop. I've already had to put up with them all for days, now it's your turn."

"Have they behaved?"

Scarlett sat back into the armchair and smiled happily. "Yes, it's actually been quite nice."

"Oh?"

Inhaling, Scarlett considered it. "I've never had that before. That sense of family. For the first time in my life, I didn't feel alone in a terrible situation. Outside of a relationship, I've never had that level of support. Even Jack has been," she ran a hand through her hair and laughed ironically, "I can't even believe I'm going to say this but, like a father."

Claudia's eyes widened. "Well, he has always been pretty good at that, even if he does get it wrong sometimes, the thought is there. I'm glad that you've all been there for each other."

"Me too, and now we're all here for you."

"I've never doubted that."

Scarlett

Chapter Thirty-Seven

Claudia cried as the police explained the details of the accident. Wiping at her face with tissues from a box the hospital supplied as the details of a large van clipping the back of the vehicle as it swerved to avoid something in the road. The collision had been at speed, and the vehicle Claudia was in had flipped and rolled into the other lane, where it was subsequently hit again by a car.

"And who, I mean, which one has—" Claudia couldn't say it.

The police officer made a show of looking through her notes, head down as she explained further, "Yourself, and the driver, a Mr Yusef Kalam, were travelling in the front of the vehicle. Airbags deploying on impact meant both of you were saved from more serious injury, however, Philip Costas and Franco Hansen were not so lucky. Unfortunately, Mr Hansen did not survive the initial crash. Mr Costas is currently still in hospital with a spinal fracture, and Mr Kalam is recovering at home with his family."

Claudia said nothing more than, "Poor Franco." The silent tears speaking volumes instead. "I didn't really know either of them very well, but we were working on a project together. I can't believe it."

"I realise that it's a difficult situation, but we really would like to know anything you remember about it?"

Looking up at her, Claudia closed her eyes and allowed the images of that night to play through her mind again. Scarlett hovered, one arm folded around her waist, the other bent, her fingers picking at her lip as she listened to the horrendous events of that night in detail, and prepared herself for worse, hearing it from Claudia's perspective.

"I remember we were discussing the meeting and everything was fine. Mr Kalam?" The officer nodded. "He indicated and moved into the middle lane. I think a vehicle then came past us, and then the next moment there was a loud bang and the front of the car moved to the left."

"So, did you notice any other vehicle hitting you?"

Claudia shook her head. "No, I was turned around slightly, facing my colleagues, it was only the sound that made me twist back in my seat and then we were rolling over. I know I screamed. I don't remember anything after that."

The officer wrote it all down in her little pad.

"Can you remember if the vehicle that overtook you was driving dangerously?"

Once again, Claudia shook her head. "No, I wasn't paying attention. We had a driver, that was his job to assess, I was completely comfortable with that. We use cars all the time."

"Okay, well that's all we need for now."

"Will you need to speak to Claudia again?" Scarlett asked.

The officer turned to her. "Possibly, but from the evidence we've gathered so far, I imagine this will be put down to a tragic accident. It doesn't appear that anyone acted in any way improper. The driver of the van said he swerved to avoid something in the road that he didn't see until he was right up on it. All we have found is a patch of paint that must have been spilled earlier in the day. In daylight you might not take much notice of it, but at night, it's dark and with tired eyes it could have appeared like something in the road to avoid."

"It's just all so tragic." Claudia wept. She yawned and her eyes began to close.

"We'll leave you to it," the officer said before heading out of the room with her partner.

When it opened again, almost thirty minutes later, Zara's head poked around it with a cheesy grin that made Scarlett return the smile.

Scarlett

"Can I come in? I brought someone to visit." She backed in through the door pulling the pushchair in after her. "I'm dropping him off with James again later but thought we'd see how Nanna is first."

"How is James coping with full-time fatherhood?" Scarlett asked.

Zara laughed. "Yeah, let's just say it was a good job we didn't want to pursue a relationship. He's good with Jacob in small doses if his mum's around to help out but I guess he is taking an interest and trying." She bent down and unbuckled Jacob from the restraints before lifting him into the air. "Look Jakey, it's Nanna."

On cue, Claudia stirred and opened her eyes once more. These numerous power naps doing wonders for her healing.

"Say hey, Nanna." Zara held his hand and waved it at Claudia.

"Na na." Jacob reached out his arms, wriggling to be allowed to get closer.

"Is he allowed?"

Claudia grunted a moan as she shifted and tried to get more comfortable. "Allowed? Of course he is. Give him here."

"She's feeling better then," Zara laughed and said to Scarlett as she lowered her son into her mother's good arm.

"Much better now." Claudia grinned and cooed at Jacob. Kissing his face and making him laugh. As he studied her bruises, however, he became upset. "It's alright, Nanna's okay."

But he didn't understand that, and the tears soon followed. In the end, he was screaming so loudly that Zara reached for him, but that just made him worse, his own little arms stretching for Claudia.

"What do I do?" Zara asked, panicked.

"He's fine, I'm fine," Claudia said, taking him back and cuddling him. "He just doesn't understand why Nanna is hurt."

"I know that. I just…I don't want to traumatise him."

Claudia rolled her eyes. "He's not going to be traumatised, Zara."

Zara looked at Scarlett for confirmation.

"If you let him settle, he learns that the emotions he feels around someone he loves being hurt are valid to have, if you take him away, he's learning we don't deal with those emotions," Scarlett explained.

"Okay," Zara responded. "Thanks, Sis."

"Anytime." Scarlett smiled, catching Claudia grinning at them both.

Scarlett

Chapter Thirty-Eight

"I'm fine, stop fussing," Claudia complained as Scarlett moved quickly to readjust a pillow on the sofa. She'd been home from the hospital for two days and already she was at her wit's end with the lot of them.

"I'm not fussing, I am loving you. If you're frustrated by that I understand, but it's where we are right now with your mobility. Scarlett stood hovering over her but lowered down onto bended knee, her voice softening. "So, take a deep breath please and try to remember that this is nobody's fault and we're making the best of it together."

Claudia did just that and took a long, deep breath before exhaling just as slowly. Glancing around the room at all of the flowers and cards, she felt guilty for her outburst.

"Sorry, you're right, I am frustrated." She reached out her good arm and palmed Scarlett's face with her hand. "I'm sorry that I'm taking it out on you."

"I'll forgive you. Now, what do you fancy for breakfast?"

"You." Claudia smirked. Looking almost back to her old self if you discounted the slight yellowing to her skin where the bruise had faded, and the sling on one arm, and who could forget the cast?

"Oh, someone's feeling better already. How about we have some breakfast and then if you're feeling up to it, I'll let ya cop a feel for a few minutes." She grinned as she stood back up.

"Tease, but fine, I'll agree to your demands." Claudia laughed. "I really do feel better, it's just this blasted broken body I'm annoyed with."

"Let's be grateful it is just a broken body we're dealing with."

The smile on Claudia's face slid off, instantly replaced with a frown. She'd been avoiding it this entire time; how close she had come to death.

"I nearly died, didn't I?"

Scarlett felt her heart break and she flopped down into the space beside her lover, arms instantly reaching around her as gently as she could.

"Yes, and so, if people need to fuss around you, let them, just for a bit."

"Okay," Claudia stuttered through the tears.

"And I don't want you bottling things up, we can talk about it, anytime, alright?"

She felt Claudia nod against her chest and kissed the top of her head.

"So, breakfast? What do you feel like? Scrambled eggs on toast?"

This time, Claudia looked up at her. Eyes still wet but the sobbing had stopped.

"That would be lovely, thank you."

Scarlett craned her neck, kissing the lips she'd missed. "Okay then. I'm going to get on with that, while you relax with your book."

As she moved about the kitchen, cracking and whisking eggs, while bread browned in the toaster, the doorbell rang. Her head fell back, and she sighed, they hadn't had a minute's peace since Claudia had come home. Flowers arrived almost hourly since the accident had become common knowledge, and her work had sent the biggest basket of fruit and goodies to cheer her up, but it was getting a bit much now and they were out of vases to use.

Scarlett walked to the door, still whisking.

Scarlett

"Hey." A grinning Bea stood as close to the door as she could get, she stepped inside the moment Scarlett moved, quickly followed by Annabelle, who smiled politely and looked about as comfortable as a three-legged chair.

"Come in why don't you." Scarlett grinned. "I'm cooking breakfast, would you like some?"

"Thanks, but we're not stopping long," Bea answered for them both. Though Annabelle looked grateful not to be having breakfast.

"She's in the lounge, I'll be in the kitchen."

Scarlett hadn't reached the kitchen door before the bell rang out again.

"For the love of—" She twisted back around, but before she reached it, it opened. Diana waltzed in carrying a large bag filled with all of the things Claudia loved.

"Hey, just dropping these off for Mum." She smiled. "Oh, what are you making? Enough for me?"

Scarlett rolled her eyes. "Yeah, sure. Go on through, she's in the lounge with Bea."

"Thanks." Diana moved and then stopped. "Oh, Dad asked if you wanted to join us for dinner at the weekend, he's taking everyone out to Joie."

"Why didn't he ask me then?" Scarlett asked, feeling like an afterthought.

Diana grinned. "He is, via me. I said I was coming over and offered to tell you."

"I'll see how your mum is, maybe."

"Great, I'll let him know, unless…you want to tell him?"

Scarlett started whisking again. "No, it's fine, you can relay back to him." She watched as Diana walked into the lounge and a round of hello's and how are you's went on, and then she headed back to the kitchen, adding more bread to the toaster and buttering the ones that had already popped. She quickly poured the eggs into the pan and stirred with more vigour than she had intended. Once cooked, she divided it up between the two plates and carried them through to Claudia, and Diana.

The doorbell rang again.

"Seriously," Scarlett said out loud.

Annabelle chuckled. "I'll get it for you."

"Thanks." Scarlett passed one plate to Diana, and then the other to Claudia. "Do you need anything else?"

"No, thank you, Sweetheart. But," she beckoned Scarlett closer, "I am feeling a little tired."

"Okay, eat that, then I'll clear everyone out and we'll have a little nap."

As she looked up, preparing to tell Bea and Diana to bugger off, she noticed Annabelle in the doorway.

"You're dad's here, Scarlett."

"My dad?" She glanced at Diana, who shrugged and made a face with her mouth that said she didn't know anything about it. Just then, a figure stepped into the room.

"Hello, Scarlett."

Two things went whizzing through Scarlett's mind in that moment. Was her mum okay, and how did he know where she lived?

"Dad?" He looked tidy, as though he had made an effort, or was going to a wedding. His hair was brushed back off his face. He was clean shaven and the suit he wore was pressed, he'd even worn a tie.

Scarlett

At the intense scrutiny, he looked around at all of the faces staring at him and looked nervous, but finally he spoke again. "I wondered if I could have a word?"

She glanced down at Claudia, who simply nodded.

"Is Mum, okay?"

Now he nodded. "Yes, she's fine, she's at home."

"Right." She marched across the room and waited for him to either move out of the way and let her pass, or step back into the hall. He moved out of the way and then followed.

Scarlett led him into the kitchen and silently thanked whichever of them had seen sense to close the lounge door.

"So, what's up?" she said, turning to face him, leaning back against the counter as casually as she could muster. "I didn't realise you knew where I live."

He fidgeted from one foot to the other before finally looking at her. "You wrote it on the back of the envelope, at Christmas. I jotted it down and put it in my wallet."

Her eyes narrowed. "Why?"

"Because despite what you think, you're my daughter and I actually do care what happens to you."

Her brow raised all by itself at that. "You'll have to forgive me if I find that difficult to believe." She turned away and picked up the kettle. "Tea?"

He nodded. "Thanks."

"So, what did you want to talk about?" she asked as she filled the kettle and plonked it back down onto the base, flicking the switch on. She turned back around and leaned against the worktop again. To anyone watching, she appeared calm, thoughtful, but inside she was a bag of nervous energy waiting to explode at the slightest shitty thing to come out of his mouth.

"I want us to start again, to put everything behind and—"

"Start again?" she scoffed. "Are you serious?"

"Very serious." He nodded, his jaw tensing under the scrutiny.

Scarlett thought for a moment before asking, "How do you envision that happening?"

He took a step forward. "Well, for a start, with you not talking to me like that."

"Like what?" she responded in the same tone.

"Like I don't matter."

She laughed. Couldn't help herself as it bubbled up from nowhere and spontaneously burst out of her mouth without permission. "That's rich, coming from the man who gave no fucks about me all these—"

"I gave fucks, I just didn't shout about it," he said, shouting about it.

She ignored the sound of the water boiling to a frenzy in the kettle, the gentle hiss as steam began to pour out of the spout. "I can't even remember the times I wished you'd given a fuck, just a tiny one, just once turned up to a school play, or sports day, or—"

He reached into his back pocket and pulled out his wallet, bulging like it always had. He walked forwards and opened it, pulling out the contents and letting them drop onto the breakfast bar. Some crumpled-up twenty-pound notes and a crisp fiver, a couple of receipts from the bookies and then photographs. An old crumpled-up and scratched picture of Scarlett, aged around five, dressed up like an angel in the school nativity.

"I was there," he said. "At the back, I was running late cos of the traffic, so I stayed at the back out of sight, didn't want to disrupt everyone. Your mum starting gassing with another parent at the end,

Scarlett

so I left, wasn't any point in waiting. I picked up fish and chips an we had them when you got home."

She picked up the photo, remembering the chips. He tosse another one down.

"That's you winning the three-legged race with that kid fro up the street, Darren? You were getting changed when I arrived. had to leave after to get to work this time. Money was short, yo needed things."

Scarlett picked up each photo and listened to how he'd bee there at every single thing she'd been proud of. And he'd carried th photos all these years. A little girl with light brown hair and freckle Each pic a different hairstyle, longer legs, but it was her in eve single one of them. Smiling, captured unawares.

"Why did you never show me these?"

"Because I was an idiot, stuck in my head with all the thoughts about what would people think, you hated me anyway, was easier to just leave it as it was."

She picked up another photo, not as old this time, of herse on stage in her cap and gown shaking hands and collecting h degree. She looked more closely at the image, two rows in front where her dad was sitting, was Claudia and Jack. Diana had been stage too, just before Scarlett.

"You came to my graduation?"

"You left the invites on the table, I wasn't gonna go, we fallen so far away from this." He showed her a photo of herse playing hockey at school years before. "We barely spoke to eac other, but it was your graduation. Your mum went and I sat the stewing for a minute before I decided I'd seen you throug everything else, I'd see you through this too. It didn't matter if v didn't like each other, you're my daughter, and I'm proud of you. S I snuck in at the back and kept out of sight, but I was there. Like was there for everything important, even if you never knew."

She could feel her eyes prick with tears but blinked them away.

"Why now? Why didn't you say all this years ago?"

"Because I thought I was too late. I thought you hated me so much you'd moved halfway across the country to get away from me. I let my pride and ego get the better of me and persuaded myself that I'd lost you so what was the point."

"And now?"

"Now, I want to fix things, I want," he exhaled, "I'm your dad. Me." He jabbed a finger at his chest. "I'm the one that clothed and fed you. It was me at all these, watching with pride. Me, I'm not giving that title up without a fight."

"So, this is about Jack?"

"No, this is despite, Jack, or whatever his name is. He might be your father, but he'll never be your dad, cos that's me. And I want another chance to put things right, to put all this sniping and griping at each other behind us."

Scarlett

When her dad finally left, Scarlett wandered into the lounge to find everybody else had gone too. Claudia had her eyes closed and Scarlett was about to turn away and leave her to rest when she spoke.

"Everything alright?"

Scarlett sat down beside her and snuggled in. "I don't know what to think if I'm honest."

"What did he want?" Claudia asked gently, opening her eyes, and blinking the sleepiness away. She couldn't deny, she was as interested as everyone else had been before she'd shooed them all off for some peace and quiet.

Scarlett puffed out her cheeks, reached up and ran both of her hands through her hair. "It would appear that I now have two fathers fighting for my affections."

"That's a turnaround."

"Hm, male pride and ego will have that effect I guess." She suddenly sat up, twisting around to look at Claudia. "Do you know, he has this wallet, right. It's always been this big old chunky thing filled with what I assumed were old receipts and bits of crap, but no."

"No?"

"It's filled with photographs. Pictures of me at all these events I didn't think he'd gone to. School plays, sports days, hockey games, my graduation. He was there, at everything. He'd sneak in at the back right before it started, watch me, take some photos, and then leave before I or my mum spotted him."

"Why didn't he just—" Claudia yawned. "Sorry, why didn't he just tell you he was there?"

"Do you need to rest?"

"Yes, but not until I've heard everything."

"You should sleep, I can fill you in on all of this later—"

Claudia grabbed at her sleeve as she went to stand up, pulling her back down again. "I said I want to hear it."

"Alright, let's compromise. We'll get you all comfy on here and then I'll climb in behind and we can snuggle while I tell you everything?"

"Can we go up to bed instead?" Claudia asked, yawning again.

"If you want to, it's a lot for you to manage though."

"I know. I just can't get comfy on here and I want to enjoy snuggling. It's been so nice sleeping in the same bed as you again, but I realise all of this gets in the way. I was thinking I could sleep on your side and that would make it easier to cuddle, my right side is pretty good."

Scarlett leaned in and kissed her quickly. "Why didn't I think of that?"

"Because it's your side of the bed, and we've always done it that way."

"True, but you're right, we can swap and that will be much easier and probably safer for you. I won't roll in the night and hit your bad arm again."

She lifted Claudia's leg down from the stool it was propped up on and reached down to help her rise up off of the sofa. Heaving her to her feet they came together, chest to chest.

"Hi." Claudia grinned. "It's been a while."

Scarlett licked her lips at the implication. "You know, I don't think we've ever gone this long without having sex, unless you've been physically out of the country."

"Well, thirty-minute nap and maybe we can remedy that?"

Scarlett

"You're supposed to be—"

"Relaxing," Claudia purred, her finger dancing across Scarlett's tight t-shirt. "And I can't think of any other thing I find more relaxing than when you make me come."

"Jesus, woman." Scarlett laughed. "Let's see how long it takes to get you upstairs before we start making sexy time plans."

Claudia was fast for a one-armed, balanced on one leg woman. Her good arm snaking around Scarlett's neck, pulling her closer to press their lips together. Firmly and eagerly, she kissed her lover until her mouth gave and allowed the intrusion of her tongue.

"Mm." Claudia moaned as she deepened the kiss and enjoyed the way that Scarlett's arms moved around her waist, supporting her "Now, that feels better already." She grinned when she finally pulled away and left Scarlett in all but a daze.

"It feels like forever since we did that." Scarlett chuckled "But I'm not sure you're well enough for—"

"Why not? It's all working perfectly fine; I'll have you know." Claudia smirked as Scarlett put that together in her head.

"When?" Scarlett frowned.

"This morning, when you were in the shower," Claudia admitted.

"You little minx. Why didn't you say anything?"

Claudia sighed. "Because it was just one of those things that needed urgent attention, and I wasn't sure if I could manage it and didn't want to get you all excited just to let you down." She shuffled in closer and placed her palm on Scarlett's chest, pressing her warm hand over her lover's heart. "But now. I'd kind of like to try."

"Alright, but nothing too adventurous."

With one arm around Scarlett, and the other hand gripping the banister, Claudia hopped one step at a time. It was an exhausting and slow process, and by the time they made it to the top, she'd all but fallen against Scarlett.

"Maybe I should have that nap first." She chuckled.

"Probably for the best," Scarlett countered as they shuffled towards the bedroom. "And a bed bath."

"Is that what we're calling it these days?"

"If ya lucks in, maybe."

Scarlett

Chapter Forty

Claudia's nap lasted a little over forty-five minutes. Sh smiled to herself as she woke and found Scarlett, sitting up in be beside her, reading from a book that had sat on the bedside table fe months untouched. When asked about it, she would always say sh was saving it for a holiday they were yet to take. A holiday mig just be in order once her leg had healed, she thought.

Rolling over onto her side took some effort, her left leg in plaster cast was heavy and cumbersome, but she just about manage it.

"You alright there?" Scarlett asked, placing the book on tl cabinet again.

"Yes. Just about." Claudia smiled, burrowing in against he Scarlett shuffled down the bed, turning to face her and holding he gaze. Staring into those eyes somehow had new meaning since tl accident. "This is nice."

"It is," Scarlett agreed, fidgeting until she was able to snal her arm around Claudia. "So, still want that bed bath?"

"Absolutely." She craned her neck to kiss Scarlett once more

"Okay. Get naked while I go get a bowl of warm water."

Claudia pouted, "Oh, you meant an actual bed bath."

"Yeah, you filthy animal. Strip, I'll be back to deal with yc in a moment." Scarlett grinned, loving the playful return to almo normalness.

"So bossy." Claudia laughed, twisting back around, ar sitting up. Her top already lifting. "Not that I'm complaining."

Scarlett scuttled off the bed and out of the room like her li depended on it. Returning moments later with a large plastic bow she stopped to notice a now very naked Claudia lounging a seductively as she could manage with one leg in plaster. Scarlett wa grateful that her stitches had all been removed, and the wounds all healing nicely, even if she didn't feel her best.

Scarlett allowed herself to stare for a moment before shaking herself from the thoughts that hurtled through her sex-starved mind.

"Still like what you see?" Claudia asked with just a hint of self-doubt. Her body had taken a beating, that was for sure.

"Oh, yeah." Scarlett licked her lips appreciatively. "Don't move."

She entered the bathroom and filled the bowl with warm water and a drop of bubble bath, swirling it to create bubbles, she dropped the washcloth into it and carried it, along with some towels, back into the bedroom.

"Right, are you ready?" She dropped the towels onto the floor beside the bed.

Claudia grinned. "God, yes. I need your hands on me."

Scarlett placed the bowl down and then picked up one of the towels from the pile. She flicked it out and grasped each end, ready to put it to use.

"Right, roll over so I can tuck this underneath you," she instructed, dropping down to her knees.

Doing as she was told, Claudia rolled to her right and revealed the other side of the damage the accident had caused.

It didn't matter how often Scarlett saw the bruises; it always shook her to her core. She was just grateful that they were now nothing more than a yellowish colour and not the vivid reds and purples from a week ago.

"The bruises have almost gone," she said, taking the washcloth and wringing it out. Gently moving it across Claudia's back and down lower until every inch had been cleaned. Claudia's soft moans turning her on. She towel-dried her off. "Okay, you can lie back now."

Claudia smirked at her. "Have we got to the good bit?"

"Sounded like you were already at the good bit," Scarlett teased as she rinsed the cloth again.

Raising her good arm up and placing it behind her head, Claudia turned her head slightly to look at Scarlett.

"Take your time."

"Oh, I intend to." Scarlett stretched up and brought the warm cloth to the underside of Claudia's breast, skimming gently across the skin as the flannel swept around and into a figure eight over her chest. "I wouldn't want to miss anything."

"I wouldn't want you to miss anything either." Claudia squirmed as the cloth made its way down and between her legs. Gasping as its rough surface rubbed against her clit and her pelvis lifted instinctively chasing the sensation. "God, I've missed you."

Scarlett pushed up and slid herself over Claudia's supine body, switching hands in the process. She levered herself up on one elbow and leaned down into a kiss, that nibbled at Claudia's lips all the while pressing harder with the fabric as her movements built and built her lover's pleasure until finally, Scarlett discarded the material and took over. Her fingers effortlessly sliding inside, curling, and pressing instantly against the one place that would usually send Claudia into a frenzy, but this time, she took it more gently. Teasing the very essence of her until all Claudia could do was go with it. Her muscles tightening, limbs stretching and retracting as she mewled with delight against her lover's mouth.

"I want to taste you," she whispered against Scarlett's ear as she caught her breath.

Scarlett leaned back, ran her hand through Claudia's hair until it was all off of her face. "Are you sure? I don't want t—"

"You won't hurt me." Claudia reached up and returned the movement. Sweeping Scarlett's long hair back and behind her ear. "Please." Pleading was always a winner, she knew that. "Please, baby."

"So underhanded." Scarlett pursed her lips but swung her leg over anyway. "I hope you know that I am going to—"

Claudia's eyes lit up. "Do what?" she teased. "What are you going to do to me?"

Scarlett slid off the bed and stripped down until she was just as naked. Her eyes firmly on Claudia as the blonde moved over into the middle of the bed.

"Don't get so excited, I was going to say that I'm going to feel very apprehensive, so don't get despondent if I don't climax." She clambered onto the bed and swung her leg over Claudia until she was hovering above her stomach.

Sliding her hand, palm up, between them, Claudia cupped her.

"I want you to relax, and enjoy, and not think about anything else other than what my fingers, and in a moment, my tongue, is doing to you."

Scarlett's eyes closed, her mouth hanging open as Claudia toyed with her. Precious moments when her head fell back, and she did all she could to clear her mind of anything, but the feeling Claudia's skilled fingers were creating. Her thoughts tumbled through the desire and need, forcing her on until her lover's voice pulled her back.

"I want you up here. I want my mouth on you." Claudia pulled her fingers away, and around her, pressing into firm buttocks, urging Scarlett to move. Knowing every move that would help get her what she wanted. "Baby…"

That was it. All it took. Just one word.

Scarlett

Scarlett slowly, tentatively moved. Her knee planting down next to Claudia's bruised and painful shoulder. She leaned forward and grabbed the bed head for support as her other leg moved and that knee dropped into place too, leaving her exposed and within reach of Claudia's intention. Scarlett looked down and locked eyes with her lover as the first sweep of a warm, curious tongue found her.

"Fuck," she cried out. "Fu—"

Claudia made it her mission to make sure Scarlett didn't get stuck in her head. Attacking her nerve endings with every swipe, teeth grazing and lips sucking. Fingertips kneading flesh. If Scarlett thought there would be any other outcome, she was in for a big surprise as Claudia brought her to the edge and pushed her over.

Scarlett's breath caught in her throat as did the strangled words that erupted with her orgasm. Still shuddering, Scarlett let herself fall to the side, away from any body part that she could hurt or injure. Her chest rising and falling as her heart rate calmed again.

Claudia lay back with a smug smile on her face, and at first, she wasn't sure she'd heard right. "What was that?" Twisting as much as she could under the circumstances.

Scarlett was staring at her, wide-eyed, a look of shock on her face, as though she couldn't believe what she'd said.

"What's wrong?" Claudia frowned. She reached down and grabbed her knee, helping her leg over so she could twist properly. "Scarlett, what did you say?"

It took a moment before Scarlett opened her mouth to speak again.

"I said, marry me."

Chapter Forty-One

It was silent in the room.

Claudia sat up and reached for her shirt, pulling it on and covering her nakedness as best she could.

Swinging her legs from the bed, Scarlett got up and came around to the pile of her own clothes. Pulling her jogging bottoms on, Scarlett kept her eyes averted.

"Scarlett, I—"

"It's fine, Claudia. I don't know why I said it."

Claudia watched her lover. Embarrassed? Humiliated? She wasn't sure.

"I just...I didn't, I mean I wasn't expecting—" Claudia rubbed her face in her hands. "I've been married, I'm not sure I want that again."

Standing upright, Scarlett pulled on her t-shirt and sighed. She turned to face Claudia and smiled sadly.

"Look, I'm not going to pretend I'm not hurt, I am. I don't know why because it isn't like I was planning this big proposal or anything. With everything that's gone on lately, I guess I've been thinking about the future more and I really didn't like having to contemplate you not being part of it, and—" She sat down on the edge of the bed. "We don't have to get married. I'm happy with things as they are."

"Really?"

"Yes, I guess it surprised us both, eh?"

Claudia chuckled. "Just a bit, yes." She reached up and stroked Scarlett's face, her hand covered instantly. "Are you sure it's, okay? I want you, you know that, right, this isn't about not wanting to be with you."

Scarlett nodded. "I know that. I have never felt so loved and wanted as I do with you, I'm not doubting it."

"Good."

"I'll process how I'm feeling." Scarlett stood up. "Now, you need another bed bath."

Scarlett took herself off for a walk the moment Bea arrived to keep Claudia company. Although Claudia had made a big deal of not needing company, that she was perfectly fine by herself on the sofa, she soon stopped complaining when Bea offered wine.

"I'm not supposed to be drinking."

"Why not?" Bea asked, holding out a small glass. "Anyway, it's weak as pish, look at it. 6%, barely any alcohol in it."

"You're a bad influence." Claudia frowned but took the glass.

"And you look like you need it, the pain bad?" Bea sat in the armchair and crossed her legs as she sipped the wine and grimaced.

Claudia sighed, putting the glass down untouched onto the side table. "Scarlett asked me to marry her."

Bea's eyes bugged. "Really, wow, congrat—"

"I said no." Claudia cut her off before she got over-excited.

"Oh." Bea's smile dropped. "Why?"

"I don't really know, I just…panicked. The thought of being married again, I don't know if I want that."

"That explains why she was so quiet when she left. I thought you'd had a row."

"God no, we rarely argue. Scarlett isn't one for letting things fester between us long enough to become a row. We bicker, which actually is quite fun." Claudia laughed. "She's gone for a walk to process everything."

"I don't think I could live with a therapist. I mean sometimes a blazing row does you good."

"I suppose, though I had enough of those with Jack, I'm quite enjoying the calmness of Scarlett."

Bea took another sip. "So, why not marry her?"

"Because I don't need to. We love each other, and we have a lovely life and there's no need to change that for what, the sake of a piece of paper that in reality means very little. Having a marriage certificate didn't stop Jack from doing exactly what he wanted, did it?"

"True, but Scarlett isn't Jack, well, not all of her." She smirked. "Sorry, that was crass."

Rolling her eyes in agreement, Claudia said, "I trust Scarlett. I have no doubts about that, and this revelation about Jack makes no difference to that," Claudia added firmly. "I just don't feel the need to get married."

"I take it she's not happy if she's walking to process it?"

Claudia smiled at the assumption. "Actually, she's processing why she felt so inclined to ask it."

"She's such a bloody grown-up." Bea laughed and swigged her drink. "This is why your age gap doesn't matter, she's the adult."

Claudia burst into laughter, gripping her ribs. "Oh, I think you're right."

"How are the injuries?"

"Getting easier. Mostly nothing hurts too badly, I've got painkillers and they take the edge off. The leg is a pain, cumbersome, I can't wait to get this cast off. But I'm not complaining, not really, not when I think of the alternative. Poor Franco." The smiles were nothing more than a sad frown on both faces. "It's the funeral next week."

"Are you going?"

"Of course, I just—" She sighed. "It doesn't seem real, but I imagine the funeral will have an impact. Scarlett will come with me, so I'll at least have her to lean on, but I feel so guilty even thinking about myself and how difficult it will be when Franco paid the ultimate price. At least I'm alive."

"Survivors guilt," Bea said knowingly. "I've read about it. People in all kinds of situations spend years feeling guilty that they lived when others perished."

"Hm, maybe I'll speak to Scarlett about it."

Chapter Forty-Two

Scarlett found herself knocking on the door before she really had time to consider if this was sensible or not. But the bus ride over hadn't made things any easier and now, here she was.

"Scarlett?" Diana said in surprise. "I wasn't expecting you. Come in, is everything alright?"

"Hey, yeah, I just needed," she blew out her cheeks, stepping inside before she said, "I need to talk about something, and I'm not sure if…it could be weird, but you're my friend and my sister, and I guess, that's who I would or could go to, right?"

Diana's eyes lit up. "Yes. Absolutely, I am here for it." Diana grabbed Scarlett's arm and pulled her further into the flat before she could change her mind and escape.

She led Scarlett into the small kitchen and picked up the kettle, because every proper conversation of importance required a cup of tea, didn't it?

"So, what's up?" Diana asked, trying not to sound too eager, but she was. This was what she lived for, and Zara and Adam rarely used her services. She was a good listener, and she gave good advice, and best of all, she could keep her gob shut.

Scarlett thought for a moment before deciding to just say it.

"Well, I asked your mum to marry me."

Diana stared at her, the kettle boiling and hissing behind her. She went to speak, and then stopped, exhaling instead before she took the three steps required to reach the other chair and sit down opposite Scarlett.

"And what…I mean, did she?"

"She said no, but that's not the issue."

"That's not—" Diana sat back and stared across at Scarlett. "So, you're upset about it and need a shoulder to cry on?"

Scarlett

Scarlett shook her head. "No, I'm good, I'm trying to work out why I asked. I mean, it's not that I wouldn't marry her, of course I would in a heartbeat, but I wasn't planning it, not yet. It hadn't even entered my mind as a conscious thought until I said it and then it was like a shock, to me and her."

"Damn, I can't believe she said no."

That made Scarlett smile. "Oh you want me as your stepmum, do you?"

Grinning back, Diana said, "There are worse options. I dunno, I just assumed that it was a natural process, you're both so in love that it's sickening."

"True, I am in love with her, and I know the feeling is mutual. There's something more there that I can't quite put my finger on. Why did I ask?"

"Maybe it's because of the accident. You almost lost her." Diana frowned. "Tea?"

Scarlett nodded. "Yeah, thanks." She thought about what Diana had suggested, remembering that was her initial thought too. "I think maybe that's part of it. I know I spent too long thinking about that fact. I didn't like it. The idea of living my life without her in it." She shuddered.

With her back to her, kettle in hand, Diana said, "A lot has happened recently. The accident was just the icing on top of a very upsetting cake."

"I mean, yes, at the time I would say there was a lot of upset but now? It's weirdly worked out quite well, hasn't it?"

Diana turned around holding two mugs, smiling broadly. "I should say so." She placed one down in front of Scarlett. "I admit, I was taken aback a little, and I'm still angry with Dad about it all, I'm working through that," she assured. "And yes, I was a little put out thinking I'd lose my spot as head of the sibling clan, but I'm okay with things now. It's quite nice having you to talk to too. Zara is

192

away with the fairies half the time. Did you know she's planning to take Jacob on a march for women's rights?"

"Sounds like Zara." Scarlett chuckled. "So, just to be clear, you'd be okay if one day your mum and I got married?"

"Absolutely." Diana sipped her tea. "And I'm pretty sure Adam and Zara would agree, not that we've discussed it." She winked.

Scarlett stared open-mouthed. "You've discussed us getting married?"

"Of course we have." Diana chuckled. "Zara is hopeful of being chief bridesmaid, obviously I'd be maid of honour and Adam would give Mum away, and oh, can you imagine how cute Jacob would look as a page boy?"

"I had no idea you were all so devious."

"I prefer invested." Diana giggled. "Anyway, she's gone and spoiled it by saying no, so we'll all just have to wait, won't we?"

"I guess we will." Scarlett picked up her mug. "I think that you're right, I think I was just overwhelmed with my emotions and the idea of losing her and all of the other dynamics and just blurted out something that made me feel safe."

"Who knew I was so good at fixing everybody's problems." Diana beamed. "Sisters are handy."

"I'm starting to understand that. It's weird because I never knew any different before, my entire life was just me. I had my parents but with those issues, I learned to depend on me, and it took a lot of work on myself to be able to lean elsewhere, I just never actually had anyone I trusted enough to really do that with."

"Until now." Diana nudged.

Scarlett smiled. "Yes, until now."

Scarlett

"It might be the perfect scenario of a Jerry Springer show and Dad might be an absolute arse for what he put Mum through, but Zara, Adam and I, we are here for you." She reached out her hand and covered Scarlett's. "We're family, and that means a hell of a lot around here."

"I definitely know that, and I hope you know that, even though these new dynamics will take some getting used to, I'm here for you too. All of you."

Diana finished her tea. "Glad to hear it, another?"

"Go on then, but I'll have to get going soon, I'm not sure how long Bea is hanging around for and I don't want to leave Claudia on her own for long."

"Oh, no need to worry, Zara is popping in with Jacob. Let her do some work for a change." Diana winked and stood up. She moved over to the kettle and flicked it on again. When she turned around she found Scarlett frowning. "What's up?"

"Nothing, I was just wondering, what does Zara do? She was teaching before Jacob came along but I know that job came to an end."

"Yep, well, she's decided she doesn't want to be a corporate slave any longer and is working to live, not living to work." She used her fingers to create quotation marks around those statements.

"Okay, I guess I can't blame her but still, she has to pay bills and look after Jacob."

"James pays her share of the rent here, that's his contribution to Jacob's care." She rolled her eyes at that. "Which Zara thinks more than generous. As well as that, she's been tutoring kids getting ready for their GCSEs and those who are just struggling. And of course, Dad throws her some cash here and there, so..." Diana shrugged with a smirk. "She seems quite content with her lot, and Jacob is loved and well looked after." The kettle finished boiling.

"So that's all that matters," Scarlett said at the same time.

"Exactly."

"Hm, well then I might have to call on her services a little more in the next few weeks, I can't keep cancelling my clients, I won't have a business left at this rate."

"Adam and I mostly work remotely now, so we can all pick up the slack when you need it. You just have to ask, remember?" Diana handed over another cup of tea.

Scarlett

Chapter Forty-Three

Franco's funeral came around far too quickly for Claudia's liking, but she got up and got ready with barely a word until they were in the car and almost there.

"Are you alright?" Scarlett asked, as she took a left turn.

Claudia stared out of the window. "Yes, in the grand scheme of things. He was so young, it just…" Her words tailed off and Scarlett indicated to turn right, stopping in the middle of the road as she waited for a space to cut across.

"I guess it's the question we never know the answer to until it happens, how much time do we have?"

Silence filled the car in response.

As they drew nearer to the crematorium, the traffic slowed to a trickle and Scarlett cast a glance in Claudia's direction. Staring straight ahead, her face completely unreadable.

There was a space to park and Scarlett pulled in.

"Ready?" she asked as she yanked on the handbrake. Reaching over, she took Claudia's hand. "I'm here, okay? Always."

Claudia finally smiled, quick and sadly, but it was an emotional response at least.

"I know, and yes, I'm ready."

Scarlett climbed out of the Beast and walked around to the passenger side, opening the door, and helping Claudia to lift her broken leg out. While Claudia straightened up, Scarlett opened the back door and grabbed her crutches.

"Okay, let's get you upright then, shall we?" She chuckled, her arm sliding under Claudia's arm and around her to help lift. Claudia used the door to gain the leverage she needed. When she was upright, Scarlett checked again, "Ready?"

"Yes, stop fussing," Claudia snapped and immediately regretted it. "Sorry, I'm sorry, that was uncalled for."

Scarlett smiled. "Yes it was, but I understand. Now, do you want both sticks or one stick and me?"

Claudia leaned forward and kissed Scarlett quickly. "I'd best take two."

They walked slowly towards the growing crowd of black that hovered around the building's entrance. A sombre waiting room in the open air for a car that would deliver the coffin, and Franco on his last journey.

It felt a little strange for Scarlett, standing there, not knowing anybody other than Claudia, but she didn't mind in the slightest. Because she'd have done anything for this woman.

Several people said hello to Claudia, and she greeted each of them with a sympathetic smile. She didn't introduce Scarlett; it wasn't the time or place yet. Conversation was sparse.

How are you? Isn't it sad? How's the leg? Was about as much as was said.

"Claudia." A tall man stepped forward from the crowd. "How are you? Did you get the flowers?"

"Gregory, yes, thank you, they were beautiful." She smiled at him before turning to Scarlett. "This is my partner, Scarlett. Gregory Thorndyke, my boss," she explained.

Scarlett reached out a hand and they shook. "Nice to meet you, sorry it's under such sad circumstances."

"Indeed. We just need to concentrate on getting you well again." He patted Claudia's arm. "We miss you at the office." He smiled once more and then he moved onto the next person to arrive. Claudia's jaw tightened but relaxed the moment she felt the warmth of Scarlett's palm on her back.

Scarlett

"I appreciate you," she whispered just loud enough that Scarlett heard.

Looking around, it was a surreal scene. Groups of people huddled together, a soft murmur of chatter, and the soft sniffles of tears all merged to create what Scarlett referred to as the funeral anthem. That silenced gradually as each person noticed the arrival of the hearse.

Six perfectly dressed men stepped forward. All in suits and around Franco's age. Brothers, cousins, friends of Franco, Scarlett guessed.

They each took their place beside the coffin and all dipped and rose simultaneously with the coffin's weight beared upon their collective shoulders.

Everyone shuffled to create a pathway, and the coffin glided through with parents and family following. Only then did everyone else slowly file into place to follow behind.

Surprisingly, the service was fun, and humorous. Franco was well-liked, happy and a joy to be around according to his brother who stood at the lectern and spoke confidently about a little brother who was always getting him into trouble with their mum and dad.

When his friend Jobi got up and spoke, it was with humour and laughter, as he reminisced about the things they'd done over the years through school, college and then down the pub.

It was heart breaking to listen to his mother, who's tears ran freely while she spoke proudly of her son, and how his loss was a void they'd never fill.

Claudia broke down and sobbed quietly into a tissue Scarlett handed her just in time.

They sang, repeated prayers and said Amen in all the right places, and then it was over, and the congregation stood, ready to file back out and leave.

"So, I was thinking—"

"Yes," Claudia interrupted with a firm affirmation, turning to face Scarlett, she repeated it. "Yes."

"You don't know what I was thinking yet." Scarlett chuckled quietly as they shuffled forward and waited their turn.

Claudia seemed to shake her thoughts clearer in her head. "No, sorry, I...I wasn't listening."

"So, I'm confused, what are you saying yes to?"

It was a difficult space to turn in with a broken leg and crutches, but somehow, Claudia managed it. Facing Scarlett, almost eye to eye she unhooked her good arm from the crutch, reaching up to palm Scarlett's cheek.

Their eyes locked and held, as other mourners filed past them, it felt like an age before she finally said.

"Marrying you."

Scarlett's eyebrows knitted together in confusion.

"Marrying me?"

Claudia nodded. "Yes. I changed my mind; I think we should do it. I want to do it." Her smile broadened. "I want to marry you."

Scarlett

Chapter Forty-Four

"I'm not saying no, I'm saying we should talk about i Scarlett was saying as she held the door open and then waited 1 Claudia to lift her good leg up the step before grasping under her a and lifting her.

"Yes, and we shall talk about it," Claudia answered on she'd got over the threshold. "I thought you wanted to get married."

"I do, I mean at some point. But you said no, and you we quite firm about it." She followed Claudia down the hall and into t kitchen. "Tea?"

"Coffee, please," Claudia answered, pulling a stool out a heaving herself up onto it.

"Please be careful, you shouldn't be sitting on those."

"Yes, Mum." Claudia winked.

Scarlett ignored her, flicked the kettle on and grabbed tw mugs.

"So, what's changed?"

"Honestly, I've been thinking about it since you asked n and I wondered if I'd been too quick to dismiss the idea, but f logically, that if I had to think about it at all then it was most like the correct decision, but now," she licked her lip and stared inten at Scarlett, "after everything, what you said in the car struck hom and then with all of the words at the funeral, I realised, I don't wa anyone else, this is it for me and why shouldn't we tell the wo about it."

Scarlett thought back to what she'd said in the car.

"When I said we never know how much time we have?"

Claudia nodded. "Exactly, I got lucky this time, Fran didn't, how easily it could have been the other way around? Life short, far too short and if the only thing stopping me from marryi the love of my life is the memory of the idiot who threw it all away the first time, then that makes me an idiot too."

"I just want to be sure that you want to do this because it's us, and not because you're upset and feeling some emotions."

Her elbows on the countertop, Claudia rested her chin in her hands. "I can see why you might think that, and I'm not going to pretend those emotions haven't helped my decision, but I'm saying this because I think about us, and the future, and I see a gold band on my finger." She smiled.

Scarlett thought about it for a moment.

"So, you want to get married?" she finally said.

"Yes."

"You want to be my wife?" Scarlett confirmed much to Claudia's amusement.

"Yes, and you mine, yes, I want that, all of that."

The kettle boiled and flicked off. It was ignored.

Scarlett grinned. "So, we're getting married then?"

Claudia matched her smile. "Yes, we're getting married."

Under normal circumstances, Scarlett would have chased a shrieking Claudia up the stairs to their room. Where she would have taken all of thirty seconds to rid her of enough clothes in order to ravish her.

This time, it took at least five minutes of giggling and falling over, as they made their way up the stairs one hop at a time, stopping to kiss and fondle before hopping the next few.

By the time they stumbled into the bedroom, they both fell backwards onto the bed laughing.

Scarlett

"Jesus, that was hard work," Scarlett continued to laugh. She managed to sit up and yank her top off. "But worth it." Turning quickly, she pounced on Claudia. Straddling across her thighs. "You really want to marry me?"

Claudia's arms reached up and wound around Scarlett's neck, pulling her in close so she could whisper against her lips, "I do."

They kissed. Firm and passionate. Tongues dancing around one another until they could barely breathe.

"This leg is so annoying." Claudia moaned, frustrated that she couldn't enjoy sex the way they usually did. "I just want to bounce on top of you and this…it's cumbersome and annoying."

"Cumbersome?" Scarlett giggled. "Cute."

"Oh, you know what I mean." Claudia slapped her playfully.

"Well, until it comes off, you're just going to have to suck it up and enjoy the vanilla kind of hanky panky. But once it's off…' Scarlett reached around and unclipped her bra. "I am going to let you ride me for a month."

"Is that a promise? I'm not going to complain."

Scarlett stopped what she was doing and thought for a moment. Her brain activating her imagination. "Hang on, wait there." She jumped off the bed and pulled their toy box out, waving Claudia's favourite in the air. "I have an idea. It's your foot that's the problem, it can't bend because of the cast, but…" She stopped talking to concentrate on stepping into the harness. "If I sit on the edge of the bed, your foot could hang off the edge."

"As much as I love your enthusiasm to make me happy, I think bouncing on my knees is still going to be awkward, and potentially damaging. I'll suck it up and enjoy the vanilla kind of hanky panky."

"Fair enough." Scarlett laughed, and pounced onto the bed making a grab for Claudia, pulling her closer. "Get over here."

Claire Highton-Stevenson

Scarlett

"When do you think we should tell them?" Claudia asked Scarlett as they lay naked together in bed.

"Whenever you're ready."

"Do you think they'll be shocked?"

Scarlett laughed. "No, I think they're expecting it, well maybe not Diana."

Claudia twisted and swore under her breath at the exhaustion of such a simple movement. "What makes you think that?" she asked once she was settled.

"Because I confided in her last week, after you turned me down, and she said she was surprised because they all thought you would say yes if I asked. So, she's under the impression you said no."

Leaning up on her elbow, Claudia said, "They've discussed it?"

Scarlett grinned. "That was my reaction, and yes, apparently they're all onboard for it."

"Oh, I thought I might have had to deal with some resistance from Adam at least."

"Nope, they've even given themselves roles on the day," Scarlett continued, amused by it all.

"They have?" Now Claudia couldn't help but grin.

"Yes, obviously, Diana will be maid of honour, and Zara chief bridesmaid."

"Aren't they the same thing?"

Scarlett shrugged. "No idea, but I'm not arguing with them over it."

Claudia dropped back down and snuggled in. "No, me either. It's a good compromise, isn't it? What about Adam?"

"He's giving you away."

"So, all we have to do now is just pick a date and turn up." Claudia chuckled.

"Sounds like a plan."

"You're getting married?" Diana said before anyone else could react. "But you said she said no." Her chin jutted towards her mother, who proudly stood next to Scarlett with their fingers entwined

Zara and Adam both swung around, beaming smiles turning to confused frowns, as they both realised, they weren't in on the action.

"How do you know that?" Zara asked.

"I—" Diana froze. Annoyed at herself for breaking a confidence, and now stuck with what to say about it.

"Alright." Claudia clapped her hands for everyone's attention. "Scarlett did ask me, and I think at the time, we were both a little shocked about it and I did say no, but now, we've talked it over again and we both agree that it's what we want, so, we're getting married."

"That still doesn't answer how she knew, and we didn't." Zara gave a sideways glance at Diana.

"Because I confided in her," Scarlett admitted. "Now, can we get back to the congratulations bit?"

Adam stepped forward and hugged Claudia, and then Scarlett.

Scarlett

"I have to admit, when you first appeared on the scene I w
pretty concerned that Mother was having some kind of mid-li
crisis, but honestly, I think you've been the best thing to happen
this family in a long time, and finding out you were my sister, we
yeah, it was a shock, but I think we've all moved past that no
haven't we?"

"Yep, what he said." Zara smiled, punching her brother
the arm with the hand that wasn't holding onto Jacob.

"Are you going to tell Dad?" Diana asked Scarlett, rath
than Claudia.

"I—I hadn't thought about it to be honest. But I suppose I
be telling him, and my parents, at some point."

"I guess it will be weird for him," Zara added.

Scarlett noticed the way that Claudia's shoulders sagged a
put her arm around her. "Honestly, his opinion doesn't matter. If i
weird for him, tough. This is about us, and we're not going to
anything take away from the happiness of it."

Claudia smiled at her grateful for the support.

"So." Adam clapped his hands. "Are we celebrating?"

"Yes. Absolutely. Let's go out and let our hair down
Scarlett agreed. "Art?"

"You want to take us to a gay bar, gay bar?" Zara sang, a
then stopped abruptly. "Uh, I'll need an hour to get James to ha
Jacob, and then get ready." She was gone before anyone could s
anything different, running up the stairs to find her bag, and t
phone inside it.

"A gay bar, huh?" Adam grinned. "Sounds fun, I'll go a
get Sunny." And he was gone like the wind too. Leaving just Dia
standing there looking a little like a deer caught in the headlights.

"You alright there, Di?" Scarlett asked.

Diana nodded. "Yes, I'm just…wow." Her face finally broke into a smile. "I'm going to be a maid of honour."

"Uh, yes, I suppose so, if we decide to have that kind of wedding, but we haven't made any plans yet," Claudia explained, trying to bring Diana's expectations back to a manageable level.

"Of course, but still, you'll need someone to take charge and make sure everything runs smoothly on the day, and I'm just saying, that I am the perfect choice," she finished, barely taking a breath.

Scarlett and Claudia both stood wide-eyed staring at her.

"Let's just enjoy the celebration today and worry about everything else later." Claudia smiled, extricating herself from Scarlett's comforting arm that now felt like a vice-like grip. "Shall we say an hour to get changed and ready then?"

"Di, come on, we need to drop Jacob off, get changed and get back," Zara said, rushing back into the lounge with Jacob giggling under her arm as he flew like an airplane.

Scarlett

Chapter Forty-Six

Claudia insisted on going to dinner first. Which in hindsight was probably for the best considering how many cocktails Adam was consuming with Zara. The pair of them on the dance floor, bouncing around to music they both knew well. Sunny sat back sipping her brightly coloured drink, getting quietly drunk, with Diana taking it easy with the glass of wine and soda she'd nursed for almost an hour. Taking her designated driver duties very seriously.

"I wish I could dance." Claudia grinned, leaning into Scarlett. She too was on the soft drinks but the excitement of the day and now, out with everyone for the first time in weeks, had given her a little boost that was missing these past few days.

"Why can't you?" Scarlett laughed. "Okay, it would be incredibly awkward, but still, you can hold on to me and sway, if you like?"

Claudia moved closer, her lips just grazing Scarlett's ear. "I'd rather conserve my energy for later."

Every time. It didn't matter what Claudia said, just the merest vibration of her lips whispering against Scarlett's ear like that would send a jolt of excitement rocketing through her nervous system, with only one target. And it never failed to hit.

She turned her face slightly until her lips were barely a brush away from Claudia. "We can leave anytime you want to."

"Darling, that would be too easy." She leaned in again, right next to her ear. "I want you begging for it."

Scarlett's cheeks must have turned the colour of her name because Diana leaned forward. "Are you alright?"

"Uh huh." She managed just as Claudia squeezed her thigh. "Yep, all good."

Diana eyed them both for a moment before her gaze moved to follow Claudia's hand. "Mother, really?"

208

Claire Highton-Stevenson

"What? It's allowed in here." Claudia winked.

"I'm going to get another drink, does anyone want one?" She stood up quickly and edged her way past them all to get out from the table.

"I'll have another one of these?" Sunny piped up, holding the almost empty glass in the air. "It's called a Rumpy Pumpy." She laughed. "I need some of that."

"Maybe you should take that up with Adam," Diana joked. "Okay, back in a minute with some Rumpy Pumpy."

"You know, you can get a Rumpy Pumpy, if you want?" Claudia said to Scarlett as they both watched Diana stand at the bar looking and clearly feeling very out of place.

"Oh, I'm planning on it." Scarlett chuckled. "Later."

They sat quietly, holding hands, enjoying the atmosphere. Completely comfortable with being themselves, which was a long way from where they'd been when they'd first met.

"Do you think she's ever going to meet anyone decent?" Claudia asked, her chin jutting towards Diana. "I do worry about her."

"Do you? I think she's content. She's happy in herself, and the right one will come along when she's ready to see it."

Claudia nudged Scarlett's shoulder. "Oh, wise one."

They both fell silent as it became obvious that Diana was talking to someone. Her drinks were on the bar, and she'd paid the girl serving.

"Who's that?" Claudia asked, craning her neck for a better look.

"I don't know. Probably just someone being friendly, you know what Diana's like, she chats to anyone given the opportunity."

Scarlett

"True." Claudia narrowed her eyes. "But what if it's someone hassling her?"

Scarlett turned to Claudia and stared. "Really? You just said you hope she meets someone, and now someone is speaking to her you've gone all, I'll kick their ass."

Claudia smiled. "Again, very true. And it isn't like Diana is interested in women, is it?"

"Exactly, she's completely fine." Scarlett glanced at Sunny. "Although this one…I'm not so sure."

Claudia turned in the same direction and giggled. Sunny was leaning against the wall, sound asleep. "I guess we're the only ones getting rumpy pumpy tonight then."

"I guess so." Scarlett laughed, but she couldn't help the last glance at Diana. Laughing at something the other woman was saying, until she felt warm fingers against her chin and her face being turned towards Claudia.

"Kiss me," she demanded.

"In public? How very daring." Scarlett grinned before doing exactly as she was told. Slowly, and reverently, as though nobody else were anywhere near them. Both of them lost in the moment.

"I love doing that," Claudia admitted when they finally pulled apart.

"Yeah, it's pretty sweet."

"I never want to stop doing that. No matter how many times we argue, or whatever else happens in life, promise me we will never stop kissing?"

Scarlett leaned closer again. "I promise," she whispered before kissing her once more.

Zara reached between the seats from the back of the car in an attempt to turn the music up as Diana drove. Sticking to the speed limit, despite it being almost 2. A.M. and, according to Zara, *she could put her foot down.*

"Zara will you put your seatbelt back on and sit quietly," Claudia scolded like she'd done twenty years earlier when Zara would push everyone's boundaries on the car ride home from anywhere.

"Aw, I just want to keep dancing. I can't believe Adam had to take Sunny home." She fell into a fit of giggles. "Drunk on Rumpy Pumpy. I'm never letting them forget that."

Scarlett smiled to herself sitting next to her. A little tipsy herself too.

"She's going to have one hell of a headache in the morning." Diana chuckled.

Zara grabbed the back of Diana's seat and pulled herself forward as much as the newly locked-in seatbelt would allow.

"And, who's your new friend?" she slurred a little.

Diana glanced back at her through the rear-view mirror. "Her name's Shannon."

All eyes turned towards her.

"What?" Diana asked, checking her face in the mirror.

"Is that all we're getting?" Claudia teased. "You met a girl in a gay bar and spent ten minutes chatting to her and then exchanged numbers—"

"Oh my god, were you all spying on me?"

Scarlett

Zara clapped her hands. "Do you have a date?"

"We weren't spying." Scarlett attempted to say before Dia glared at her through the mirror and she sat back, trying her harde to keep a straight face.

"It's not a date." Diana straightened up and prepared for t turning into their street. "We're just going to have a coffee and ta about—"

"It's a date." They all shouted gleefully.

Chapter Forty-Seven

It dawned on Claudia that she didn't actually know the first names of the two people sitting on the couch in her living room. Which seemed quite odd now, seeing as Scarlett had been living here the best part of a year.

They'd just been her parents whenever they'd been spoken about. She'd only met them once each. The day Scarlett had moved out and she'd had words with Scarlett's dad, and once in town when they'd bumped into her mum.

Now though, the woman sitting demurely opposite her was also the same woman who had cheated with her soon-to-be husband. And it was cheating! It was a known fact that it was a stag night, his stag night. It rankled Claudia somewhat, and yet, she couldn't quite find it in her to dislike the woman. She'd been young, stupid, and drunk, and Jack was a good-looking charmer, and she should know after all, she'd fallen for him hook line and sinker too.

The cups of tea were steaming on the coffee table when Scarlett stood up and turned to them.

"So, I asked you here for two reasons. One, I think its time to put all of our differences aside and for you both to be part of my life, a life that includes Claudia, and two, because my life with Claudia is going to be celebrated. We're getting married."

"Married?" her mum exclaimed before her face broke out into a smile. "Oh, that is wonderful news, isn't it?" She nudged her husband.

Her dad drew in a deep breath before answering, "Yes, I...congratulations." He smiled. He was trying, Claudia thought. "Both of you."

"So, when is the big day?" her mum asked excitedly.

Scarlett

"Uh, we haven't decided yet, we want to make sure Claudia is out of her cast and any other potential walking issues first," Scarlett answered.

Her dad was quiet, which didn't surprise her in the slightest. They might be trying to put things right, but his personality wouldn't change, he was a quiet man in general. Which was why she was surprised when he sat forward and said, "Is it a church wedding?"

"Oh, we've not even thought about it," Claudia chipped in.

"Well, whatever you decide, it's all very exciting," Scarlett's mum added before picking up her cup.

"But it will be me giving you away, though, right?" her dad asked.

Scarlett stared at him. "I don't—"

"As I said," Claudia interjected, "we haven't talked about what kind of wedding we want."

Her dad nodded slowly, his gaze firmly on Scarlett despite it being Claudia who was speaking.

"Scarlett, could you help me get up. I need to—"

"Of course." Scarlett was on her feet instantly. "I won't be a minute, more tea?"

"Would love one, thank you." Her mum smiled at the pair of them as Claudia leaned one side on Scarlett, the other on her crutch.

When they were out in the hall Scarlett whispered, "Bloody hell, I didn't even think about that."

"And you don't have to think about it now," Claudia said pushing the door to the toilet open. "By the way, what are your parents' names?"

"Oh." Scarlett laughed. "I've never thought to tell you, my mum is Brenda, and dad is Terry."

"Where are we going?" Claudia asked once Scarlett's parents had waved goodbye and she was settled into their car. Scarlett kissed her as she leaned in for the seatbelt. "I can put that on myself, you know, you don't need an excuse to kiss me."

Scarlett chuckled. "I like excuses."

She shut the door and came around to the driver's side, opened the door and climbed in.

"So?" Claudia said, "Where are we going?"

"You'll find out when we get there," Scarlett answered mysteriously.

As they drove it became apparently clear that wherever they were going, it was a drive out to the countryside. And as they neared where Scarlett was heading, Claudia suddenly recognised something.

"Are we going to where I think we're going?"

Scarlett smiled. "That depends on where you think we're going?"

Claudia grinned at her. "The spa hotel where we spent our entire time hiding away from the girls?" She laughed at the memory. "That was crazy."

They rounded a bend and the big hotel loomed up in front of them.

"We are," she exclaimed. "Oh, but we didn't bring any clothes and—"

"Didn't we?" Scarlett wriggled her brows as she pulled into the space marked with a disabled sign. She jumped out and scrambled around to assist Claudia. "Now, careful, this gravel isn't the best for walking on." She handed Claudia her crutches.

Scarlett

From the other side of the car, someone shouted, "You can't park there."

Leaving Claudia for a moment, Scarlett edged towards the back of the Jeep and peered around to see a woman in her sixties leaning out of the window of a small metallic pink hatchback. Scarlett frowned in confusion at her.

"I said, you can't park there."

"Why not?" Scarlett asked, stepping around the Jeep completely.

The woman huffed. "It's a disabled bay, have you got a badge?"

"No, we don't have a badge."

"Then you'll have to move, somebody will need that space at some point."

Scarlett nodded. "Yes, I'll be moving once we've got inside with all of our things."

"That's not how it works." The woman glared. "You need to be someone with a disability, not an able and fit young woman like yourself, it's very self—"

She stopped speaking as Claudia hobbled around on her crutches. One leg hanging in the air to keep the weight off it. "What's going on?"

"Oh, I didn't realise." The woman became a little embarrassed.

"Probably should have been the first question you asked, or maybe just mind your own business?" Scarlett snarked.

"Sweetheart, it's fine," Claudia soothed. "We will be moving the car, it's just temporary while I get inside." She smiled and the woman looked away. "Have a lovely day," Claudia added before

216

hopping away. The woman's window closed, and she drove off without another word.

"Bloody cheek," Scarlett muttered, opening the back space, and pulling out a holdall that she slung over her shoulder. She glanced once more at the retreating car before turning and bounding in after Claudia. "Nobody had better ruin this visit."

"You booked the same room?" Claudia gasped as Scarlett opened the door.

"Yeah, well we did get to know it pretty well before." She smiled as Claudia hobbled inside. Following, Scarlett dropped the bag onto the desk. "I know you can't use all of the spa options, but I thought it would be a nice way to spend a couple of nights together before you start working again."

Claudia chuckled. "I'm only going to be on the sofa with my laptop." She held out a hand for Scarlett to take, pulling her closer the moment their fingers interlocked. "This is a wonderful idea."

"Good, I'm glad you feel that way. So, shall we get changed and then head down to dinner?"

"Yes. Oh, I have nothing to wear."

Scarlett grinned and unzipped the heavy bag. "If you don't like the choices, blame Zara, she picked your outfits."

Scarlett

Chapter Forty-Eight

"You look amazing," Scarlett gushed when she came out the shower to find Claudia ready. A summery dress that fell to t[] floor and covered the plaster cast perfectly. Thin straps showed off tanned and muscular set of shoulders and arms that Scarlett had pla[] to explore more later.

"I think I could wear a bin bag and you'd still say the rig[] thing." Claudia giggled.

Scarlett rubbed at her hair with a towel. "That is becau[] you'd make a bin bag look great." She leaned in and stole a kiss. won't be long."

Claudia sat down on the edge of the bed. "It's okay, take yo[] time. I can enjoy the view."

Scarlett twirled and then let the towel wrapped around h[] torso drop to the floor. Lean and a little tanned from the summer su[] every inch of her appealing to Claudia.

"You can enjoy this anytime you want."

"It's hard to imagine that there was a time when I would ha[] run from you."

"Yep, was kind of ridiculous." Scarlett winked. "But we'[] here now, and that is all that matters." She moved in closer, kissi[] Claudia slow and gently. Pulling away, she grinned. "Now, st[] distracting me."

"Spoilsport." Claudia laughed but leaned back on her pal[] and watched as Scarlett moved about the room pulling on clothes a[] drying her hair quickly. When she put lipstick on, Claudia w[] intrigued. It wasn't often that Scarlett bothered. As she looked at h[] she realised that she had more than bothered.

"Right, I'm ready," Scarlett said with one more look []
herself in the mirror. She wore a dark suit. A woman's tailored a[]

fitted-to-perfection suit with a dark red shirt beneath it. Her hair hung loosely around her face.

"You look gorgeous."

"Scrub up alright, don't we?" Scarlett held out her hand and helped Claudia to her feet.

Fingering the collar of the suit, Claudia hummed. "I think I'd like you wearing a suit at our wedding."

"Really, you don't want me in a huge frilly Cinderella style—"

Laughing, Claudia playfully slapped against her chest. "No, absolutely not. That's what I'm wearing."

"Oh goody, I can't wait to unwrap those layers." Scarlett reached for Claudia's crutches. "You good, need a hand?"

Sliding her arms into the hole, Claudia smirked. "Let's save your energy for later, you're going to need it."

"Promises, promises." She laughed, opening the door for Claudia. "Oh, go on, I can't remember if I turned the straighteners off."

Claudia rolled her eyes with a smile. "I'm sure you can catch me up."

Scarlett watched her walk away for a moment, before turning back to the room, ignoring the straighteners that she already knew were off. Instead, she opened a pocket on the front of the bag and reached in for the small box inside.

Double-checking for the fiftieth time that the ring was still inside, she clapped it shut and shoved it into her pocket. Grinning to herself, she left the room, and jogged down the hall to where Claudia was waiting at the lifts.

"Okay?"

Scarlett

"Yes, all good. They were off," Scarlett said, leaning forward and pressing the button again.

They rode the short lift ride down in silence. When the doors opened, Scarlett waited for Claudia to step forward, and then followed.

"I assume we're eating here?" Claudia asked, turning towards the dining room.

"You assume correctly."

The Maître D welcomed them with gusto, and took them through the dining room, and out into the orangery, where only one table sat in the centre. Candles burning and a bottle of champagne on ice.

Claudia glanced quickly at Scarlett, but her lover looked nonplussed as they were seated.

"This is all—"

"Perfect?" Scarlett offered.

"Yes, it is. But why are we out here?"

"Well, I was going to wait until dessert but—" Scarlett stood up and came around the table, dropping down onto one knee as she reached into her pocket and produced the box, opening it to a gasp from Claudia. "I didn't think asking you to marry me while lying in bed, with no thought or romance, was adequate for what I feel about you. You're the love of my life, the woman I want to spend that life with. It's your face I want to see when I wake up every morning and the last face I want to see before I drift off to sleep at night." She smiled and took Claudia's hand. "So, I'm asking again if you Claudia Maddox, would do me the honour of becoming my wife and spending the rest of whatever time on this planet we have left, with me?"

"Yes, you already know that. I will spend every moment of my life loving you and being loved by you. Yes, absolutely I will marry you."

Scarlett slid the ring onto her finger. A simple gold band with an emerald-cut diamond in the centre. Claudia stared at it for just a second before she reached out and pulled Scarlett closer and kissed her.

"I can't wait for you to be my wife."

"Then let's set a date," Claudia said before kissing her again.

Scarlett

Chapter Forty-Nine

"This is ridiculous," Claudia complained disconnecting the call with Diana. "Every date we come up with there's someone who can't make it."

Scarlett shuffled over on the sofa and patted the space next to her.

"There's no rush, babe."

Claudia hopped over and sat down in the space, sighing in the process. "I want to marry you." Her head falling against Scarlett.

"I know, I asked first remember!" Scarlett smiled and kissed the side of her lover's head. "Why don't we call a family meeting get everyone to come over and bring their diaries and then we can thrash it out."

"We could do that; it would make sense."

"Yep, if we can manage with all of them in the same room at the same time. I'd have to invite my parents."

Claudia twisted around to face her. A look of seriousness on her face. "What about Jack?"

"I dunno, hadn't thought about that."

"I mean, he is…well, I'd imagine he'd want to be there if you wanted him there."

Scarlett fidgeted. Picking at the material of her sleeve. "How would you feel about that?"

Smiling, Claudia took her hand, "A little bit weird, but I think we've buried the hatchet now. He's doing his best to make changes and I think he really wants to be a part of your life."

"I know. He's been texting, and I have to admit he was really supportive when you were in hospital. But, how do I manage this

My dad isn't going to want him there. My mum is going to be embarrassed. It's going to be awkward whatever I do."

"Yes, I suppose so." She patted Scarlett's leg. "Then maybe inviting him to the family meeting is the opportunity to get that all done with so everyone can enjoy the wedding and we don't have to worry about a full-scale riot taking place at the reception."

Scarlett laughed. "Yes, maybe you're right."

"It will be fine, sweetheart. I'll referee." She picked up her phone and tapped out a text. "Okay, I've informed the kids to come over tonight. I'll leave you to deal with your parents, and Jack."

"Gee, thanks." Scarlett laughed. "I'm going to make a cup of tea, do you want one?"

Claudia watched as she stood up. "No, I'm fine." She had a feeling Scarlett didn't want a cup of tea either, just the privacy to get her thoughts together and call her folks.

"You mean, Dad's coming over, and so are Letty's parents?" Diana whispered.

Claudia nodded. "Yes, so it's going to be awkward enough. I want you three to stay out of it and be on best behaviour."

Adam rolled his eyes. "Trust me, I'm not getting involved. I don't even want to speak to him."

"Oh Adam, I really wish you could find some common ground with him again." Claudia ran her hand up and down his arm. "I know he's—"

"A lying, cheating bastard."

"Zara!" Claudia turned and glared at her youngest.

Scarlett

"Well, that's what he was going to say, and we all kno
that's true, but at the end of the day he's still Dad, and you're gettin
too old for this tantrum anytime he upsets you." Zara crossed h
arms and blew out her cheeks. "It's getting boring."

"For goodness' sake." Claudia huffed. "Just sit down the
of you and behave."

In unison, they did as they were told, and under any oth
circumstance, it might have made Claudia giggle. Instead, she turne
and hopped her way out of the room to where Scarlett was placi
champagne flutes on a tray.

"Right, they've been warned, and they're all on be
behaviour." Claudia leaned in and kissed her cheek, just as t
doorbell rang. "Go on, you get it, I'll finish off here."

"You should have your foot up," Scarlett argued.

"And you should do as you're told." Claudia smiled as t
doorbell rang again.

Opening the door, Scarlett found three faces staring at h
Her parents, and Bea.

"Alright love bird." Bea winked, strolling in like she own
the place. Brenda smiled at her antics. "This your mum and dad
Bea asked, turning back to them.

"Uh, yes. Brenda and Terry." Scarlett turned back to h
parents. "This is Claudia's best friend, Bea."

They all said their hello's and followed Scarlett in. At t
door to the lounge, Scarlett let Bea pass but stopped her paren
"Look, you need to know that Jack will be here too."

"What?" Her dad glared. "Why?"

"Because I asked him, you're my dad, but I can't ignore t
fact that he's...you know, and he's their dad, and has history wi
Claudia and he's about to be a father again, and that kid will be n
sibling too, so I can't...I don't want to ignore that."

"Still putting it about, is he?" Her dad sneered.

"Terry, we have to face this one way or another," Brenda said reaching for his hand, but he shook her off.

"Don't...don't tell me that I've got to be okay with this."

"You don't have to be okay with it. You don't have to like it, but I'm asking you to understand it from my perspective. I don't want to be forced to choose. I want to marry Claudia and to have all of the people we want there, but if I'm forced to choose, I'll choose her, and we'll go and get married without any of you."

He looked close to tears, and she felt the weight of his emotions hit her like a brick.

"You're my dad, okay? Nothing changes that."

"It's like it's being rubbed in my face, Scarlett."

"I can see why you'd feel that way. And I'm going to do my best to make sure that there is limited contact for you both, if that's how it needs to be, but that's kind of why I'm doing this now, so I can work out how this might work."

"It's difficult enough walking in there to a room full of people that we don't know—"

"You don't know them because for the last year you've been stubbornly refusing to be part of my life, Dad, if you want that to change like you've said you do, then it is going to require uncomfortable situations at times."

Pulling his shoulders back and taking a deep breath, he said, "Fine. Let's get it over with, shall we?"

Her mum smiled sympathetically.

Without another word, Scarlett opened the door and led them in. Conversation came to a halt as all heads turned towards the newcomers.

Scarlett

"Hey, everyone this is my mum and dad, Brenda and Terry," Scarlett announced. A unanimous chorus of hello, welcome, hi, rang out. Claudia pushed herself up from her chair and hobbled across to greet them both with an uncomfortable hug.

"It's good to see you both, please, come in and make yourselves at home. These are my children, Zara, Adam, and on the end there is Diana." Claudia smiled proudly at each of them as they all said hello again.

And then the doorbell rang.

Chapter Fifty

Scarlett walked slowly to the front door, her heart in her mouth. The shadow of Jack in the glass made her feel suddenly unwell. Was this the right way to do this? She really didn't know, but it was the only way she could think of.

"Jack." She tried a smile as she opened the door wide.

"Hey, you alright?" He reached forward with his palm and placed it warmly on her bicep as he stepped inside. "We missed you at dinner the other night."

"Yeah, sorry had other plans." She felt the awkwardness of it all weighing her down. "Look, my parents are here too."

He nodded. "I assumed they would be."

"Yeah, and it's just…it's hard for my dad, you know, with you here too."

"Do you want me to go?" he offered.

Scarlett shook her head. "No, I want… Claudia and I both want you and Maisie at the wedding. You're part of this family, and…I just—"

"I get it. I'm not here to cause any trouble or to make your dad uncomfortable. I'm your father though, and I want our relationship to grow, being part of your wedding is an honour, but I totally understand if you need me to stay away."

In some ways, she wished Jack was still the arsehole he'd been when she first met him, instead of this new man. It would have been so much easier to dislike him and be done with. Therapy looked good on some people, and he was one of them.

"Come on." She led him inside and into the lounge where the hushed hub bub of chatter came to an instant halt. The silence deafening until one person stood up and moved slowly across the room, despite the outstretched arm of another, who tried to stop her.

Scarlett

"Jack, I'm Scarlett's mum, Brenda. This is her dad, Terry." She turned to her husband and beckoned him with her fingers. He rolled his eyes and for a moment, Scarlett was certain he would get up and storm out, but to her surprise, he stood slowly. Adjusted his tie and held his head up as he closed the gap between them all reaching out his hand. Jack was taller by half a foot, but her dad was broad and stocky, if they kicked off, Scarlett wasn't sure she'd want to bet on who'd win.

"I won't say it's a pleasure, but I'm here for Scarlett, *my daughter,* so we'll put pleasantries at the forefront and be amicable for the foreseeable," Terry said, his chin up, jaw clenched.

"Indeed, I think that's exactly what we should do. Scarlett's needs far outweigh our own ego's, right?" Jack took his hand and shook vigorously.

"Right, well that's the awkward thing out of the way." Brenda smiled. "Shall we get on with what we came here for?"

Terry was about to turn and walk away when he stopped. He glanced back at Jack. "If anyone is giving her away, it will be me just so we're clear."

"Dad—" Scarlett started but Jack held up a hand.

"I think that's something only Scarlett can decide."

Terry pursed his lips, taking another step towards Jack, Brenda pulling his arm back. "Terry, not now," she warned.

"Don't think that after all of these years, you get to waltz in here with ya fancy suit and just take whatever you want. Not happening. She's, my daughter."

"Enough," Scarlett shouted at the pair of them just as Jack squared up ready for the fight that was brewing. "Neither of you will be giving me away. I'm not a possession, and I'm not a traditionalist either, whatever *we* decide to do, you are invited to attend and celebrate with us, but if all you're going to do is squabble and but heads, you can both leave." She pointed to the door. "Right now."

When neither man moved, she added, "Or go and sit down and help us work out a date that suits everyone, otherwise, I swear to god we will just elope and leave you all here."

"Oh," Diana said, "But I can come, right? I mean, I'm Matron—" The glare from Claudia meant she stopped speaking instantly.

Brenda dragged Terry back to their seats, and Scarlett pointed out a chair at the other end of the room for Jack to sit in.

"Okay then." Claudia smiled and lifted her diary onto her lap, pen in hand. "Shall we work out when is the best date?"

Bea jumped in, a voice that settled Claudia and had nothing to do with the drama that surrounded them all. "Okay, what month are you thinking? Let's narrow it down a little and start from there."

Claudia smiled. "Good idea. So, we were thinking about September."

"Oh, that quickly?" Diana chipped in.

Scarlett turned to her. "No time like the present, why? Is there a problem with that?"

"Well, no, it's just finding a venue and a celebrant might be difficult, that's all. People plan these events years in advance, don't they?"

"Yes, I guess they do," Claudia said sadly. "You're right, we were so excited we didn't think about that.

"Do it in the garden," Bea suggested.

Claudia and Scarlett both stared at her. "In the garden?" Claudia finally responded.

"Yes. Lots of people do it now. You just need to get officially married at a registry office, and then you can have a celebrant come to the house and give you the wedding you both want."

"You seem to know a lot about it." Scarlett chuckled.

Bea blushed a little. "Well, I looked into it once when I w thinking about marrying Rick, but that never happened. Basicall anyone can act as the celebrant on the day, so you could slip off the morning and do the official, legally binding bit, then come hor and have everyone here to enjoy the actual ceremony."

"I think that sounds lovely," Brenda piped up. "Don't yo Terry?"

Her dad glanced around the room quickly at all the eyes no on him. "I think whatever Scarlett and Claudia want, is what v should all be happy with."

Scarlett's eyebrow raised a little. *Who was this man?*

"I think it sounds perfect, actually. I mean, I've done t whole church wedding, and I know you're not that bothered abo it," she said to Scarlett. "We could see about booking a regist office, and then have all of our friends here."

"I like it too." Scarlett grinned. "So, date?"

Everyone had left, except for Scarlett's parents. Terry w using the toilet and Scarlett had taken the mugs and glasses out to tl kitchen, and that left Brenda alone in the lounge with Claudia.

"Claudia, I," Brenda moved along the couch a little, wanted to apologise for—"

"There's nothing to apologise for, Brenda." Claudia tried smile, knowing this was a conversation that was probably a long tin coming. "Really, it was all a long time ago."

"I think there is. I've carried that guilt with me for a lo time, it was a moment of—" She looked away, embarrassed. "V were drunk, and I know that's no excuse."

Claudia nodded and took her hand. "I won't say that it didn't hurt to discover Jack's indiscretion, but it wasn't the first, or the last. I can forgive a naïve, drunk girl on a night out. And without it, I wouldn't be marrying the most wonderful woman I could ever have met, So shall we call it quits and let the past go?"

Brenda smiled. "Yes, oh yes, I would love that and move forward."

"Good, then all is forgiven and forgotten, alright?"

They hugged, just as the door opened and in walked Terry. "Right, you ready to—oh, well, in a minute then." He backed out and found Scarlett in the kitchen loading the dishwasher. "We're off, your mum and Claudia are just having a heart-to-heart."

"Right, I guess that's probably long overdue."

He nodded but didn't speak.

Scarlett grabbed a tea towel and wiped her hands dry. "Dad, I just wanted to say thank you. I know how much that took for you to be here tonight, and for us to even be trying to get our relationship back on track. I appreciate that."

He looked up at her, eyes wet with emotion. "I shouldn't have let it get this far in the first place. Claudia was right." He chuckled at Scarlett's look of confusion. "When you moved in here and you brought her round to get all your stuff, she told me I was an idiot and that one day I'd regret my decisions, she was right."

"She told you that?"

"Yep, once you'd gone inside to open the garage. I didn't appreciate it then, and I'm ashamed to say that it took all of this to bring me to my senses, but I promise you this, I'll never let that distance build between us again."

He stepped forward and held his arms out, open, a hopeful look on his face that turned into tears through a smile when Scarlett

Scarlett

stepped forward and met him halfway, allowing her dad to hug her properly for the first time in over a decade.

Chapter Fifty-One

Scarlett bounded up the stairs and into the bedroom like a tornado of excitement as she flopped down onto the bed beside Claudia. Staring up at the ceiling, she giggled like a child before rolling over to find Claudia watching her.

"That went well then?" Claudia said, smiling at her girlfriend's exuberance.

"Uh huh. Can you imagine that all it would take for my dad to stop being an arse and start being the dad I always wanted, was for me to find out he isn't my dad?"

"Yes, and I think talking with your mother was something I needed to do too." Claudia pulled Scarlett closer as she spoke.

"What did she say?"

"That she was sorry, and that she had carried the guilt of that night with her ever since. And of course, she had no idea about my connection with Jack."

"And you're alright with that?" Scarlett asked, stroking her cheek.

Claudia nodded. "Yes, I think it's water under the bridge now. I can't very well be angry about the one thing that brought you into the world, can I?" She smiled up at Scarlett. "I'm glad you're happy, darling."

Scarlett swung a leg over Claudia's waist and leaned down, ready to kiss her.

"I've never been happier."

"Me either and we have a date. Another few weeks and you'll be—" She stopped speaking and gazed up quizzically. "What are we going to do about names?"

"How do you mean?"

"Well, when I married Jack, I became Claudia Maddox, and although we're now divorced, I never thought about reverting to my maiden name, but if I'm marrying you, whose name is taken?"

"Oh." Scarlett grinned. "I have to be honest; I hadn't thought about it. I mean do you want to become a Taylor? Or a double barrelled? Or?" She frowned. "What is your maiden name?"

"Clarke." She grinned. "Nothing exciting. But I suppose Taylor-Clarke would work."

"Bit of a mouthful though, isn't it?"

"Yes. And I guess I like having the same name as my children."

Scarlett sighed and sat up on her knees.

"What's wrong?" Claudia asked.

"It's just…Jack is my father, legally I could take his name and marry you and you'd still have the same name without having to change anything."

Claudia stared at her. Unsure if she was being serious or not until the smile on her face cracked.

"Seriously, can you imagine the drama that would kick off if I took his name?"

"God, I hadn't thought of that, but you're right. Maybe we can get creative and come up with something different?"

"Oh, I like creative." Scarlett purred as she swooped down again, this time taking the kiss that she had planned on a moment ago. "Tell me more."

Claudia laughed as warm lips moved to her neck. "Well, what about Taydox? Madlor?" She could feel the movement of Scarlett chuckling against her skin and the sensation sent a shiver of delight along her spine.

"How about we toss the patriarchy out of the window and just keep our own names?" Scarlett said lifting up and staring down into green eyes that looked almost black in the dim light. "I love you."

"I love you." Claudia reached up and pulled her back into a searing hot kiss that sent a pulse of pleasure on a direct course to her clit. "Make love with me."

"Always."

Scarlett peeled back the covers and revealed a very naked woman and a plaster cast. "I know I'll be promising to love you in sickness and in health, but I really can't wait for this to be gone."

"Me either, but right now, my only focus is putting my mouth on you." She yanked Scarlett down, her heart rate increasing as her tongue slid easily into the mouth of her lover. Swirling and twisting until she felt the pressure of deft fingers slip between her folds and meet her need with a gentle stroke across the very tip of her clit.

Claudia gasped, her head dropping backwards as the touch grew more intense, more pressure, speeding up and then slowing down again into that delicious tease that had stars floating inside her head exploding one by one. Scarlett was inside of her pressing and pulling, coaxing her body to do the very thing it needed to.

"So, wet." Scarlett's voice gruff against her ear, her breath tickling. "I make you like this."

"Yes." Claudia barely managed between the, "Oh fuck," and the "More, please, more."

Always one to please, Scarlett gave her what she needed. That fullness of three digits keeping the rhythm her hips dictated as they rose and fell in unison.

Her arms pulled tightly around Scarlett's shoulders. Fingernails slicing into her skin. "Yes, yes, oh god, yes...don't...keep, fuck yes. Like that. like that."

Scarlett

Heavy breathing against her ear, sweat dripping fro Scarlett's neck, all of it turning her on and edging her closer to th place only Scarlett seemed capable of taking her. It started in h extremities, in her fingers and toes before it raced around her boc thrusting into her hips and thighs as every muscle and sine ligament and nerve found itself in action. Clenching, releasin chasing the sensations that all focused on those fingers working h up and up and up until she could do nothing more than release it and enjoy the ride.

"I don't like to brag." Scarlett grinned when Claudia final stopped shaking.

"Oh, you can brag about it. But I'm having my turn."

"Yeah? Where do you want me?"

Claudia smirked. "Right up here. Suffocate me."

Scarlett laughed, leaned in, and kissed those lips once mor "I'll grind hard enough to."

"You do that." Claudia licked her lips. "I'm sure there a worse ways to die."

Chapter Fifty-Two

"I was thinking," Claudia said, looking at Scarlett over the top of her reading glasses as she sat up in bed the following morning. "Do you have much on today?"

Scarlett stopped towel drying her hair and thought for a moment. "No, I've clients tomorrow and Wednesday, but nothing I can't change today. Why? What did you want to do?"

Claudia closed the book and placed it in her lap before she removed her glasses and gazed at Scarlett's near-naked frame. "When I look at you all I want to do is stay in bed." She smiled. "But I was thinking that maybe we could take a drive. I'd really love to get out of the house."

Walking towards her, Scarlett let the towel drop. "I guess we could...do both?"

"No." Claudia giggled. "You kept me up half the night."

"I kept you up?" Scarlett gasped. "The cheek of it." She laughed at her lover. "I am pretty sure, no, I know for a fact," she said climbing onto the bed and straddling Claudia. "That it wasn't me begging." She mimicked Claudia, *"Please, Scarlett, please, right there, don't stop, don't' stop."*

Laughing Claudia pulled her close enough to kiss.

"Alright, you win. I never want you to stop." She kissed her quickly. "But right now, I don't want you to start." She continued to laugh.

"Tease." Scarlett smirked before climbing off of her and walking over to the chest of drawers to retrieve her underwear. "So, where do you want to go?"

"How about the beach?"

Glancing out of the window at the blue sky, Scarlett said, "Yes. Let's do that." She opened a different drawer and pulled out her swimwear. "We can take one of the shower wraps for your leg so you can dip your toes in the water, if you like."

Claudia threw the covers back. "And can we take a picnic make a day of it?"

"Of course. I'll run around to the café and get us some sandwiches while you get dressed." Pulling on her clothes.

"Are you not going to wear your bikini?" Claudia asked, a slight tilt of her head as she considered the image in her mind. "Might be easier to put it on now and wear it under your clothes than try and get changed on the beach."

Scarlett eyed her with just a hint of suspicion. "You really do just want to see me naked today, don't you?" She smiled, pulling off the t-shirt she'd just pulled on. "Fine, have it your way."

"Oh, I think we've both established I like it my way." Claudia smirked, sitting back on her hands to watch the lithe body taut nipples and pert breasts, and those legs that wrapped around her in a vice-like grip at times. "And take your time. I'm somewhat enjoying all of this edging."

"Seriously, sometimes I don't know what I unleashed." She covered her breasts with the scanty piece of yellow material before turning and backing up to Claudia for her to tie the strings. She shivered when she felt warm lips press against the bare skin of her back.

"Sometimes I wonder how it was never unleashed before."

Scarlett glanced over her shoulder. "The less said about that the better."

Claudia laughed. "Yes, sorry,"

The mention of Jack brought up a thought that Scarlett gave voice to. "He was quiet last night, wasn't he?"

"Once your dad and him sat down, yes. Very." Claudia continued speaking as Scarlett sat down on the edge of the bed beside her. "It's so strange to see him, so…different these days. When I first met him, he was all cock sure of himself, and I guess that was the attraction. Part of it at least, he was handsome of course, and charming too, but as time went on, I started to see through the façade, at the man he tried so very hard to hide, selfish and blasé, running around like he was the only thing that mattered, other than the kids. He tried to be there for them."

"But not you?"

"No, not me, oh don't get me wrong, he wasn't a bad man, just no longer attentive, not in the way that I needed, wanted."

"It must have been difficult."

Claudia shrugged. "Yes and no. I had three children to keep me busy but at night, when it was just me watching tv or lying in bed alone, that's when I really felt it. But this new Jack, he's someone entirely different. And it looks good on him. He seems much calmer, more balanced and I think he might finally have grown-up."

Scarlett stared down at the floor. "I have to confess, every interaction with him lately leaves me feeling like I want to get to know him."

Reaching out with her hand to rub Scarlett's back, Claudia said, "Then you could do that."

Scarlett breathed deeply, and then stood up quickly. "Maybe, but first, you need to get dressed, and I need to go and scavenge us some food for our picnic and get the car packed up with everything that's in the shed."

"Good plan, you do that." Claudia watched Scarlett yank on a pair of long shorts. "Scarlett, having two dads could be a blessing."

"Or a curse." She laughed as she exited the room.

Scarlett

Chapter Fifty-Three

Music blared from the car's stereo speakers as Scarlett hit the accelerator and The Beast joined the motorway traffic. Picking up speed as she sang along to a pumped-up version of, *I will survive* she indicated and weaved into the middle lane in order to overtake a vehicle before swinging back in again and cruising at the speed limit. Enjoying nothing but the day and what it would bring.

As the song moved into the famous chorus, Scarlett grinned and swayed in her seat. Until the music was cut off and a terrified Claudia screamed, unbuckling her seat belt with fingers that couldn't quite work fast enough for the way her brain was reacting.

The first coherent thing Claudia could say was, "I need to get out." She began reaching for the handle of the door. Erratic breathing, one hand gripping her chest. She was having a panic attack that much Scarlett was certain of.

"Claudia, stop it." Scarlett reacted quickly, now equally terrified that her lover was about to jump from the car travelling at a little over 70mph. "Babe, hold on." She hit the button on her own door that would lock the car, and then reached for Claudia while simultaneously pressing the brake and indicating to pull over onto the hard shoulder.

When the car finally came to a halt, Scarlett unbuckled her seatbelt, twisting in her seat until she faced Claudia.

"Claudia? Look at me, babe. Claudia?" she repeated until finally her words managed to seep through the panic and help her to ground herself. "Claudia, look at me, it's Scarlett." Scarlett pressed the button that would open the window and allow some air in, while keeping the door firmly locked. The last thing she wanted was a panicked Claudia hobbling about on a motorway.

Slowly, Claudia's head turned, her breathing still heavy, chest heaving as she sucked in quick short breaths.

240

"It's okay, you're okay, we're okay." Scarlett kept her voice calm and steady, her eyes firmly fixed onto Claudia's. "You're okay."

"What happened?" Claudia asked, her eyes darting around at their surroundings.

"You're having a panic attack. We're in the car going to the beach."

"The beach?" She looked confused. "I had...I thought." Her breathing had slowed a little but was still far too erratic for Scarlett's liking.

"It's okay. You're okay." Her hands were shaking, and Scarlett reached for one and let Claudia clutch at her fingers. "That's my hand, can you feel that?"

Claudia nodded.

"Can you tell me something else you can feel?"

For a moment Claudia just breathed, jumping slightly when the slipstream of a passing lorry made the car rock.

"The seat, I can feel the seat."

"That's good, and something else?"

Claudia searched her mind and body for something else she could feel. "The cast, on my leg, I can feel that."

"Perfect. Just keep breathing," Scarlett encouraged. "Can you smell anything?"

"What?" Claudia looked at her in confusion. "Smell? I'm alright, I promise, I just—" She looked around them, parked on the side of the road with traffic flying past. "I just had a flashback to that night. I...I felt it, the collision. I hadn't realised until now, but I felt it happen. The driver overtook a car and then we—something hit us, and we spun out of control. It was terrifying." She sobbed.

Scarlett

"I'm going to get us off the motorway so we can park somewhere safer, okay? Do you think you can manage that?"

Claudia closed her eyes and nodded. "Yes," she whispered and Scarlett felt her heart tear at the sight of her fiancé in so much turmoil.

"Okay." Scarlett leaned across her. "Need to put your seatbelt back on, alright?"

Again, Claudia nodded, but this time said nothing as Scarlett leaned across her and pushed the buckle into the slot until it clicked into place. Then did the same with her own. She checked her mirror and waited, too many cars coming to make a gentle return to the road.

"Okay, here we go," she said when eventually a gap opened up and she could edge the car back into the lane. Thankful that a sign appeared almost immediately indicating a service area a few miles ahead. "I'll pull in there and we can get a cup of coffee and you can get out of the car and catch your breath."

Claudia remained silent, staring out at the blur of passing trees, ignoring the traffic that passed by every few seconds. Scarlett considered putting the radio back on but decided against it. Instead she focused on the road and keeping the car a steady 60mph. Breathing a sigh of relief when she saw the markers indicating the slip road to the services were 300 yards, 200 yards, 100 yards. Slowing to 30mph she turned the steering wheel left and took them away from the speeding traffic and the noise of the motorway and into the car park of the roadside services.

They'd been parked a full minute when Scarlett opened the doors and got out, walking quickly around to the passenger side, she opened Claudia's door.

"Okay? What do you need?"

"Just some fresh air and to get out of the car for a moment." Claudia tried to smile. "I'm sorry if I scared you."

Scarlett blew a breath. "For a minute there I was worried. If you'd got that door open——" She shook her head not wanting to say it out loud or imagine it in her head again. She helped Claudia out of the car and passed her the crutches from the back seat.

"I don't understand why that just happened. I've been in the car lots of times since the accident."

"Yeah, but not on the motorway, or at speed."

"Even now my heart is still racing." Claudia sighed a stuttered breath. "I'm sorry I've ruined the day."

"Hey, come on, that's not the case at all." Scarlett looked around before turning back to Claudia. "I tell you what, why don't we go and get a cup of coffee, and then you can decide if you want to carry on, or head back home?"

"You're so supportive, I don't know what I'd do without you." Claudia smiled, this time feeling it.

"Yes well, I've been known to be a superstar now and then." Scarlett grinned back. "But I think we do a good job of supporting each other, don't we?"

"I guess you're right, we do." Claudia took a step forward, and then another, Scarlett bouncing along beside her. "I might even treat you to a chocolate muffin."

"Oh, now you're talking." Scarlett chuckled. "And you thought you'd ruined the day? Not a chance."

Scarlett

Chapter Fifty-Four

"How are you feeling?" Scarlett asked while plumping cushions and generally fussing over Claudia.

Leg up on the sofa, Claudia smiled up at her. "I'm fine honestly. Obviously, the accident hit harder than I thought, and I'm going to take up work's offer of some therapy as well as the physio."

"That's a good plan." Scarlett finally sat down, lifting Claudia's plastered leg up onto her lap. "It won't be long until this is off too, and you can start thinking about what you want to do next."

"Next?" Claudia quizzed.

Scarlett turned towards her. "Yeah, like when you go back to work at the office, if you go back."

"Why wouldn't I go back?"

"No reason, I'm just saying that if it was difficult—"

"I'm going back to work, Scarlett. That's a given, when is the question I need to work out. They've been very accommodating allowing me to do a few hours from home, and aren't pushing at all—"

"Well, they can't, can they, it happened on their watch. You'd have been home hours earlier if you hadn't had to stay on and finish that meeting."

Claudia noted the tone of Scarlett's voice, a little angry and hurt. She sat forward and took Scarlett's hand, interlocking their fingers.

"It was an accident, Sweetheart."

Scarlett was silent.

"I'm sorry, I've been so wrapped up in how this affected me that I didn't think about the impact it had on you, or anyone else."

Scarlett turned slowly, her eyes wet. "I almost lost you, and for what? A meeting? Someone else died because that meeting couldn't wait. What was so important that it had to be finished that night? It makes me so mad that that happened."

"I guess I hadn't thought of it that way before. I was just doing my job so I could get home to you."

"We had a date. That night, the job was more important than me, and it almost cost us. So, I know you want to go back, and I support that. You're an independent woman and I love that about you, but I am aware that I'm concerned about it. Because it's not the first time. It impacted our anniversary, Zara's birthday and two of Adam's family get-togethers."

Now it was Claudia who remained silent.

"All I'm asking is that you don't rush back. And if you do go back, maybe you could consider that."

"Alright, I think that's fair. I'll speak with Gregory about the specifics of my job and see if we can find a more structured way to deal with these things, but this is the corporate world, darling, it's what's expected in this kind of role. It's what I signed up for, we discussed it."

Scarlett nodded. "Yes, we did, and I honestly didn't think it would be a problem. I can deal with missing a few dates here and there, but I can't deal with losing you, or having you hurt because you're having to travel late at night due to a meeting that has run on longer than expected. It's a hotel consortium, it's not like they can't put everyone up for the night and continue the following day with fresh eyes."

"Why have you never said any of this before?"

"Because you didn't almost die before. I didn't want to be that kind of girlfriend who complained about your job. I didn't want you to feel like I needed you here with me all the time. That's not it. I'm not co-dependant. But I value our time."

Scarlett

"And you think I don't?" Claudia snarked.

"That's not what I'm—"

"It sounds like that is what you're saying," Claudia snapped, looking away.

Scarlett shifted her position, reaching out and taking Claudia's chin in her hand. "Look at me." She waited until Claudia did just that. "Have I ever done or said anything that would suggest don't think this is a relationship that both of us are equally involved in?" Claudia sighed. "I love you. I love everything about you, and us, and I want us to have the best opportunity to spend as much time as we can loving each other and enjoying life together, for as long as we can."

"And I want to make sure I can provide that, that financially we are able to enjoy that time, doing what we want. Your business is still new, it's growing, and in the meantime, I can—"

"We don't need money to be happy."

"We don't? So, should I sell the house? The car, no holidays or spa weekends?" Her voice rose with her frustration. "I want to live a lifestyle that requires paying for, Scarlett. I like spa days and nice restaurants and 5-star hotels."

"I'm not saying—" Scarlett blew out her cheeks. "Can we please not argue. That wasn't my intention with this conversation I'm feeling resentment, I acknowledge that. I clearly needed to vent and I'm sorry that it's turned into you having to defend your career choices."

Claudia lifted her leg down and shuffled across, pushing herself against the warmth of Scarlett. "I'm sorry too, I took your pain personally, and I know that wasn't what you were trying to express. It's been a long and exhausting day emotionally, and I think I just…all I want to do is get married, and spend the rest of my life with you, making memories."

"We're going to do that," Scarlett agreed, pressing her lips against their counterparts. "I promise."

Scarlett

Chapter Fifty-Five

Scarlett bounded up the stairs and into the bedroom, whe
she found Claudia fully dressed, laying on top of the covers, readi
her book. Exactly where she had left her two hours ago before she
popped into town.

"It's done." Scarlett grinned and flung herself into the spa
beside Claudia.

Snapping the book shut, Claudia took off her glasses a
turned, smiling. "Really? The date was available?"

Nodding, Scarlett couldn't take the grin off of her face. "Ye
There was actually a cancellation. Looks like the universe is on o
side. We've got two and a half months, and then we will be arrivi
at the registry office at 10 a.m. to officially get married. Then t
following day we will have the ceremony in the garden as planned.'

"Remind me why we're not doing it all on the same day
Claudia grinned and rolled towards her.

"Because I am greedy and want two wedding nights."

"Oh, yes, that was it."

They kissed, slowly. Hands edging beneath clothing until t
need to breathe took over.

"Do you think it's a jinx though?" Claudia asked once she
gotten her breath back.

"A jinx?"

"Yes, taking the spot someone else cancelled."

Shaking her head, Scarlett said, "No, I think that's t
universe telling them they weren't ready, and we are."

"I guess so." Claudia smiled. "I am excited about it."

Scarlett stared dreamily at her. "So, we have a lot to do next week. You get this cast off, and we could find us some outfits and organise the food."

"I was thinking of speaking with Liz about that. She started up a small sandwich business when we left Quango, I bet it wouldn't take much for her to expand herself for one day."

"Good plan, especially at such short notice, worst case, we drag your children in and do it all ourselves."

Claudia laughed. "Do you really think that's wise?"

Scarlett manoeuvred up onto her knees and grinned down at Claudia. "Maybe not but needs must."

"I'll call Liz," Claudia confirmed.

Claudia had moved downstairs. She still had the book when Diana arrived as planned for mothersitting duties. Much to Claudia's irritation. Scarlett had insisted, despite Claudia's protestation that she was quite capable of sitting on the sofa for a few hours by herself.

"Is she still grumpy?" Diana asked Scarlett when they met at the door.

Scarlett picked up her satchel and slung it over her shoulder. "A little, but she will be fine once she sees this one." She reached out and tickled Jacob's red cheek. "Still teething?"

"It's on and off. No sooner one comes through, and he's settled, another one starts. He seems fine at the moment though."

"Great, well I've got to go, I have three clients this afternoon and then dinner with Jack, so…" She shrugged a shoulder.

"Dad said he's looking forward to it." She grabbed Jacob's hand. "Wave bye bye to Aunty Scarlett."

"bu bu," he said giggling.

Diana closed the door. "Right, shall we go and surprise Nanna?"

Jacob's legs kicked excitedly. "Na na."

They crept down the hall towards the lounge, pushing the door open just enough that Diana could poke her head around.

"Hi Mum, you okay?"

Looking up, Claudia smiled, before putting her attention back into the book. "Yes, thank you."

"Still cranky," Diana whispered to Jacob. Opening the door, she stepped inside and waited.

For a long moment, nothing happened, until finally Claudia said, without looking up, "Are you going to hover in the doorway all afternoon?"

"Maybe," Diana answered back, smiling as she waited a little longer for her mother to realise, she wasn't alone. Jacob, however, had other plans and squealed.

Claudia's gaze flicked up instantly, the book tossed to one side and her arms stretched out. "You didn't say you had Jacob."

"Well, in all honesty, I thought my presence would be enough, but obviously not."

Diana handed Jacob off, and Claudia pulled him close, smattering his cheeks in kisses and cooing at him as though she hadn't seen him for months.

"Right, well I'll leave you to it and make myself useful, shall I?" Diana said without much of a response.

"Okay."

"Now I know how Zara feels." Diana chuckled and left Claudia singing to Jacob. She found her bag and pulled out her apron, wrapping it around her waist as she surveyed the tidy kitchen, she had a storm to cook up if Scarlett had ordered the things she'd asked for.

"Diana?" Claudia called out just as Diana opened the fridge.

"Yes?" she replied brightly, heading back to the lounge, and poking her head back around the door again.

"Come and sit down with us."

Doing as she was asked, Diana took a seat in the armchair. "Don't you want a cup of tea?"

Claudia shook her head. "No, I'm all tea'd out. Scarlett has been very attentive to my needs." She made a face at Jacob, and he giggled again.

"Not sure that's information I need." Diana smiled and sat back, getting comfortable in the chair now that she didn't need to get up immediately to make tea.

"What happened to your generation? Always finding sex in every conversation. I just meant that I am being looked after."

"I should think so, too," Diana responded. After a moment she asked, "Mum?"

"Hm hm." Claudia lifted Jacob into the air.

"Can I ask something that might be...well, it's unusual, for me and I'm worried about what it might mean."

Jacob landed back in Claudia's lap instantly as her eyes were drawn to her eldest daughter. "Of course, you can ask me anything, and you can tell me anything too, you know that."

"I know, I just, well, I'm not even sure what I'm asking."

"You have me intrigued, go on."

Scarlett

"It's just that, Shannon called and asked me to go to dinner with her again and I'm not sure how I feel about it."

"Shannon? The woman you met at Art?" Claudia confirmed because nothing more had been said about that since that night.

Diana swallowed and her cheeks went red. "Yes, that's the one."

"Did you say yes?"

Diana nodded slowly. "I did, yes, but I'm not sure." She sighed. "I don't know why I said yes. We have sent a few texts back and forth since we had coffee, and I get the impression that she's...*interested* in me...that way."

Claudia bit her lip to stop herself from interrupting.

"And the thing is. Sometimes when we're talking, I feel like...I'm interested too."

"Would that be a bad thing?" Claudia asked, "To explore side of you that maybe you hadn't considered before?"

"But that's the thing, I have considered it. At university. was hanging out with Letty and other gay people, and I thought they all seemed to be having fun, maybe I could be part of it, but then met Jason, and I knew that that was where my interests lay, and I've been quite content with that...until now."

"So, what's the problem?"

"I guess I'm worrying that it's a reaction to Jason and the rubbish dates I've been on recently. I feel like I'm going to end up on the shelf."

Claudia laughed. "Oh, Sweetheart, that won't happen, you're a catch and maybe, you haven't cast your net wide enough." She thought for a moment, "It's just a date, just dinner with someone who you like spending time with. Overthinking it will only take you down a path that gets you lost. Enjoy it for what it is, and if you feel like you want to do it again, then do that, and if not," she shrugged, "at least you won't have any what ifs."

"Is that how you did it with Scarlett?"

"Not quite." Claudia looked a little sheepish. "In all honesty, Scarlett was a surprise that came from a lot of alcohol and a very real lack of any intimacy for years. I didn't have an opportunity to really consider it until after the fact and by then I was…" She blushed. "Let's just say that my mind was blown."

"It was that good?" Diana asked quietly, as though Scarlett might walk in at any moment.

Claudia looked Diana in the eye and nodded. "Better, I'd never experienced anything like it in my life, not that I—"

"I get it." Diana cut her off before this got anymore embarrassing for them both.

"Just go into it with an open heart, and mind, Diana. You'll know if it's for you or not."

Scarlett

Jack had booked a table at Joie which was predictab Scarlett almost refused the opportunity to have dinner with him, b he'd been quite persistent and if anything, she could use it to put h boundaries in place with regard to how much of her time he cou expect.

He noticed her first, standing up from his seat to wave acro the heads of other diners. Scarlett smiled and was headed in I direction when she noticed someone else standing up to greet her, h dad.

The two men in her life stood awkwardly at the round tab almost side by side, smiling nervously at her as she joined them. Ja dressed in shirt and tie, the matching suit jacket hanging in t cloakroom no doubt. Her dad looked equally as smart in a bla cotton slacks and a thin long-sleeved jumper. Jack balding, her dac full head of hair brushed and neat. They'd made an effort that w for sure.

"What's this then?" she asked, moving in to kiss her dac cheek and then reaching out a hand to Jack, she wasn't quite the yet for informal greetings with him.

"I invited Terry to join us, I hoped that we could find sor common ground and that things between us might become a lit less—"

"Awkward," Terry finished. Which was absolutely the wo for it.

"Right." Scarlett sat down and the two men followed h lead. "So, you've been talking to each other then?"

"We've had a conversation," Terry started. "We agreed th we have a couple of months to get to know each other and put o issues aside in time for the wedding."

"And we decided that we need to accept the role each of might be allowed to play in your life moving forward."

"Alright. Well, that's preferable to a punch up, I suppose."

The waitress arrived and took Scarlett's drink order, as both of her fathers already had one.

"How was your day?" Terry asked. "Your mum said to give you a hug from her."

"Give her a hug back then." Scarlett smiled. "My day's been nice. We've officially set the date. They had an opening so, that's all good. We'll do the official bit on the Friday as planned and then everyone can come over on the Saturday for the ceremony."

"And do you have someone in mind to officiate?" Jack asked while casually perusing the menu.

"We have someone in mind but not asked them yet."

"One of us could do it," Terry spurted quickly. "I mean, if you—I know we haven't always seen eye to eye—"

Scarlett placed her menu down and sat back in her chair. "You mean all the years you wished I was a boy and not a lesbian?"

Terry followed suit; his menu landed with a slap. "I didn't wish for that, you decided that was the case. I never said that."

"You said, and I quote, you could at least have been a boy if you're going to shag women."

His face went red. "That isn't the same as wishing you were—"

Jack held his hands up. "Alright, can we all agree that whatever was said in the past is water under the bridge now, we either forgive and forget or we give up."

Scarlett sat up and breathed deeply. "You're right, I'm sorry."

Terry swigged his drink. "I'm sorry that I ever said that to you. I've never wanted you any differently to who you are, I just...I felt so out of my depth with everything and I'm not a man who finds opening up easy."

She reached out and placed her hand on top of his. "I think you're doing a great job of it now."

"Thanks," he mumbled with a shy smile as he looked back to the menu and picked it up.

When their order was complete and the waiter had removed the unnecessary glasses and cutlery, Jack spoke again. "Usually the Father of the Bride would be paying for the wedding, but we both know that neither yourself or Claudia would want that, but Terry and I wondered if there was something we could do. Something you both would feel comfortable with of course."

"Yeah, like your honeymoon, have you planned anywhere yet? We thought we could chip in, or—"

Scarlett held her hands up. "Woah, thanks, it's very thoughtful but honestly, we don't need anything. Claudia's job gives her access to a whole heap of hotels around the world, and we've already picked out the one we want to go to." She watched them both sink a little in their seats, shoulders sagging. "I think it's really great that you both are so interested in me and my life, I really do, but the days of needing you to financially provide for me are long gone." She looked from one to the other. "What I need is…what I want is to work on relationships with both of you. But I don't know what that looks like right now, it's going to take time, but I'm willing to work on it."

"I think that's more than I can ask for," Jack acknowledged.

Terry nodded. "I know that I've let you down in the past. I know that you deserved better, I'm trying to change that now."

The waiter reappeared carrying plates that were deftly placed onto the table in front of them. Scarlett wondered if they had an in built ability to know just when to interrupt a conversation, or whether it was pure luck each time, but she felt grateful for the opportunity to gather herself.

She watched them both more closely, tucking into steaks and chips smothered in sauces. How alike they actually were was quite comical, clearly her mother had a type. But it was definitely Jack that Scarlett noticed she favoured, subtlety, though enough to notice and she wondered how hard that must be for her dad to sit here with the both of them reminding him. She'd been considering dying her hair black again, maybe this was a good reason. Mousy brown like Jack's was pretty boring after all, and her dad's darker brown, flecked with grey around the temples, made her consider how much longer she could get away with dying her hair that dark.

"Maisie is looking forward to seeing everyone." Jack was saying when Scarlett's mind cleared, and she realised she was being spoken to.

"Uh, well, we're all looking forward to that too." She wasn't quite sure how her siblings felt about Maisie, but everyone was at least polite. "She must be starting to show now."

"Oh, yes, indeed. Almost five months now, won't be long until you've another brother or sister to fuss over," he said proudly, and she wondered how he would have sounded hearing about her impending birth. One look at Terry staring at her told her how proud he'd been. After a moment, he reached into his back pocket and pulled out a white envelope. He passed it across the table to Jack as though something secret was held inside.

"We thought you might like to have these." He smiled quickly at Scarlett and winked before turning his attention back to Jack as he opened the envelope.

Pulling out a stack of photos, Jack sucked in a breath, his eyes instantly filling with tears. "These are—"

"Of Scarlett, yes, when she was a baby and growing up. I had copies made."

Scarlett

Staring incredulously between the two of them Scarlett chuckled. "Seriously, I'm going to need to check that you've not been taken over by some form of alien life."

Terry grinned and slapped Jack on the back. "Between us, we did something right." And Scarlett wondered what kind of parallel universe she'd slipped into.

Chapter Fifty-Seven

"Everything alright?" Claudia called out once Scarlett had entered the house and shut the door behind her. The muffled sounds of coat and shoes being removed filtered into the room and she smiled to herself as she watched the lounge door for her lover to appear.

"I just had dinner with Jack," Claudia nodded, she knew that information already, "and my dad."

Confused, Claudia said, "You went to dinner twice?" She checked the clock, there had been barely enough time to enjoy one meal, let alone two. "How?"

"Just the one dinner." Scarlett lifted her leg and slid in underneath it. "Jack invited my dad, apparently, they've been talking and working things out."

"That's—"

"Weird?"

Claudia chuckled. "Well, yes, but I was going to say wonderful. It makes things a whole lot easier for you, doesn't it?"

"Of course." Scarlett's head hit the back of the couch and turned slowly until she faced Claudia. "It just wasn't something I expected I suppose and now, I'm not sure how I feel about it."

"Do you not want them to be friends?"

"Seriously, what do they have in common? Jack's a successful businessman who moves in circles that would have my dad feeling intimidated. My dad's idea of a good time is an afternoon in the bookies and a night down the pub playing darts."

"You. They have you in common." Claudia held her gaze. "And maybe that will be enough."

Scarlett didn't look convinced, but she smiled anyway. "Did you have dinner?"

"Yes, Diana cooked. She only left an hour ago. And there a leftovers that need to go into the fridge once they're cooled down."

Checking her watch, Scarlett frowned, it wasn't that late, b she felt like the day was done. "Did you want to watch some TV go up?"

"You're asking if I want to watch television or go upstai get naked and climb into bed with you for a snuggle?"

"That is indeed what I am asking." Scarlett grinned, feelr suddenly more alert.

"Hm, I suppose we could do that, and then I can fill you in."

"There's gossip to be had?" Scarlett asked with mischievous look on her face. She lifted Claudia's leg and clamber out from under it to stand before her and reached out a hand.

"Gossip and information, yes."

"Oh, the excitement is off the chart." Scarlett laughe "Right, you head up, I'll deal with the leftovers." She made sure tl Claudia was steady on her crutches and scurried off.

"I'll be happy when this is off on Monday." Claudia call after her. Had it really been six weeks since the accident? She cou scarcely believe it. Time moved so fast these days.

She'd only gotten up two stairs when the kitchen lig switched off and Scarlett appeared behind her carrying two glasses water.

"No rush," she whispered as she followed, step by ste behind Claudia as they made their way to the top.

"Remind me when I'm old to have one of those lifts put in Claudia giggled.

Playfully, Scarlett slapped her behind. "When you're old, l carry you up."

260

"I'll hold you to that." Claudia hauled herself up the next stair.

"You better."

They'd made it almost to the top when Claudia said, "Diana is questioning her sexuality."

Scarlett stopped in her tracks. "Shut the front door."

Claudia laughed. "You sounded just like Zara then." She heaved up the next, and then the next and finally, she was at the top and turning around to find Scarlett open mouthed.

"We might have to stop them coming around so often if I'm picking up her linguistic talents," Scarlett joked. "And Diana is picking up…" She winked. "I have to admit though, that's not what I was expecting."

"I know." Claudia grinned all excitedly. "It's strange isn't it how you watch your children grow and even though you try not to, you often end up imagining how you think they'll turn out." She grabbed hold of Scarlett's lapels when she finally took the last step up to meet her. "I always assumed Diana would be the first to get married and have a baby, and I'd have laid money on Zara being the experimental bisexual who'd marry someone from another culture. I'd never have picked Adam for that; he's always been so set in his ways and somewhat traditional, and yet, he found the most wonderful partner in Sunila."

"I guess it just goes to show, that if you bring them up right, they'll be full of amazing surprises. But James is mixed race, so you got that half right." Scarlett giggled.

"Yes, I did," Claudia said, pleased with herself. "I am so very proud of them all, they turned out to be decent, kind, loving human beings, and that was all I wanted."

Scarlett

"Success looks good on you. Now, fill me in and do not leave out any details." Scarlett turned her and guided them both gently to the bedroom.

Chapter Fifty-Eight

The kitchen was a mess. Not the kind that it usually had on the days when Zara and Jacob stayed over, but the kind planning a wedding in a short space of time created. None of that mattered though, not now that Claudia was free of the plaster cast and about to dive in and start tasting.

Claudia's friend Liz stood in the centre of it all. Nearly every countertop laden with a serving tray of nibbles, sandwiches, and quiche. Bite sized fondant fancies and cheesecake covered the breakfast bar and Scarlett had her fingers ready to dive into it all.

"So, I was thinking we don't have time for anything too fancy, and I know you wouldn't want that. No matter how posh everyone says you are, I know different." The Yorkshire woman winked. "But that doesn't mean we can't make it fancier."

"Right, and what are you proposing?" Claudia asked, taking another bite of the sausage roll that didn't quite live up to the usual flavour.

"Well, for a start, as you can probably tell by now, that isn't a sausage roll, it's actually a goat's cheese and tomato stuffed pastry in the guise of a sausage roll."

Claudia nodded. "I like it, it's different and kind of messes with your mind and taste buds. You're expecting one thing and get something completely different."

"Exactly, nothing is as it seems. That's not cheesecake." Liz said quickly as Scarlett was about to bite into it. The spoon hovering an inch from her mouth, she sniffed it and frowned, trying to work out what it was. "Salmon mousse," Liz announced proudly. "On a Blini."

"Diana is going to be flummoxed," Scarlett said once she'd finished chewing, she moved around the room and pulled out a stool, staring at Claudia until she took the hint and sat down. "You still need to rest," she whispered.

Scarlett

"Hm, I think most people will be confused by it. I love it all, I really do. The flavours are exquisite, are you happy?" Claudia said to Scarlett as she casually picked up what looked like a fondant fancy and stared at it quizzically.

"Cheese and pineapple," Liz stated as Scarlett bit into it.

"This is bloody genius." Scarlett laughed. "Yes, I'm really happy with it."

"That's settled then, Liz, you've got the job."

Liz beamed. "Really, I mean, this is the first wedding I've done, so...I can't believe it, you really like it all?"

Scarlett wiped her fingers. "Absolutely, it's like what we were saying the other day about how people assume and expect and then it never turns out the way you thought it would."

"Gosh, well, I'm pleased, and grateful that you thought of me."

"Of course, first name that came to mind, and you'll stay and enjoy the day with us, right?"

"Yes, that would be...wow, I can hardly believe it. All those months ago, who would have thought a night out on the razz would have ended with one of us getting married and one of us cavorting their way around said gay bar. I'm just glad I've got me sandwich round to keep me busy." Liz laughed. "Seriously though, congratulations. I'm made up for ya, I really am."

"Thanks, Liz." Scarlett smiled before shoving another fake fondant fancy into her mouth.

Scarlett stared in through the window and sighed. This was the bit she wasn't really looking forward to. Shopping for an outfit. It had been a busy morning what with taking Claudia for her check-up and plaster removal, and then rushing back so she could shower and shave her leg before Liz arrived. The sound of which had Scarlett wondering if Claudia was alone in there. Six weeks without a proper shower, yeah, she could relax and let Claudia enjoy it.

The food tasting though had been exceptionally fun, and she chuckled to herself imagining Bea, and Jack, and her dad all trying to get their heads around it. But now it was her turn to get her head around the fact that she had no idea what she wanted to wear.

Claudia and Diana had gone off to buy her outfit, leaving Scarlett with Zara for help, which was probably not a bad choice, her youngest sister had that knack for putting an outfit together, even if nobody else would be seen dead in it.

"Dress or suit," Zara had asked twice before Scarlett heard her.

"Oh, I dunno, I was thinking..." What was she thinking? Nothing, her mind was blank. The truth was, she had never envisioned herself getting married. She'd never had that dream outfit already picked out in her mind. This was all just new.

"I gotta be honest, I've seen you in a dress and it's out of this world," Zara said, earning red cheeks from Scarlett. "But, I've also seen you in a suit and I've seen the way Mum looked at you in that suit and quite frankly it was obscene."

Scarlett stared down at her like a deer caught in headlights and hit.

"I mean, we've got a couple of months to—"

"Really," Zara reaffirmed. "That time is going to whizz by, so, I say we go in here and check out some of these sexy options and see what we think." She didn't give Scarlett any time to argue as she yanked her arm and pulled her along. "Now, Sis."

Scarlett

On the other side of the mall, Claudia was already in t[ ] dressing room, stripped down to her underwear and slipping into o[ ] of the two dresses she'd already picked out, and Diana had found third.

"Mum, I found this. It's a bit different, I'm not sure it's y[ ] but worth trying on." Diana passed it through past the curtain a[ ] held it until Claudia grabbed it and added to the collection. "Or y[ ] could always wear a suit."

"I did consider it, but I don't know. I just never envisag[ ] myself walking down the aisle in a suit," Claudia called out as s[ ] shimmied into the second dress, already discarding the first as t[ ] frumpy.

"Technically, you're not walking down the aisle, you'[ ] heading to the registry office and then standing in the garden, I thi[ ] you can probably wear whatever you want."

"Yes, I suppose you're right. Let's see how we get on fir[ ] oh, and I need something sexy for bedtime. Two bedtimes."

"Christ on a bike, how did I end up with this job." Dia[ ] blushed.

"You said you were Matron of Honour." Claudia giggl[ ] imagining what kind of sexy Diana would find for her.

Chapter Fifty-Nine

Scarlett came out of the bathroom towel drying her newly dyed black hair. She'd dressed in her pyjama's once the dye was rinsed out, and now she was perplexed as she caught sight of Claudia sitting on the bottom of the bed, wrapped in a towel, pouting.

"What?" Scarlett asked, looking around to see what was so upsetting.

Claudia shrugged, stood up and glared at her again before passing her and heading into the bathroom herself. Mystified, Scarlett lifted the covers and climbed into bed, assuming whatever was bothering Claudia would be worked out in the shower, or she'd communicate it once she was done.

But it still rankled with her. It wasn't like Claudia to sulk.

Scarlett threw the covers off and got out of bed, moving back to the bathroom.

"Are you going to tell me what's up, or do I have to guess?" Scarlett asked, leaning casually against the door frame as she watched Claudia's naked form.

It was steamy from the hot water, but she could still make out the shape of her lover behind the glass, her back to her, perfectly shaped buttocks on display.

"You made me a promise," Claudia said over her shoulder before continuing to soap her body.

"A promise?" Scarlett racked her brains to think what she could have promised and forgotten about, but nothing sprang to mind. "Wanna give me a clue?"

Claudia turned, still under the water until she was facing Scarlett.

"No. I don't think I do." She smirked and ran her soapy hands over her breasts, holding Scarlett's attention. "I'm sure you'll work i out."

"Alright." Scarlett turned away and wandered back into the bedroom, her mind whizzing through conversations and topics that might have involved her promising something. It had been a bus day; anything could have been said and slipped from her consciousness. She sat down on the bed and worked backwards.

They'd gone clothes shopping and she knew for a fact that wasn't it, because they barely saw one another until it was time to leave. Liz had come over with the food and there were definitely no promises then. Before that, they'd only been up to the hospital to get Claudia's cast removed.

Oh, wait. Scarlett thought about that. What had Claudia said once it was off and the young man had left the room to get some more cleaning wipes?

"Rodeo time." Scarlett hadn't had a chance to ask her what she meant before the man returned, but now it sparked another memory. *"But once it's off, I'm going to let you ride me for a month."*

Scarlett grinned. "Oh, that promise," she muttered to herself.

She jumped up and quickly grabbed the toy box from its hiding place and pulled out the harness, slipping her pyjama bottoms off, she looked up at the sound of the shower cutting off. Speedily she yanked it up, attached the dildo and tightened it around her waist

Fast as lightning, she ran around the bed and jumped under the covers, just in time for Claudia to walk back into the room covered in the smallest towel they owned.

The pout remained as she viewed Scarlett sitting upright in bed, still in pyjamas and now reaching for her book.

Waiting at the bottom of the bed, Claudia glared at Scarlett until eventually, her bedmate looked up. When she had her attention she let the towel drop to the floor to reveal a very bare area between her legs. One hand on hip, she raised a brow at Scarlett.

"Nice," Scarlett said in response. "What brought that about?"

"I just felt like a change, I've been so...limited until now." Her fingertips moved down her torso slowly, followed by Scarlett's eyes until they lightly brushed the bare skin. "I'm wet."

Scarlett nodded. "Showers will do that." She had no idea how she managed to keep such a straight face, but she did.

Not one to give up so easily, Claudia opened herself and teased her clit with the tip of her finger. Never once taking her eyes off of Scarlett. "Shame to let it go to waste."

"I'm sure you can think of something to do to avoid that."

Her finger moved freely, tight circles that had her hips jerk and buck. "Do you want to watch, is that it?"

"Not from that distance. Come here." The smirk on Scarlett's face almost gave her away.

"I don't think I should give you what you want, when you can't keep—"

Scarlett tossed the cover back and revealed the dildo. Claudia's favourite one that they'd picked out together a few months ago on a trip into London.

"Oh." Was all Claudia managed before Scarlett was on her knees, crawling towards the end of the bed until she was close enough to reach out and pull Claudia up onto the mattress.

"I said come here."

"I like it when you demand." Claudia giggled, face to face. Her hand now reached for the dildo. Wrapping tightly around it. "You know how much I want this?"

Scarlett

"Hm," Scarlett answered, nudging her lips with her own "And you can have it…when you've come for me."

She moved away, back to the pillows where she sat back an relaxed.

"Show me," she said, her eyes descending back dow between Claudia's legs. "I want to hear you come. I want to watc' and when you do, I'll reward you." She stroked the dildo an enjoyed the way that Claudia's eyes dilated.

"You're going to do that anyway." Claudia smirked, but di as Scarlett demanded, getting comfortable as her fingers stroke herself. Teasing herself. "A promise…is a promise." She sighed a her head fell back, her hips thrusting forwards.

Scarlett smiled; it was true after all.

"A promise is indeed…" Scarlett held out a hand and waitec When Claudia finally noticed and took it, she was propelle forwards. "A promise. Climb aboard."

Epilogue The First Bit

Claudia woke with a start. The dream she'd been having had left an imprint as she moved from sleeping to conscious. A feeling of dread and despair filled her senses. Which really wasn't how she'd planned to wake up this morning. On the day she would be legally marrying her person. The sleeping peacefully, happy, gorgeous being in the bed beside her.

"Scarlett, wake up." She gently tried to coax her awake. "Scarlett, I need to—" She sat up and glanced around the room feeling suddenly suffocated by it all. "Scarlett, I can't...I don't think I can—" She pulled the covers back and escaped the hand that reached out for her.

"Mm babe, come back to bed," Scarlett mumbled as she rolled towards where Claudia had been.

Pacing the room, Claudia felt her heart begin to race. Feeling off balance, she slipped to the floor. "Scarlett." She all but pleaded and this time the dark head in the bed raised up and looked around.

"Claudia, what's wrong?" Scarlett was up and moving in an instant. Sinking down to the floor beside Claudia, she moved in as close as she could get without overwhelming her.

"I don't—" Claudia grabbed her chest, her breathing becoming more difficult. "I can't—breathe."

Scarlett reached for her. "It's okay, I'm here. Can you feel my hand?" She began going through the motions of bringing Claudia out of the panic attack, a not-too-often issue that had hit a few times since the accident, an issue Scarlett had hoped they had a handle on, but maybe not.

When Claudia was calm again, and able to breathe without the panic or impending doom looming over her, she relaxed and began to sob.

Scarlett

Stroking her hair and pulling her closer to her chest, Scarl[
asked gently, "Hey, what's brought all this on?"

Claudia continued to breathe deeply. "I don't know, I had
dream and it—I felt like everything was going to go wrong."

"What was the dream about?"

"I'm not sure," she replied vaguely. "I was running, we we
in a castle or I don't know a big building, old, with bars on [
window and all I knew was that I had to escape. I had to get out a[
away."

"Are you having doubts about today?"

"No," Claudia said quickly. "I don't think so. I want to [
with you for the rest of my life."

"Yeah, but that isn't the same thing as being married to [
for the rest of your life," Scarlett said reaching out to cup her chee[
"And if you don't want to get married, that's okay."

"No, I do. I want to marry you." Claudia covered the hand [
her face. "I just…I don't think until right now that I'd really allow[
myself to think about it. It's all been such a whirlwind of organisi[
everything that—" She looked into Scarlett's eyes and saw nothi[
but love there staring back at her. "I want to be your wife. I do[
want to be *just the wife*."

"Oh Sweetheart, you could never be just anything. There w[
never be a time when you are just the wife, you'll always be r[
wife, and my wife is a smart, professional, independe[
sophisticated, witty, beautiful—"

"Okay, okay." Claudia laughed and leaned in to kiss her. [
get it."

"Do you? I mean, I need to be sure you understand. You'[
fabulous, and creative, and fun, and—"

"Shut up."

Her words were cut off by the lips that sealed eagerly against her own.

"May I have the rings please?" The celebrant smiled at them both as Adam and Diana stepped forward to place the rings onto a small velvet blue cushion that Zara carried and held out for her mother and Scarlett to take when it was their turn.

Scarlett took the ring that would be Claudia's. Turning to her, she took it all in again. How radiant and beautiful she looked. "You're gorgeous," she whispered.

Zara's gentle cough broke her from her reverie.

"I give you this ring, that you may wear it, as a symbol of our partnership and as a token of my love and the promises we have made this day." She read aloud from the card, trying to be serious but incapable of not smiling in the moment.

She slid the ring onto the finger of the hand she held. Smiling so widely she knew her cheeks would ache later, but it would be worth it. She listened intently as Claudia repeated the same words back to her, and just as happily pushed the ring Scarlett would wear onto her finger.

She barely heard the words the celebrant said affirming the marriage, only just managing to catch when her name was said. So wrapped up in the reality of being married to this goddess who had picked her out of all of the people in the world.

"Scarlett and Claudia, you have made a statement to those around you of the relationship you wish to cherish and share together. A good partnership is formed by love and friendship, compromise and taking care of one another. Today marks the beginning for you both as legal partners in marriage and I am delighted to announce that from this day forward, you are now joined together as partners in marriage." She smiled at them both. "You may kiss your bride."

At the same time, they both leaned in, aware of the smiles and tears of Zara, Adam, and Diana. "I love you," whispered Scarlett seconds before their lips met.

"I love you," whispered Claudia the moment their lips parted.

Claudia kicked off her trainers and hung up her jacket following Scarlett into the house that was now their marital home.

She laughed as she caught sight of herself in the mirror. After her panic attack that morning, Scarlett had insisted they took all of the pressure off. Instead of the summer dresses they'd both picked for today's official engagement, they'd gone in jeans and a t-shirt topping it all off with a pair of trainers.

"Do you think everyone was surprised when we turned up looking like this?" she asked watching Scarlett open a bottle of champagne from the kitchen doorway.

"I think Diana might have had a shit fit. Did you see her face?" Scarlett laughed. "But Zara soon sorted that out." She popped the cork and just about managed to stop it from spilling onto the floor. Pouring two glasses, she placed the bottle on the counter and picked up the flutes, handing one to Claudia. "You look beautiful whatever you're wearing, or not wearing." She winked and clinked their glasses together. "And tonight, and the rest of this afternoon, we get to spend in whatever state of dress we want."

"Hm, I like your thinking. And we should probably make the most of it because tomorrow we will most likely be too tired."

"Too tired?" Scarlett faked shock. Sipping her drink once more before she took the glass from Claudia and put them both to the side. "You know, I recall way back when we were still hiding this that I did some unspeakable things with you, right here." She gripped Claudia's buttocks and lifted her onto the counter.

"I seem to remember we were celebrating then too." Claudia tilted her neck just as Scarlett's lips met the crease of her shoulder. "Mm, I love when you kiss my neck."

"You know, I worked that out a long time ago," Scarlett mumbled between kisses.

"Mm, as much as I love the memory of being fucked senseless on the counter, I have plans."

Scarlett stopped her movements and stood upright. Narrowed eyes accompanied a knowing smirk. "Plans, huh?"

Claudia licked her lips slowly as she nodded. "Yes, so I'm going to go up and you can follow in fifteen minutes." She jumped down and placed a peck against Scarlett's cheek. "And bring snacks."

"Bring snacks?" Scarlett laughed as she watched Claudia saunter away, hips swaying. If Scarlett was honest, that backside might actually be her favourite thing. She growled as she considered what was coming.

Scarlett kicked the door open with her foot and almost dropped the tray she was holding when Claudia came into view. Lit up by the sunlight coming through the windows.

"Holy hell." Scarlett gasped, moving towards the bedside table to place the tray down without taking her eyes off of her wife. With the snacks off her hands, she turned back to stare at Claudia.

She was naked, that much was clear, beneath the black lace of intricate roses in the design. Off the shoulders, and down to mid-thigh, arms covered, it was sexy as hell.

Scarlett

"Do you like it?" Claudia asked almost shyly. "I wasn't sure but Diana said—"

Scarlett took two steps, awestruck. "It's...wow." A breath shuddered out. "You look awesome."

Claudia smiled wolfishly. "Take your clothes off."

"Yes, Ma'am." Scarlett grinned, already lifting her t-shirt to reveal her own black lace. Claudia watched, one arm across her stomach, the elbow of the other balanced on it, her chin cradled by her thumb, as she considered all of the things she wanted to do to the body that was slowly revealing itself.

When Scarlett was stripped of her jeans and standing only in her underwear, Claudia beckoned her over, turning slowly as she neared and backing up against her. Enjoying the feeling of Scarlett's fingertips on her waist. She twisted her neck to the left. "This is the first time you'll make love to me as my wife. I want you to know how much that means to me. How very special this moment is."

"I don't think there has been a moment when I haven't felt that way. Being in this, with you, has been the most—" Scarlett nuzzled in against her neck. "I've loved every minute of it and I'm going to do everything I can to make sure that nothing changes, no matter what we come up against." Her palm flattened out as it smoothed across Claudia's stomach, to pinch gently at the material gathering it inch by inch until Claudia's bareness was available to her.

Her arm raised, Claudia reached up and wrapped her finger into Scarlett's hair, tightening just as her wife's fingertip found her hardening clit. "God, yes." She sighed and relaxed into the touch "I...so good, I..." She couldn't find her words. All cognitive thought leaving her body as she gave herself over to Scarlett's deft touch.

When she knew she was wet, she reached for Scarlett's hand and guided her to the bed. "I need you inside of me." She sat on the bed and scooted backwards, legs open, inviting.

Scarlett gazed down at her. Wanton and seductive, open, and available. She climbed onto the bed on all fours and crawled towards her. Her mouth teasing a nipple through the lace as Claudia writhed and begged. Her chest pushing upward, hips jerking.

"Please…I need…"

"Me." Scarlett chuckled as she did exactly what she was asked and gave her everything. All of her.

Scarlett

Epilogue The Second Half

"Mother!!" Diana hollered from the house. Scarlett looked and over at Claudia who raised a brow and smirked.

"Yes, sweetheart."

Diana appeared at the patio doors looking harried. "Zara running late."

"Okay, well, we can just wait till she arrives, there's schedule really Diana. It's our garden, nobody is shutting us down it's not over and done within the hour."

"That's not the point, honestly, does nobody have any ser of doing things like they said they would?" Diana continued to h before turning and walking back into the house.

Scarlett wandered over, wrapping her arms around Claudi shoulders, and instantly reminded of the night before. "Shall I go a have a word?"

"Would you, you're far more diplomatic than I'll be."

Bea walked out carrying a tray of glasses. "Where do y want these?"

"Over on the table, would be my first guess." Clau grinned.

"Oo snarky, I like it. Lacking sleep, are we?" Bea threw ba with a giggle.

"Actually, yes," Claudia said, as Scarlett took that as her c to go and sort out Diana.

It wasn't difficult to find her sister, sitting on the sofa w her legs curled up, frowning while stroking Truffle vigorously.

"You alright?" Scarlett asked, sitting down in the armch opposite.

Diana stared at her. "Yes, sorry, I'm just having a moment."

"Clearly." Scarlett smiled. "Want to talk about it?"

Huffing Diana uncurled and sat up. "I've been…seeing someone," she said slowly, trying to gauge whether her mother had shared the information with Scarlett or not.

"Uh huh, and what's the problem," Scarlett asked, giving nothing away.

"Well, we've had a bit of a row."

"About?"

Diana crossed her arms defiantly. "Because I said that—" She stared at Scarlett, "I said she couldn't come today and now she thinks that I'm ashamed of her and that's unfair because I've been very honest about my feelings and where my head is at and even though we cleared it up, it's bothering me."."

"Why couldn't she come today?" Scarlett asked as casually as she could. Not wanting to make a big deal out of it and embarrass her.

"Because it's yours and Mum's big day and not the time for me to announce to everyone that I'm exploring options other than men." She sighed again. "I am not going to be the centre of attention on your big day."

"Well, that is pretty magnanimous of you. If it wasn't our big day, would you feel ready to introduce her to everyone?"

"I'm not sure. It's only been a few weeks and we've barely…we're not sleeping together!" The outburst almost made Scarlett snort, but she held it together.

"So, what I'm hearing is that you have a new friend and she's someone who you like and who might potentially be around for a while, and you'd quite like to see how the family feels about her, and you potentially being in a relationship of some sorts with her?"

Scarlett

"I suppose so." Diana scrunched her nose up. "I know it's ridiculous needing validation from you all, but I do. Shannon is—' The smile that lit up her face told Scarlett all she needed to know "Well, she's fun and I like her a lot and we're getting closer, more intimate. She's being such a sweetheart going at my pace, and I fee badly for not inviting her as my plus one, because let's face it, if she were a man, I wouldn't have thought about it at all."

Scarlett held her gaze and waited.

"So, I should invite her, shouldn't I? I should ask her to come over and then just go with the flow, which is extremely out of my comfort zone."

"Zara is running late, which means you've got time to cal Shannon and invite her. If that's what you want to do."

"But it's your—"

"Every day with Claudia is special, you're part of that. Invite your friend." She winked, got up and went back into the garden to finish helping with the set up.

"Everything alright?" Claudia asked, pinching Scarlett's bun as she sidled up next to her.

"Oi, hands off. You've got another ceremony before you ge your mitts on me again." Scarlett winked. "Unless you want to sneal off for a few minutes?" she whispered before landing a big smool on her lips.

"I want more than a few minutes, I'll wait." Her smile turnec serious. "But is Diana alright?"

"Yep. She's got lady troubles." Scarlett smirked. "Whether to invite her lady or not troubles."

"Oh, and what was decided?"

"Let's just say you might be meeting your future daughter-in law this afternoon."

Claudia's eyes widened. "Are they that serious?"

"Not yet, but take it from me, the way that Diana's face lit up just talking about her, that's either turning into love, or a major heartbreak. But this is a woman, not a man we're talking about, so I'm hedging my bets towards love."

"Oh my, well this is going to be eventful, isn't it?"

"Hopefully." Scarlett grinned.

"Hey, love birds?" Bea called out, pointing to the new arrival. "Liz is here with the grub."

"I'll go sort that," Claudia said, allowing her palm to stroke Scarlett's bum again.

Scarlett raised a brow. "Obsessed, much?"

Claudia turned back to her. "I don't know why, but it's my new favourite thing."

"I'm not complaining."

Bea waved at them. "Seriously, you've got the rest of your lives for this flirting."

"I'm coming." Claudia grinned making her way towards them to greet Liz with a kiss to her cheek and a hug. "Thank you again for this, I really appreciate it."

"No, thank you, I hadn't considered branching out to events before." She looked around the kitchen. "I take it I'm setting up in here?"

"Yes, that would be great."

The doorbell rang and a moment later a whirlwind arrived down the hallway. "Mum, Mum? I'm here, sorry we're late, James couldn't find his shoes." She pointed over her shoulder to the light-skinned black man they'd only been introduced to a handful of times, despite him being Jacob's dad.

Scarlett

"Hi, Mrs—"

"James, nice to see you again. It's still Maddox for now, bu
please, call me Claudia." Claudia said leaning past Zara to kiss hi
reddening cheek. "And my beautiful grandson." She swooped in an
snatched him from Zara. "Hello, darling." She finally got round t
kissing Zara.

"Oh well that is charming isn't it." Zara laughed. "Come on
James, I'll introduce you to everyone again."

"I'm pretty sure I can remember them." He was saying as hi
hand was grabbed and he was yanked forwards.

"Yes, sweetie, but I need to escape Diana's glare and it wa
incoming." She glanced back at him, as he glanced back to see Dian
staring at Zara. "See."

"Oh, got ya." He laughed. "Come on then, let's escape."

Soft music played in the background and the sun shone dow
through white fluffy clouds. The chairs they'd leased were lined u
either side of an impromptu aisle. Each wrapped in satin bows. The
guests seated and waiting. Even Truffle had wandered out and foun
a lap to sit in. Jack's.

It was perfect.

As two o'clock approached, surprisingly to most, it wa
Claudia who appeared first. Dressed in a pale-yellow dress tha
hugged her curves and exposed her shoulders. She was barefoote
and had her hair pulled back into a simple ponytail. Alone, sh
stepped out and waited just a moment before Scarlett appeared in th
doorway, Zara still faffing with her hair.

Zara leaned in. "See, I told you. Look at the way she'
looking at you in this suit." She quickly moved past them and too

her seat before Scarlett stepped out and almost tripped over her own feet at the sight of Claudia in front of her.

For a moment, Scarlett was speechless. Forget what she looked like in this suit, her wife looked like a goddess. "Beautiful," Scarlett muttered to herself, walking towards Claudia with purpose.

Face to face, Claudia smiled. "If I didn't fancy you before…" She chuckled as Scarlett blushed.

"You're stunning," Scarlett said. "Absolutely stunning."

"Shall we do this?" Claudia offered her arm, and Scarlett linked through without hesitation.

They had nobody walk them down the aisle, no bridesmaids, or matrons of honour. It was just them and Bea, who would be officiating the ceremony, and their families and friends. It was all they needed.

"It seems fitting really," Bea began, "that it should be me up here doing this, because as some of you may not know, I'm to blame." She grinned when that got the inevitable laughter from the audience. "You see, we were just three bored women in our 50s who fancied a night out, but Claudia had a condition." She nodded as Claudia laughed and looked around at the guests all waiting for the story. "Claudia said, I don't care where we go, just make sure we're not going to be harassed by horny young men looking for a milf for the night."

There was more laughter from the guests and Scarlett's cheeks had definitely turned a little red.

"So, I took us to Art. A delightful little bar and club in town where we danced and drank and all agreed that what happened in Art, stayed in Art. Isn't that right, bestie?"

"It's true," Liz shouted.

Scarlett looked around at all of the smiling faces. Their family, their friends. Their love for one another had done this,

brought all of these people together. Her mum and dad looking mo
together than they had for years. Jack and Adam finally getting
Even Zara had decided that James deserved a chance, and then the
was the newbie, Shannon. Sitting beside Diana, sneaking glances
her.

"So, there were no horny young men…but Scarlett here F
other ideas about that." Bea saying her name brought her out of I
revelry. "A lot of ideas according to Claudia the following day."

Groans mixed with laughter as those who didn't need
added information cottoned onto the innuendo.

"So, I feel privileged and honoured to have been the catal
to creating this, this love affair that might have surprised a few of
but has proven to be something amazing, for both Claudia a
Scarlett. Now, I know that all of the legalities have been cover
yesterday and as such, these two are already married and enjoyi
the honeymoon."

More sniggers and laughing came from the audience and E
smiled to herself, after all, it was her job to be entertaining, wasn't

"Today we are all gathered together to share in
celebration of that love by listening to them tell us, but first, I'll ha
over to Diana who wants to speak on behalf of herself and I
siblings."

Standing Diana looked back down at Shannon and got
reassuring smile she needed, before she turned her attention back
her mother and sister. Smiling she said, "Well, I never expected to
here doing this a year ago." She took a calming breath befo
continuing, "My mum is our hero."

"Aw." Came the unanimous response.

"She really is, throughout our lives she has been our consta
never failing to be there when we needed her, and when my c
left." She didn't turn to look at Jack, but Scarlett did. His thin-lip
smile said he felt and accepted the dig. "We didn't know if M

would survive it, but she did. She got up every day and kept us all going, never once complaining. And we worried for her, we worried that she wouldn't find anyone else to love her like she deserved because she was so focused on us. But we needn't have been concerned, because somehow, she wound up exactly where she needed to be, on a night out with Bea and Liz, where she met Scarlett. Someone I knew from university, and I can't lie and say that I wasn't shocked. But I'm thankful every day, because all we've ever wanted is for Mum to be happy, and Scarlett does that. I've never seen Mum more happy, and of course, it wouldn't be the Maddox family without a little drama mixed in, because now Scarlett is more family than she ever imagined she would be, and that's what brings me to speak about Scarlett, our sister."

That brought more laughter from those in the know and a few gasps of surprise from those who didn't. Diana grinned as Claudia mouthed, *I love you.*

"Scarlett has become a very much-loved member of our family, and in some ways, it's hard to imagine a time when you weren't. You've brought your sense of calmness and your unconditional love into all of our lives, not just Mum's, and any doubts we may have had have all dissipated. We only have to spend an hour in your company to know just how in love you are with each other, and in the words of my baby sister, we're here for it."

Diana did a quick bow and sat down. Scarlett smiled to herself as she watched Shannon reach out and pat Diana's leg. *Yeah, that was love growing,* she thought to herself.

"Now I guess we should get to the good bit so we can go and eat." She winked at Adam. She turned to Claudia and Scarlett. "Ready?"

They looked at one another before nodding at Bea.

"We have come together to bear witness as Scarlett and Claudia share their own vows with one another."

Scarlett

Claudia decided she would go first. After all, she was the oldest, she'd told Scarlett during their discussion.

"Firstly, thank you all for coming. We both really appreciate the support and love from you all. I uh—" She turned back to Scarlett and held out her hand, Scarlett took it and squeezed. "You once told me that I was like a song, on a loop, playing in your head." She smiled. "And I remember thinking, that must be the soundtrack to the movie playing in mine, but back then I dare not tell you in case I jinxed it, then I forgot about it until I started to think about what I'd say right now." Claudia looked at her children, then back at Scarlett. "That movie was a what if, a series of scenes that ended with me right here, in front of you, saying 'I do'. And back then, I thought that was crazy, we barely knew one another, and I was too terrified to even tell anyone about you, and yet, I already saw my future with you." Her eyes went misty, and Scarlett's followed suit. "I promise to never stop seeing you. And to love you with all that I am. You have my heart."

A small round of applause and aw's and oo's rang out as Claudia leaned in to kiss Scarlett's cheek. It took a moment for the excitement to quieten down enough that Scarlett could have her turn.

"Well, I'm not sure how I follow that up, but I'll give it a go." She laughed. "For the record, I didn't go out that night as the horny equivalent to Bea's young man looking for a milf, seriously Bea?" She chuckled some more, as Bea shrugged theatrically. "I had no idea that I'd be walking into the night that changed my life. I was about to leave, actually, when I saw this beautiful woman standing alone and I said to myself, if she turns me down, I'll go home, but if she says yes, I'll stay and dance. Like a fool, she said yes." Everyone joined in with the laughter, when it went quiet again, Scarlett stared into Claudia's eyes. "And like a fool, I was smitten. Because let's face it, who wouldn't be." She turned to the audience and made sure not to look at Jack. "Have you seen her? She's stunning, and not just because you are gorgeous, but because you're a decent, kind, loving and generous human being, who stands up for those who can't defend themselves. You are the most amazing human being, and

286

am grateful for every day that I get to share with you. My heart sings your name, my soul hears a melody only you play, and my promise to you is that I will sing your song for as long as you'll have me."

There was another round of applause and woops and aw's from everyone as this time, Claudia leaned in and the kiss they shared was nothing less than the passion they felt for one another.

"Alright, alright, can we get on with it, people are starving," Bea jokingly interjected before Zara could shout, 'get a room'. Claudia blushed as they pulled apart but stood close together, an arm around each other, grinning like idiots as everyone snapped away on their phones. Truffle came over for a sniff and then walked away again. "So, before we all disperse and start eating and drinking, which let's face it, is the real reason most of us are here."

"Bea!" Claudia exclaimed laughing.

"What? It's true." She winked. "Seriously though, I want to say, and I think I speak on behalf of everyone here, that we all wish you a wonderful life together. With all of the love, respect, and joy you can offer each other." She reached out and took a hand from them both. "And whenever there is a moment when one or the other is upset, remember how you felt on this day, remind yourself how much love you have for one another and speak accordingly. Never go to bed on an argument, and whatever happens, enjoy it." Letting hands go, she turned to everyone else. "Now, where's the wine?"

Their guests all rose to their feet and clapped, rose petals were thrown and shouts of woohoo could be heard coming from Zara and James. It had been just perfect.

As the night was drawing to a close and many of their guests had left, Claudia pinned Scarlett to the wall in the utility room.

Scarlett

"Can we just go to sleep?" she said when she'd finishe kissing her.

Scarlett smirked. "See, and this is why I said we needed tw wedding nights."

"I know." Claudia stifled the yawn. "Would it be rude if w just snuck off?"

Raising her arm, and waving the new bottle of prosecco ε her, Scarlett said, "Probably not, once I give this to Zara."

"I knew it was a good idea to let them all have their rooms fc the night, they can see everyone off. Did Bea pass out already?"

Scarlett chuckled. "Yep, Annabelle helped her up to Adam' old room. I doubt we will see her before morning now."

Claudia moved in, wrapping her arms around Scarlett, an resting her head against her wife's shoulder. "I can't wait to se where our life takes us."

"On another adventure, I hope." Scarlett kissed the top of he head. "Because that is where all the fun is."

Looking up into her eyes, Claudia grinned. "And we do lik fun, don't we?"

"Hm, we do. Still sleepy?"

Claudia stepped back and opened the door. "Come up an find out."

"I'll follow you wherever you take me."

The end

If you enjoyed this book, or any other of Claire's books, then please consider leaving a review, https://mybook.to/

or why not sign up to Claire's monthly eMag and Newsletters for all the up-to-date information on new releases and what Claire is up to?

Subscribe here: https://bit.ly/Scarlett2CHS

If you want to connect more with Claire, you can follow her on social media.

Facebook:

https://www.facebook.com/groups/ClaireHightonStevenson

Twitter:

https://twitter.com/ClaStevOfficial

Instagram:

https://www.instagram.com/itsclastevofficial/

TikTok:

@ItsClaStevOfficial

Website:

http://www.itsclastevofficial.co.uk

Printed in Great Britain
by Amazon